PRAISE FOR P.D. SINGER

Fire on the Mountain —Rainbow Awards Jury's Choice Honorable Mention

"This was a well written, engrossing story and I can't wait to see where this series goes from here."
—Pants Off Reviews

"…a sexy and fun and sweet story."
—Under the Covers

Snow on the Mountain

"I highly recommend *Snow on the Mountain* to anyone who likes a romance mixed with misunderstanding, scandal, adventure, a little possessiveness, and a secret cabin in the mountains. It is as fun as it is sweet."
—Joyfully Jay

"…another treat from Ms. Singer and I really enjoyed it."
—Mrs. Condit Reads

Blood on the Mountain — Rainbow Awards Finalist, Honorable Mention (5*) — Elisa Rolle

Read it for a cracking plot, and a wonderful couple that deserve their Happy Ever After.
—Mrs. Condit Reads

Blood on the Mountain

P.D. SINGER

ROCKY RIDGE BOOKS

COPYRIGHT

Blood on the Mountain
Copyright © 2020 by P.D. Singer
Cover Art by Cosmic Letterz

"In Flanders Fields" (1915) written by John Alexander McCrae (11-30-1872—1-28-1918) Public domain

Print ISBN: 978-1-62622-087-4

First edition Dreamspinner Press 2012

Published 2020 2nd Edition

Rocky Ridge Books
Box 6922
Broomfield, CO 80021

ALSO BY P.D. SINGER

Thanks to Eden, Lynda, and Angie,
who keep me going when the going gets tough.

Blood on the *MOUNTAIN*

ONE

I sighted down the arrow nocked against the bowstring, trying to focus on the target instead of the chill breeze blowing across my bare ass.

Quite aside from the fact that I was shivering alone, I would *not* allow Kurt to have the last laugh in this little contest. He remained admirably silent in spite of watching my attempts to aim between shudders, although I knew he was dying to bust out laughing and demand another piece of clothing as forfeit. I was running out of things to take off.

Taking advantage of a lull in the breeze, both for my comfort and for my aim, I released my arrow. It flew with a slight upward curve, slicing through the air and coming down in perfect alignment with the gold ring in the near center of the target. The *znng* of the bowstring still hissed near my ear when the arrow struck—I'd learned to hold my stance those extra seconds to avoid introducing a bad vector to my shot.

"Good one, Jake!"

Kurt Carlson, my lover, my self-appointed archery coach, and my current opponent, had spent a big chunk of last summer's ranger season chivvying me into a semblance of competence with his long bow, which was both shorter and with a heavier draw weight than I needed. This year, I was armed, literally, with a bow that suited my reach, and my prowess had increased by leaps and bounds.

Not enough to keep me dressed in our game of strip archery, though. Even with well-fitted equipment and improved skills, I was standing at the shooting line wearing nothing but socks and boots. Kurt still had his ranger-green T-shirt and utility pants on, though my one very good shot cost him his hat.

My hat, utilities, shirt, and underwear lay in a ranger-green heap near a clump of mountain mahogany. At this point, I could only hope that the sight of my near-naked body would distract Kurt into muffing his shot. So far it wasn't working—he'd seen me often enough in the last year that the novelty had to have worn off a little, although his enthusiasm for the view certainly hadn't. Maybe if I was rubbing against him, or was slightly erect, but the breeze had raised a couple of goose bumps on my back end and done that shrinkage business in front. A safety measure, really. The last thing I needed was a close encounter between my dick and the bowstring.

"Your shot." I ceded the shooting line to him, prepared to lose a sock.

He lifted his bow, arrow to the string, the late afternoon light filtering through the trees that ringed our little meadow to tip the ends of his blond hair with gold. With his back to me, his arm holding out the bow, and his face in profile, all he needed was a hunting horn to turn our Colorado mountain into Sherwood Forest. Looking at him, I knew I was lucky to have won even one round.

In spite of the stakes, we played fair; he didn't laugh at me, and I didn't cough or otherwise distract him. But should I warn him about the fly?

Not knowing if it was the biting sort, though it was big, dark, and not flying in a straight line, I held my tongue. Kurt pulled his bowstring back. I covered my groin.

It whizzed at me, veering off when I swatted at it with my free hand. Cutting past Kurt's ear, it *bzz*ed away without stopping for a taste.

But the damage was done.

Kurt danced sideways to avoid the fly at the exact moment he released the bowstring. The arrow arced up and came down near a low clump of yellow flowers, yards from the hay bales that supported our target.

"Agh!" He waved his bow to chase away the fly, and then an even louder, "*Agh!*" when he realized how badly he'd shot. "Interference."

"Natural hazard." I grinned at him. A puff of wind had stolen one of my earlier shots out of the gold ring and onto the edge of the red ring, costing me my utilities, so I wasn't exactly sympathetic.

"Where'd it go?" He scanned the meadow. The pink fletching that should have made the arrow easy to find made the arrow look like a wildflower now, though the columbines, closest in shape and color, preferred the shade of the aspens.

"I shot an arrow in the air; where it fell I knew not where," I quoted. "The bad shot will make me go bare, the arrow landed over there." Between mangling Longfellow and pointing, I earned one of Kurt's glares, his Colorado-sky-blue eyes slitted against the sun and bad rhymes. "Shirt. Off."

"I'm still ahead," he mumbled through the cotton he dragged over his head. He tossed his T-shirt at the pile of clothing.

"We both win," I pointed out reasonably. "Could be worse." I slid one hand over my chest and down to my hip, my sense of fair play succumbing to the magnificent sight of his exposed, muscular torso. If my next shot was going to be tougher because of his naked chest, I'd even up the distraction.

"More bare skin for the fly." Kurt trailed one finger over his nipple.

Okay, two could play at that game, but since I was six feet of exposed hide, less a few inches protected by my work boots, I was feeling a little more vulnerable. I shook my ass, making my equipment swing. Even with the shrinkage, there was a fair amount of me flapping. "If it comes back, I'll swat it for you."

"You'd knock it into next week." Kurt's dimple, there at the right corner of his mouth, made an appearance. "If you were hard. I could help with that."

He most certainly could, and was. Except.... "Two more shots finishes this. Three, maybe."

I had two socks yet as my stake—we'd agreed that boots were safety, not clothing, when it came to strip archery. We couldn't afford to be less than effective from something as stupid and avoidable as stepping on a sharp rock barefooted. Not when we'd have a fire to fight sooner or later, or wildlife to evade. Danger in the Uncompahgre National Forest came in more than one flavor.

"Two." He grinned at me. "If you need to take it to the bitter end."

Bastard. Okay, I have a competitive streak, not quite as wide as Kurt's, but it's still there, and I didn't plan to give up so easily. I'd make him work for it—with a little luck, I could stretch this out to four shots. I didn't have any real hope of winning, but a man has his pride.

Besides, I felt the need to test myself under pressure. Last year, when Kurt had been attacked by a biker, I'd driven the guy off by shooting him in the Harley. Since I'd been trying to skewer his big beer belly, nailing his gas tank had to be considered pure dumb luck, both for the hit and for running him off. I didn't intend to depend on luck like that ever again. Kurt was far too precious to me.

Which didn't mean that he wasn't a distraction now. I willed my mind back to driving my eyes and hands instead of my cock. Being very, very careful not to bring the bow near enough to catch on my bobbing semierection, I took position, aimed, and fired.

"Bull's-eye!" Kurt licked his lips and took his own shooting stance. I'd hit the gold center circle, but it was two inches across —he could possibly come nearer the exact middle.

Thwap!

He did, eying me archly. I balanced against him to pull my boot off. I waved my sock at him, because there had to be some upside to losing again, stuffed my bare foot back into the boot, and added his winnings to the pile of clothing. One last chance to delay defeat.

His hand was warm on my back. "We don't have to play this all the way out, Jake." He slid his hand lower, cupping my ass.

"We don't," I agreed, pulling him close and finding his mouth. Another game two could play at. I let him sink against me, and for a moment, I was tempted to just call it good right there, break off the competition, and slide my hand under the olive-green denim covering his ass. "But we're going to." I finished the kiss with a pop. "You shoot first this time."

"Not fair." He was as hard as I was, proving it by thrusting his groin against mine, and I cursed the clothing and my competitiveness. "We shoot at the same time."

Still not exactly equal: one of us would be in line of sight of the other. I'd do my best to ignore him. "Fair enough." My arrows had blue fletching; there wouldn't be any issue knowing which arrow flew truest.

He turned his back to me, selecting an arrow and settling his feet at shoulder's width apart. Kurt was only two inches shorter than I, which meant that his wide shoulders stayed in my field of vision, and if I dropped my eyes to his narrow butt, I might as well unstring my bow right then and declare him the winner.

With arrow to string, I told him, "Fire at will."

If Will had been strapped to the bull's-eye, he'd have been perfectly safe. My arrow hit the edge of the hay, but Kurt's went wild. Had the fly come back? Surely I hadn't rattled him that much with a smooch and a grope.

"You okay?"

"Yeah," Kurt told me, standing abruptly straighter with his chin upthrust. Guess I had shaken his concentration, but I had won the round, even if my shot was lousy.

"Utilities." Such was the penalty for distraction. Then I had to look away when the globes of his ass thrust out at me as he bent to pull off his boots and slide his britches off. Something heavy sagged the cargo pockets on each trouser leg. His folding knife on one side, probably, but I hadn't seen him slip anything else in. Kurt tended to go prepared for all eventualities. Better not think about that too hard.... With laces flapping, he poked his feet back into his boots, leaving his utilities in a puddle on the ground. He would have to choose today to go commando.

"One more arrow." I really didn't think I could win another round to tie it. Not when I was shooting against a man with more skill and enough aggression to make the US Ski Team, and facing his bare behind.

"One more."

If I was going to go down, I would do it in style. Regulating my breathing so my body's motions wouldn't influence my projectile, I tried to calm myself enough to shoot between heartbeats. Good luck with that, but the blue ring of the target and my arrowhead lined up, with the expectation that gravity would pull it down the few inches to the gold bull's-eye. I'd learned to aim above what I expected to hit at this range.

"Fire at will." Kurt gave the signal this time, something I heard only distantly; all my focus was thirty yards away.

Becoming the arrow was beyond me, but this might be the closest I'd ever come to Zen archery. I watched the arrows fly, with time slowed enough to see that one trailed the other slightly, pink fletching to the rear, and when they hit, they seemed to hit together. I came back to myself.

"Can you tell from here?" The fletchings looked like they touched.

"Nope." Kurt looked surprised. Well, if he was expecting to rattle me with the sight of his naked backside, I'd messed with his perceptions. I should have insisted we swap off who stood to the right.

We wouldn't be shooting again, so another kiss and cuddle before we went down range to collect our arrows wouldn't have made a difference, but Kurt strode off, collecting the arrow he'd lost to the fly's attack. He examined the yellow flowers carefully before marching on.

"Something weird about the plant?" I asked. It was low growing with grayish-green leaves, and I didn't have a name for it.

"Just checking to see if it's a native. We were told to keep an eye out for invasive species, remember?"

I did recall, but my ability to tell one gray-green plant with yellow flowers from another was pretty limited—this could be one of three species. "Is it?" I looked closely, trying to decide what the identifying characteristics were.

"Yes, it's alpine avens. I thought it might be California poppy, but the flowers are smaller and the petals shaped differently. Besides, it's kind of hard to tell what the home range for California poppy is. That's found all over the West." Kurt bent to collect his wild arrow, which had fallen short of the target by several paces. He tucked it between his fingers, careful not to foul the fletching on the arrow he already held.

"I thought poppies were red."

"The garden kind comes in all sorts of colors, but California poppies are yellow, and prickly poppies are white. Those are native around here. There's a huge stand of them by the scarp. About knee-high."

Did we have a field of morphine plants in the middle of our national forest? Nah.

We reached the target and started to remove the arrows, starting with the ones farthest from center, mostly mine. We halted on the last two projectiles, one fletched blue, one fletched pink, that straddled the line between the center gold circle and the gold ring just outside it that made the bulls-eye. Mine was a few millimeters closer to the center. I blinked, unsure of what I was seeing.

Kurt pulled back a fraction of an inch. "Pretty good shooting, Jake."

"Uh, I guess you owe me a sock." I touched the arrows again, just to be sure I'd really accomplished this feat, before pulling one out of the target. Faced with nothing but the evidence of really good shooting, no distractions or insects helping, I wasn't sure what to make of this. Besting Kurt by even this fraction just didn't match my perceptions. Staying in hailing distance, yes. Beating him, no. I lay the arrow on top of the hay, ready to pull out the evidence.

"I guess I do." He toed off a boot.

"No, don't. Not here. You'll only lose it." Not anywhere. I yanked out the second arrow. Kurt's socks led a life of their own, since he couldn't seem to hit a laundry basket with them, but I didn't want an escapee on the archery range.

"Looks like a tie." He touched the holes in the target's fabric and turned to me, his face tilted enough to reach my lips.

"No, you still won. You didn't have any underwear on." That thought steadied me a little.

"Don't worry about it, Jake. It's okay." He brushed his mouth across mine. "That last arrow should take all." He slipped his hands around my waist to pull me close—I took his shoulders and nuzzled back. "I'm declaring you the winner." Picking up where he left off earlier, he rubbed his nude body against mine.

"Kurt, what are you doing?" I asked when he dropped out of kissing range, licking a trail down my chest, my belly, to my cock, which perked up under his breath.

"Going down in defeat, Hot Stuff."

TWO

My hand slipped to Kurt's head, stroking his hair while he sucked me into his mouth. I never got tired of him doing this—it was the first way we'd ever touched each other and still one of my favorites. He had a lot to suck on and made the most of it, sometimes coming off me to rub his lips down my shaft, and keeping up a soft massage against my balls with his hand. I flopped backward against the target, needing support to stay upright.

Reaching around to cup my butt with his other hand, Kurt took me deeply again. Between seeing eight inches of cock disappear between his lips and feeling the wet warmth of his tongue and throat, I trembled against the target, the perforations and the hay scraping my back lightly. Small moans escaped me to mingle with the rustling of the aspen leaves at the edge of the meadow.

Watching him was a pleasure second only to feeling what he was doing—the world got very narrow, big enough only to contain us. Kurt closed his eyes while his head bobbed before me, slowing so he could swirl his tongue around my glans for a moment before wrapping his hand around my shaft. He worked me a little harder, coaxing the tension and tingling deep inside me into a full explosion that doubled me over, both hands to his back for support. The waves crashed over me, and he swallowed them down, never taking his hands from me, even when I could finally stand upright again.

Kurt didn't let me go, but turned slightly to rest his cheek against my belly, letting me soften in his mouth. A time or two he swiped his tongue against my cock, bringing a shiver and gasp. His chest was warm against my thigh, his hand a small comfort against my buttock. I went back to stroking his hair, shorn short for the summer.

"Wonderful," I breathed. It always was. I hoped it always would be, in whatever way or place that my lover and I would find. I wanted to spend the rest of my life finding out. Kurt and I had one year together out of the twenty-three I'd lived, and it was the best year ever. If wanting fifty or sixty more was greedy, then yeah, I had both hands out.

I could feel more than see his smile, which let me slip away from his mouth. Kurt lipped a little kiss onto the base of my cock and rose to press against me, his own cock still hard and needing. "What for you?" I breathed between the slow kisses.

"I have lube in my pocket, but my pocket's over there, and you're over here." The way Kurt pulled closer and rasped his groin against mine, a thirty-yard journey wasn't going to happen. Didn't feel like a hike myself, not when I could reach down to take a big handful of his warm cock and still thrust my tongue into his willing mouth.

He was my armful, my mouthful, and my handful—I wasn't letting go of him for anything short of a bear wandering by, and I might not even notice the bruin the way Kurt wormed against me, thrusting into my hand and sucking on my lower lip.

Somewhere in there I thought to slide to my knees and take his cock in my mouth, but his arms were like iron—the change wasn't okay with him. He turned his head a bit sideways, grinding our mouths together almost frantically, his tongue needy, his thrusts faster. I was pleasing him; I'd do it his way, and it wasn't long before he twisted his hips just enough to spatter the fox grass and mariposa lilies instead of me. I held him through his climax, trying to meld us together and still let him breathe.

The tiny aftershocks made him twitch in my hand—I didn't care to let him go afterward any more than he'd wanted to release me. Kurt brushed my lips a last time before dropping his face into the crook of my neck, sucking in gouts of air and leaning on me.

Kurt sagged in my arms while he recovered. I did let go of his cock, the better to run my fingertips up and down his back while he caught his breath, and he replied in kind with one hand at the base of my spine, all he could reach since I still leaned against the target.

We stayed like that while the light faded around us, the sky going aqua and indigo, and if the warning *zee* of a mosquito hadn't made me grab at it, we might have stayed a while yet. "Come on, mosquito chow, let's find our clothes and some dinner."

Kurt unwrapped himself slowly, but not before taking one last, leisurely sip at my mouth. Then he slapped his thigh. "Guess we better."

We gathered the arrows, holding them like prickly

bouquets, and once back at the shooting line, we shrugged back into our clothing before any more little flyers tasted us. Dinner was quick, boiled up on the propane camp stove, and silent, and our shower, taken together under the tank of water that the sun spent all day warming for us, was even quicker.

Out here in the wilderness of the Colorado Rockies, we rose and set with the daylight. No electricity and no need to light the lantern if we could spend our darkness cuddled together. Still, I took a good long look at the sky from the stoop of our cabin, the Milky Way blazing over the dark forest, obscured by a few wisps of cloud.

I loved this life, far away from the hustle and bustle of civilization. I loved the land, its trees and the flowers that had few names for me beyond "yellow spiky" or "white triangle," its animals, its weather. And here, come to kiss me once more under the stars, was Kurt Carlson, whom I loved best of all.

We lay together on the queen-size mattress that was most definitely not part of the standard ranger cabin equipment. We'd dragged our bed up to the cabin in the back of our tanker, hidden, mostly, by the equipment compartments, because there was no way either of us wanted to sleep in the narrow folding cots the Forest Service issued. We'd probably have deer mice in the ticking by August. Something rustled under the yards of heavy plastic swathing my big green trash-picked couch. We'd pushed the couch to the far end of the cabin, in case whatever wanted to nest in there had relatives. The rest of our town lives, like ski clothing and my laptop, occupied some big cartons, and a few more cartons stayed in the storage shed in town, keeping Kurt's motorcycle company.

"What was that all about earlier?" I mumbled to Kurt, whose head lay against my shoulder. "You never let me win." I'd had time to get a little miffed about being treated like a five-year-old playing cards with the grown-ups.

"Didn't let you this time, either." Kurt's thumb stopped its little strokes against my side. "Hard to fake a shot like that."

"You put those arrows any damned place you want them, Kurt. Maybe my one shot was that good, but when you don't even hit the target... twice." He always hit the target when it was stationary and inanimate, and usually nailed it when it was live and ran away if it was startled. We'd eaten a lot of ground elk last winter.

"You try shooting while a horsefly sails past your nose."

Horseflies definitely were the biting sort. "And the other time?"

"That. Um...."

I waited, but no explanations followed. "Um?" I prodded him with a word and a finger to his side. He jumped but didn't speak. "Um?" I prompted again.

"I was struck by a thought." He pulled me tighter, making me think of the way he'd clung out on the target range.

"Hard enough to make you miss a shot?" I had no idea what that would be.

"Yeah, just... that I had to appreciate everything we were doing, because it's not going to last. Bad time to shoot."

"What do you mean, it's not going to last?" Sure, summer would turn to fall, and we'd go back to Wapiti Creek, where I might get to be a good enough skier to tackle the black diamond slopes, but....

"Jake, you know it's not going to last. You aren't going to be here through the end of fire season."

"Like hell I'm not. I told the Chief—" I twisted us around

so I was looking down into his face, even if it was too dark to see him.

"I know what you told the Chief, and you were an idiot to tell him that, because your ass is going to be off this mountain and in Denver by the first of September." His breath was hot in my face.

"Don't you think that's my decision to make!" It wasn't a question.

"Yeah, and you made it, a long time before you ever met me. I shouldn't have even agreed to come up here for another ranger season with you."

Every certainty I had melted away with his words. "What were we going to do? Stay in Wapiti Creek and caddy golf? Or are you just sorry you're with me?"

"I'm only sorry to be with you if it means you give up your dreams!"

I might have only heard part of that—"You're sorry to be with me?"

"No, Jake, I didn't say that!" Damn, he sounded as hurt as I felt. "You are not going to give up going to pharmacy school. You can't—you sweated bullets to get in, and you've worked your ass off to pay for it. You have state residency now, and they won't save you a space indefinitely. You have to go."

"You mean I have to leave you."

"You're the smartest idiot I know, Jake Landon!" He reached up to nip my shoulder, making me leap away. "You aren't leaving me. You're just going to leave the mountain for a while."

"And you're not."

"Not yet, Jake. I have to finish the season. You don't."

"Yes, I do." Except why? If Kurt was sorry to be with me? If I thought last year was going to be awkward if he hadn't turned out to be as interested in me as I was in him, I hadn't even considered what it would be like if he changed his mind this much later.

"I already told the Chief you were leaving midseason as you originally planned."

"Fuck, Kurt!" I was on my feet now, yelling. "You don't get to plan my life!" Or throw me out without talking to me, without trying to make it work. I thought we were working pretty damned good, until now.

"You planned your life, Jake! And yeah, it should be us planning our life, but you're trying to make some decisions that are going to change everything, you know that?" He was on his feet now too, and we faced off in the dark.

I could only place him by the anger in his voice, but I yelled toward it. "I'm trying to plan to be with you, but it sounds like you don't want me!"

"And I'm trying to plan so you get everything you want, including me, and you're trying to fuck it up!"

"You hate cities, Kurt. You hate crowds and traffic and indoor jobs. What the hell are you going to do in Denver for four years?" If I put it off another year, we'd have time to work something out he'd like better. Maybe I could get into pharmacy school in Montana? Or Wyoming? Residency would be an issue all over again, and out of state tuition would be a bitch, but we could work Jackson Hole or Big Sky this winter....

"I'll figure something out. Okay?" He'd stopped shouting at me at least. "I just don't want us to turn around one day and discover that we're fifty-year-old ski bums one paycheck away from eating out of dumpsters because you blew off the biggest opportunity of your life, all because you thought I hated cities."

"You do hate cities." I quit shouting, because it was enough to hate knowing that I was right.

"Yeah, I do hate cities. But, Jake—" Kurt bumped into me

in the dark and found me with an embrace. "I do love you." He rubbed his cheek against mine.

We got back into bed, cautiously this time, and I doubt either of us could have slept until we'd made love, face to face, Kurt on top. I needed him in me, because I couldn't bear it any other way.

THREE

Even July couldn't warm our snowmelt lake enough to make it useless as a refrigerator. I lowered the plastic carton back into the water after breakfast; ten feet below the surface, it would probably be safe from marauders. This wilderness fridge had been my big contribution to comfort last year, and life was much nicer with cold milk and fresh meat. Kurt had offered to trap a rabbit for dinner last year when I'd moaned, but I was still a bit too much of a city boy for that.

We loaded into the tanker, ready to start patrolling our stretch of the forest. Still subdued from last night's fight, we didn't say much over the rumble of the big diesel engine, but Kurt kept his hand on my leg between shifting gears. I covered his hand with mine. I didn't take it back, even when the two men in a blue pickup rattled right up to our tailgate. We'd seen them several times in the last few weeks. A mile or two of that was damned annoying, and getting to one of our regular over-looks with a pullout came as a relief. The pickup roared past, raising a cloud of dust. I wondered where they were camping—they had to like the distance from civilization, and we hadn't found them yet. Since the camping rules for the forest were not more than fourteen days in one place, and not closer than 100 feet to lakes or streams, we probably should find them soon and roust them. If we didn't have other things to do right now, we could just follow them.

Our route took us through the area west of the scarp that had burned last year. The flames had chased us from the original ignition site all the way to the cave in the scarp, and we'd survived only by the grace of the rains. We'd waited to die in the cave, and while we waited, we'd touched each other for the first time. A lot had happened in the year and some since then.

"I can have the admissions packet filled out and sent to U of Montana by next week." That still seemed to be the best idea. Instead of craning my neck trying to find the cave, I peeked at Kurt from the corner of my eye.

"Nope." He looked straight ahead, but a muscle jumped in his jaw.

"Yup. It'll work. I'll send applications to the University of Wyoming, too, just to be on the safe side. No big, I can recycle the essay I used before."

"And spend half a year waiting to find out, and then another year on residency, and then another six months for classes to start when you can have your butt in a chair in two months. Not gonna work, Jake."

"Sure it will." I was so proud of myself for finding a way to make us both happy. "The extra time is hardly anything."

"It's two years out of my life too. What if I hate Laramie or Missoula worse than I hate Denver? Then what?" Kurt's knuckles whitened on the steering wheel. "Or worse, what if Laramie or Missoula hates us worse than I hate Denver?"

I hadn't thought of that. "College towns tend to be pretty liberal, Kurt."

He slammed on the brakes and jammed the truck into neutral. "That's what Matthew Shepard said."

I stuttered for an answer on that one. "Time has passed since then," I finally babbled.

"But has enough time passed? Have enough things changed? Are you gonna stuff me back into the closet because you think I can't handle four street lights in a row?" He was yelling as loud as he had last night, only this was worse because we were in a smaller space. "Do you think so little of me—that I can't cope with something necessary just because I don't *like* it?" Kurt struck the steering wheel with the heel of his hand. "I lived there for a year because I chose to. I can do it again."

I felt it like the blow had really been aimed for me—he'd told me about sharing an apartment with a friend. "I'm not questioning your manhood, Kurt. I'm trying to change the situation so we're both okay with it."

"Nothing is gonna make Denver be anything but Denver, and spending two more years fucking around waiting is only going to make you think you can put it off more. Then you'll have another reason, and another reason, and another reason why you aren't going back to school. Somewhere in there the school will decide not to hold your place. And then there we are, the fifty-year-old ski bums."

We'd been living on the low end of the food chain since we'd known each other, and it hadn't been an issue. "Is that what bothers you? That I'm not going to be a professional and support you in the manner to which you'd like to become accustomed?"

"Damn it! That is *not* what I said!" He pulled off his Smokey Bear hat with the blue jay feather in the band to run one hand through his hair in his agitation. "You showed up for a summer's work, and you were a man with a plan. You were going to enjoy yourself, make some money, and get back to school. And I thought it was great—you were a guy going places. What did I get you for Christmas, Jake?" He swatted my thighs with his hat.

I remembered perfectly well. "A textbook." A ten-pound textbook that I'd been delighted to take from his hands. Then.

"Damned right." He glowered at me so hard that if he'd had that copy of *Remington's Pharmaceutical Sciences* in grabbing distance, he'd probably have tried to smack me with that instead of his relatively painless ranger flat brim. "Did that give you any clue at all that I was on board with your plans? That I'd seen the path you needed to go down and was planning to go with you?"

A meadowlark trilled its entire ditty before I could answer that. "Yeah."

"Do you think I didn't know where the pharmacy school was and where we'd be?"

Kurt always knew where he was—it made him the skier, rock climber, and ranger that he was. I nodded my head.

"So quit fucking worrying about where we spend the next four years." He cut the motor on the tanker and slammed out the driver's door, crushing the brim of his hat. I heard him wrench open an equipment compartment and clang out some equipment. Kurt never used that kind of language—twice in one conversation meant he was more riled than I'd ever seen him. He hadn't been that angry even when Mark had brought me home drunk last winter. He wasn't ready to quit yelling at me. "Get out here and grab your shovel, Jake."

I followed him slowly. I'd only been trying to think of him, trying to make it easier on him while I spent four years immersed in a graduate program. Denver might as well have been in a different universe, not a hundred seventy miles away

22

on the road, or a hundred miles as the crow flies. Out here the sky was so blue it hurt to look at it, the air smelled of sage and pine, not exhaust, and no one was going to pull up behind the tanker on this single-tracked dirt road that was the only way back into the Flattops, and honk to let them through. And too bad if they did—they'd have to follow or back up to a turn-around spot, because gambel oak and sage four feet high on either side of the road wasn't going to let anyone, not even us in our medium-duty tanker, cut around. That dirt road was as narrow and direct as Kurt's vision of my future.

With my shovel on my shoulder and a canteen slung around my neck, I followed Kurt through the brush and up a ridge, where we stopped to look for signs of fire in the swale below. Taking my turns with the binoculars, I didn't so much look for smoke as at the land around us, the greens and grays of the scrubby oaks merging into the green of the pine forest, turning green-black on the more distant slopes. Wildflowers bloomed in the sparse open areas, the snowy drifts of prickly poppy dancing in the breeze above the pink haze of prairie smoke. The wind blew the larks' songs away in little puffs, the music sweet in the bright sun. A break in the trees where the aspens fluttered their leaves signaled water and a place where fire had been, ten or twelve years before. We were specks in the wilderness and not the most important beings here.

Kurt let the binoculars hang from the lanyard around his neck to slip one arm around my waist. His cooler temper was as refreshing as the water in my canteen. I dared to lay my arm across his shoulder—he leaned into me.

"Won't you miss this? I murmured into the side of his head.

He brushed his mouth across mine before he answered. "Not as much as I'd miss you."

FOUR

We patrolled the forest for the next few days without mentioning school. A minor fire from a dry lightning strike kept us busy one day, though we didn't need to call in any reinforcements as it hadn't really gotten past the smoldery stage. I felt like we'd done something real and concrete, something that seemed very far from textbooks and tests. We fell into bed with well-earned exhaustion.

Before we fell asleep, I thought about our next trip into town; groceries were getting a bit low, and the laundry pile a bit high. Once Kurt captured all the errant socks currently lurking under the bed, it might be overflowing.

I curled against Kurt's back, contemplating reaching around to his front. "Payday's Friday, isn't it?"

He nodded. "Money, groceries, and hot showers. We could catch a movie if you wanted."

Even in a town as small as Meeker, the theater still sucked up several dollars for the show, and more for the popcorn and sodas than the occasion seemed to require. And I was looking at the bank balance and thinking about tuition. The two figures were awfully far apart.

Every time I tried to make some economy like skipping a movie in favor of going home and getting naked, Kurt would just nod, agree with me, and pay my way. Awkward. I loved that he wanted to give me the tiny luxuries that I didn't feel I should be spending my slender resources on, but things were getting really one-sided that way. Being able to treat him to anything we could think of once I was out of school was too abstract to make me feel right about it. "I'm not sure there's anything playing we'd want to see." I could hope for some three-hanky chick flick.

"Steampunk Norse gods, I think," he mumbled. "It's third run now, or fifth, and gotten all the way to the wilds of Colorado. You'll like it."

I probably would. But. I made some noncommittal noise.

Kurt lifted my hand to his lips. "It will be a date. We just won't tell the good citizens of Meeker that I'm holding your hand in the dark."

I stroked his cheek, appreciating the thought. One day we'd walk into the theater with our fingers already entwined, and no one would say a word. That day was going to come a lot sooner if we were in Denver, because we'd need another decade or two of ranger seasons to do it. Kurt's vision of fifty-year-old ski bums holding popcorn and each other's hands loomed up at me.

"Urm." I reached down to tickle the lightly furred skin at the base of his cock.

"Urm what?" He flexed into my fingertips and reached back to grip my thigh.

"Urm, University of Wyoming wouldn't be quite so expensive, and I'd have more time to save up."

"Thought we went over this once already, Jake. And besides, by the time you get into the classroom, tuition will have gone up there too. It won't be a net gain on money, and it will be a net loss on time."

"I really don't have enough saved, Kurt." I could borrow the rest—I'd probably have to borrow a lot, but it did seem like twice as much as I'd planned when I'd thought out this scheme. I stopped stroking him, put off by the nosebleed-inducing numbers in my head.

"Are you counting Jorey and Ted's contributions to the scholarship fund?" He sounded braced for an answer he wouldn't like.

"After you made them cough up over this and that?" I thought back to the first time I'd seen Kurt performing this sort of wealth transfer, last winter at Wapiti Creek.

Kurt pulled up by the base of my ski lift with something under his arm, which he used to flag down the nearly nude ski racer. Had to be chilly wearing not much besides briefs and shin guards. Looked like Kurt was waving long underwear.

"What are you doing?" I demanded, when the racer turned out to be Jorey Taylor. I nearly said "What the fuck are you doing?" and it would have been appropriate, but I was working and you didn't say stuff like that in front of the skiers at this posh resort.

"Winning a bet," Jorey told me grimly when I asked again what he was doing. "Carlson! I want my clothes back!"

I bet he did. The exertion of his run had made Jorey sweat; he was steaming slightly. Kurt waved a handful of spandex and microfiber, taunting his erstwhile teammate.

"Come on, Kurt, let him dress. He's making everyone's goggles fog up." I could understand it—Jorey was unrelentingly hetero and inclined to pursue every attractive female in sight, and both handsome and famous enough to succeed fairly often. Not that I was interested, mind you, it's just that I'm not blind.

Kurt tossed Jorey's clothes at him. "All the way down Hotdog Bun, through the slalom gates, and now at the lift line, this close to naked and no one's come to warm you up. Admit it, Jorey, you suck at being a chick magnet."

Jorey looked like he'd bitten into a quince. "I admit no such thing." He stepped out of his ski boots, trying to stand on his skis and not put his stocking feet on the snow. Getting into his clothes with all the grace of a platypus on ice, he seemed to dawdle putting the jacket on, as if zipping the zipper would seal his lost wager.

"Brrr, I'm cold just looking at you!" A woman with cinnamon hair and a lemon-yellow jacket bypassed the lift line to approach him, reminding me that I should be getting people on and off the lift. "Have you turned into a giant icicle?"

"I'm in imminent danger of it." Jorey put on what had to be the most fake puppy-dog eyes ever, completely absurd on a man who stood six foot two and was as solidly muscular as the mountain. "Please warm me up."

She laughed at his pleading, which covered the stray gagging noise that might have slipped out of me. He'd tried this sort of tactic on our friends and been shot down more than once; the tourist looked considerably more susceptible to his beseeching. She probably knew him only as a champion skier and a trophy.

"I have a hot tub at my place—we can soak the frostbite out of you," she suggested, ignoring us the way she ignored the trees.

"Perfect!" He aimed a smirk at Kurt over her head, and the pair skied off to what would surely be a tale to tell for each of them. I went back to my loading zone, leaving Kurt wearing a long face.

"You about ready to shut that down for the evening, Jake?" He looked at the lift. Two skiers were offloading, and the rest of the chairs were empty. I pulled the lever after checking with the operator at the top, and we headed home. Kurt's mood had miraculously changed: now he was laughing to himself and once inside our apartment, he pounced on me.

Being pounced on by Kurt was a damned fine thing. Parkas and snow boots went flying, snow pants came down, and he slid his tongue into my mouth with the kind of wild abandon that sent us to the carpet almost before the door was shut. Rolling and nipping, kissing and squeezing, and we ended up with my cock in Kurt's mouth. I would have offered him some encouragement, but my mouth was kind of full.

Later that night, I snuggled against him on our big ugly couch. A fire would have been really romantic, but fireplaces were amenities not found in the resort's employee housing. Neither were little delights like hot tubs and room service, which Jorey was no doubt enjoying to the fullest with his ladylove *du jour* at her hotel. At least the starlight through the window was free.

"Okay, Kurt, what did you bet Jorey, and what did you lose?"

"I bet him that I could ski down the mountain and collect a partner before he did, even if he peeled down to do it." He kissed me rather thoroughly, and went on. "Jorey owed me a hundred bucks the minute I pulled up next to you."

Our budget would be completely broken if he lost a hundred bucks, which could only mean that Jorey didn't have a clue about us as us. "You've certainly won, but how are you going to prove it?"

Kurt looked stricken. "I didn't think about that."

I bit his ear, hard. "I'll vouch for you, but, Kurt, don't put me in this sort of position again." I wasn't the happiest guy about being gay in public, although I'd tried to ease up among friends in Wapiti Creek.

"Ouch. I won't. But if he was even halfway observant, he'd know already." He rubbed his ear, looking contrite.

"He's too busy looking at Julie and Kim to notice us." And getting shot down every time—our buddies didn't have a lot of patience for Jorey's girl-in-every-resort ways.

"Wonder what else Jorey hasn't noticed?" If Kurt chuckled that evilly about me, I'd be heading for the hills.

Jorey met us at the base of the lift the next morning, a huge grin on his face and all his clothing on. "Pay up, Carlson. Veronica and I had a lovely evening." Lovely had about seven syllables. "I won." He rubbed his fingers together in the universal money sign, then held out his cupped hand.

"Fork over, Jorey." Kurt regarded him steadily. "I won."

"Oh, you did not." Jorey laughed. "Veronica and I left you two… standing… there…." He trickled to a halt and stared at me.

"You owe him, Jorey." My face was so hot my eyebrows were probably on fire. I wouldn't look directly at either of them.

"You. Him." Jorey looked from Kurt to me and back again. "Well, what do you know? Treat him good, Jake, or I'll shove you down Dynamite Alley."

He'd seen us together, not that we made a big hand-holding deal of ourselves. Jorey'd known Kurt a lot longer than I had—he only sounded surprised about me. I guess I'd just come out to someone. Not someone I especially gave a rat's ass about, but… the earth wasn't quaking nor lightning flashing. Huh.

"Money, Jorey." Kurt reached out, palm up.

"Damn it, Carlson, one of these days I am going to win a bet with you." He dug in his pocket. "You know, Jake, it's almost worth the hundred bucks just to see you blushing like a teenage girl." He grinned widely, losing a few degrees of smile with every twenty he counted into Kurt's hand. "At least I can still kick your ass down the mountain." Jorey poled off, grumbling. I wondered how often Kurt had lightened his wallet over the years, and how.

"You'd think he'd learn." Kurt made no effort to tuck the money away. "Take it, Jake."

"Your bet, your winnings." I didn't reach for the money.

"Ill-gotten gains. I'll have to spend it on you. Frivolously."

"Don't do that!" Kurt would make good on that threat—I accepted his offering.

"Put it toward your therapeutics class." He watched with approval while I zipped the cash into a pocket. "I shouldn't have put you on the spot like that. It's just, Jorey and I make these bets that he thinks are sewn up tight, and I always walk away with his money. In fact, I have another idea for Jorey's next contribution to the scholarship fund, and it doesn't involve you or us at all, just a bit of set up…." Kurt broke into a huge grin. "Oh, Jake, this one is gonna be good!"

Over the winter, Kurt had tapped his old buddies on the US Ski Team every time they had a training session at Wapiti Creek. He'd turn over the boodle to me, saying, "Here's your medicinal chemistry class," or "lab fees." Two years of enriching him before he left the team ought to have taught them something, but Kurt kept handing me wads of pro skiers' cash.

"Even counting that, it's going to be tight." I couldn't rely on any more windfalls.

He relaxed a little under my hand. "We'll figure something out."

I nestled a little closer. Knowing Kurt was with me on this helped, but he shouldn't have to feel like he had to put me through school.

"Jake, maybe we should skip the movie." Did he sense how the expenditure made me uncomfortable? Kurt twisted to kiss me over his shoulder, and his voice went unexpectedly playful. "Ever been to the rodeo?"

Ranger headquarters doubled as the Chiefs' living room, and our weekly visits were a bit of lifeline to civilization. We'd report in, get a hot shower with indoor plumbing and a reminder that people cared what we were doing out in the wilderness. Mrs. Chief was the Forest Service's "other mother"; she greeted her rangers with smiles and homemade treats on our weekly trips to town. Snickerdoodles and banana bread went a long way to taking the sting out of the primitive cooking most of the teams did, more out of skill than supplies. Other teams had copied our "fridge" in the lake with varying success, depending on how many pulley-bearing trees stuck out over the water. Our good fortune didn't keep our hands out of the brownie dish. She chuckled and poured a second glass of milk for each of us.

"Thanks, Mom." Kurt drank deeply and came out of the glass with a white moustache.

"You're welcome, sweetie." She ruffled his softly bristled head.

Mrs. Chief played the "mom" game more with Kurt than with me, since he'd passed his third ranger season and was officially considered housebroken enough to finalize his "adoption." I was still on probation that way, but she'd also seen our records and knew that my own mother was still alive to "mom" me herself. Kurt had been without that kind of attention since he was ten. If I could just get past this "tell the family I'm gay" crap, I'd share my mother with him. She'd love him and fuss over him and…. If she still loved me after I told her.

"Save a couple of those brownies for Terry, boys," Mrs. Chief admonished us. "He's coming by in a bit to chat with Harold."

Harold. Oh, right. His wife could actually use the Chief's name. "If he's not a ranger, does he get brownies?" The remaining squares of fudgy goodness taunted me from the plate.

"Special Agent Souder most certainly does get brownies, Jake. You must be one of my other sons, because I'll have to teach you about sharing." With a gentle hand, she pulled me to sitting upright, incidentally putting the plate out of reach.

"Special agent, like FBI?" I asked, treats momentarily forgotten. Did we have FBI-type problems brewing?

"No, he's Forest Service, like us, only the law enforcement end, not the fires and shovels end," Kurt said before taking another sip of milk. I relaxed and noticed the brownies with both eyes again.

"Exactly," Mrs. Chief agreed. "He's responsible for three national forests and a grassland on the Western Slope, but there's no reason for you to have met him so far. Although—" She swatted my hand playfully when I reached into the plate, not stealthily enough to avoid detection. "—he might arrest you for stealing all the brownies."

When the Chief joined us, he wanted to know about moisture levels, lightning strikes, and traffic patterns. "Find that blue pickup, boys. If they overstay the camping limit, it will take years for the vegetation to recover."

I hadn't thought of conservation issues as much as I'd thought about squatters using federal lands as home. "They always come by when we have our hands full with something else."

The Chief snorted. "Seems the way of it. Triage what you're doing next time you see them. Odd that you haven't found at least the truck on your rounds, though. The camp should be back from the road at least a hundred feet, and if it isn't, feel free to roust them no matter how short a time they've been there."

Ranger matters were the easy part. While Kurt was taking his turn in the shower, I got hit with the hard questions.

"Are you heading out over Labor Day weekend, or the Tuesday following?" Coming from him, grizzled and weathered, with a khaki ranger's uniform that made him look carved from the granite, there didn't seem to be any other choices.

"I expected to finish fire season, Chief." I still had no idea about the rest of it.

"I thought you might say that, son." He'd swiveled away from the topographical map spread over his desk. "But I think you're making a mistake."

I looked up at the man who'd defined authority for me for most of the last year. "But you need an intact team for patrolling."

"I do, but there's more than one way to have it. Jake," the Chief said, leaning forward, "you have this opportunity, and you hired on with the expectation that you'd pursue it. I planned for it, rather than lose you both this season. You and Kurt make a good ranger team, I admit, but this isn't what you've spent your academic career working toward. What's changed your mind?"

I didn't have a good answer for that—the doubts and concerns that I'd spoken out loud seemed pretty pitiful compared to the enormity of abandoning the profession I hadn't really begun yet. "I haven't changed my mind, sir. I'm... I just need another year. Or two."

"No, Jake, you don't." The Chief held my eyes with his, reminding me of my father, and even more of Gramps. I never liked disappointing either of them, and they'd probably appreciate the Chief acting as their proxy. I squirmed and looked at my feet. "The longer you stay out of the classroom, the harder it will be to go back. It's seductive, being out in the world where there's a paycheck and work ends when the sun goes down instead of when you can't keep your eyes open any longer. But that isn't the way to your larger goal, now is it?"

"Even the Forest Service requires that much when there's a fire, sir."

"Then you'll be used to it, and no getting grimy in the process." The Chief came to his feet, bringing me to mine. He gripped my upper arm firmly. "I won't actually fire you on August 31, but I believe you should be leaving us by then."

"I'll... I'll think about it, sir." This wasn't fair, getting tag teamed by my partner and my boss, and this was the biggest concession I was prepared to make.

"Don't be thinking about it, Jake. Just keep on with your plan." He hadn't let go of my arm yet, and gave me one last squeeze. "This is what I'd advise my own son. Don't derail yourself. The forest, and the Forest Service, will manage."

I could only nod—making an actual promise about it was too big right now. Kurt collected me from the doorway, his hair still damp. I don't know how much he heard, but he said nothing apart from good-byes to the Chiefs.

Once we retrieved our laundry, Kurt headed my elderly dirt-brown Toyota down the highway toward Glenwood Springs and the county fair with its rodeo.

"It'll be fun, Jake," Kurt assured me on the narrow road south. "Saddle broncs, bulls. Prize-winning pigs and well-groomed cattle."

I'd take his word on it, and he sounded so excited that I'd give it a shot, though it did sound terribly agricultural to me. With funnel cakes in hand, we watched a couple of sheep dogs work a balky flock in the trials, meandered out before the chuck wagon races, and took a quick trip through the exhibition halls. Prize quilts and 4-H projects didn't keep us longer than it took to pass through, although we paused at tables of high-grade fleeces. I didn't know fleeces competed without a sheep underneath. Kurt ambled toward the barns back of the stock pens, where we watched twelve-year-olds tease their steers' tails into big puffballs.

"They're taking this really seriously," I mused aloud.

"You bet they are," he told me. "Those kids are grooming their college money—they sell the animals at auction after the competition. You should have started with a calf about ten, twelve years ago."

Maybe I should have. Livestock would have caused a certain stir in the suburban Detroit neighborhood where I'd grown up. Pushing that thought aside, I followed Kurt to look at pygmy goats, and it was all good fun.

Or, I should say, it was fun until Kurt led me somewhere I was pretty sure we weren't supposed to go.

FIVE

"Kurt, that sign said 'No Unauthorized Personnel'."

Kurt eeled past the barricade anyway. I followed, quite sure that we were exactly the people the barrier was meant to keep out. The public didn't belong among the roughstock at a rodeo.

"So it does, Jake, but I want to check it out, and until someone throws me out, I'm here." Kurt checked out the stalls filled with horses that shifted and stamped. Every one of them had wilder eyes than I was used to seeing on the trail horses at the Rendezvous Lake Lodge stables, but those horses had to be gentle and quiet. These horses were here to buck.

The cowboys moving among the horses gave us sideways looks, and a few stared, openly hostile. We certainly stuck out amongst the Wrangler jeans and pearl-snapped shirts, dressed as we were in ranger-green T-shirts and utility pants. Our boots were the heavy-soled, fire-stomping variety, not the tall, heavily tooled cowboy boots that didn't have treads to catch whatever crap their owners walked in. We didn't belong here, and I concurred with the cowboys, we ought to go. I'm a decent-sized guy, six feet tall with some muscle, and Kurt's only a few inches shorter and made of whipcord, so I hoped we looked like people not to mess with. Some of these guys were as big or bigger, and there were an awful lot more of them. "Are they going to object, uh, strenuously, to us being here?"

Kurt inspected the corral like he knew what he was looking for and showed no signs of leaving. Okay, he'd grown up in Jackson Hole, Wyoming, and cut a lot of hay for his brother-in-law, he'd told me, but not everyone from Wyoming was a cowboy. He'd been back to Jackson for a week earlier this spring when I'd flown to Detroit to see my family—had that given him delusions of cowboyhood?

"We'll be okay. This ain't my first rodeo." Kurt grabbed my arm and drew me away from the middle of the open area. A cowboy led a saddled horse into a chute to our left, and I wondered nervously if one of us was going to get kicked. The cowboy climbed the rails to get out of the chute, leaving the animal to shift uneasily in the confined area and blow a flapping sigh.

"Pete's up first, then Dale. Cal third." An official in a white Stetson ticked names off the clipboard. "Get the broncos loaded, two in the chute, third out here. Keep one on deck; we need to make this march."

We watched the second horse protest going into the narrow enclosure, bumping into the metal railings and rattling the gates before agreeing to enter. More cowboys in jeans and battered hats vaulted onto the railings and one settled on the saddle of the first horse. He looked partly determined, partly scared shit-less, and the way the horse was moving, I was a bit concerned he'd get a leg crushed against the gate before he ever had a chance to show his stuff. A rodeo clown in ripped overalls and white face paint with red features ran past us and vaulted over the fence into the arena. The horse stamped in his wake.

"Eight seconds and a good score, that's what he wants," Kurt said in a low voice. His eyes hadn't left the horse in the gate.

"Score?" Eight seconds on a horse that intended to behave like a trampoline wasn't adequate?

"Yeah. Two judges, right and left, for the horse, and the same for the rider. Add the four of them."

"How do you know that, Kurt?"

But Kurt wasn't listening—he was gawking at the horse waiting impatiently on deck. "Oh, wow."

Too bad he wasn't listening to the crap in the background. I was hearing things that made me want to get out of the stock area and back among a crowd that would object to ass-kickings for innocuous bystanders.

Like: "Who are those two clowns?"

"Them? Forest Service fags," followed by a hack and a spit.

"Leave 'em be, they're okay." I wanted to hug that person. Well, not exactly, but you know what I mean. Now all the cowboys would be wondering if we were checking out their asses, if they took that seriously, or just thinking we were truck-bound wusses if it was a general insult.

Hell, no, I wasn't checking out their asses, although one or two men had jeans that sat just right on their hips. That was incidental; I was much more interested in whatever objects were lying around that I could use for a weapon if it came to that. I didn't belong there, I wanted to get out of there, and I wouldn't let anybody pound on me or Kurt while we escaped. Before, we were just idiot tourists that had wandered where we didn't belong; now we were objects of scorn.

Why the hell did he want to be in here, anyway? "Kurt, I think we should get out of here."

"Not yet. Oh man, look…." Kurt's voice trailed away.

"It's a horse with an attitude. Let's go." I spoke low, not wanting to attract any more attention than necessary.

"It's not just a horse, it's—"

The announcer barked his spiel over the loudspeaker, punctuated with squeals and pops. "And now, ladies and gentlemen, the Glenwood Springs Fair and Rodeo Saddle Bronc event you've all been waiting for! Give them a big hand!" The crowd dutifully applauded and the cowboys got tenser, their moments of truth nearly at hand. "First out of the chute: from Glenrock, Wyoming, Pete Colbertson, riding Hammerhead! This is his first season on the circuit—Pete, that is—Hammerhead's been to every rodeo worth the name on the Western Slope. Let's see what he can do!"

A buzzer sounded, the front gate on the chute opened, and the horse bounded out, springing in directions that no well-mannered horse should attempt. The cowboy bounced on its back, arm flailing wildly, and he was down in the groomed dirt of the arena before the bronco had kicked up his heels a fourth time. The buzzer went off long after the cowboy had come out of the saddle; he hadn't managed his eight seconds.

I didn't know eight seconds could last so long, and I wasn't even on the horse.

"Mack, on deck with Limbo, and get Dale into the saddle!" The official looked around to see if everyone was ready.

"A big old goose-egg for Pete. Better luck next time. Next up, Dale Vernon, from Rifle, Colorado, on Dilly Dally, with a fresh Bronco of the Year award from the Torrington Rodeo!"

Kurt looked entranced. In fact, the last time he'd been so enchanted with anything we'd been buck naked and I'd been trying something I'd only read about on the Internet. Just so we'd be in any condition to do it again, I elbowed him. "Kurt, let's go. Now!" I didn't like the sidelong glances we were getting, and matters might have turned ugly already if the cowboys didn't have so much to do.

Again the buzzer sounded, and the horse did its best to put foolhardy Dale Vernon on the ground. Leaping around in contortions I didn't think a horse could do, Dilly Dally didn't part ways with Dale until the eight second buzzer went off. Then it wasn't so much that the rider got off as he went flying. The rodeo clown ran at the horse, waving and doing whatever it was that distracted horses from putting their metal-shod feet on top of fallen cowboys. Dale got up from the dirt, with brown streaks on his face and the need to hork soil out of his mouth while the horse danced away.

"That ride was good for a score of sixty-one. Not Dale's best, but not his worst, either, and he's got the first valid score of the afternoon." I had to strain to understand the voice on the loudspeaker, and didn't want to divert too much attention to it, just in case things went as badly as one cowboy's sullen glare suggested it might. The mixed scents of leather, sweat, and horse soured in my nostrils.

"Is that good?" I asked quietly.

"It won't win, even at a little rodeo like this one, but it's above where he can ask for a re-ride. Something in the seventies will take the belt buckle tonight. Eighties and even low nineties to win at the really important rodeos like the Cheyenne Frontier Days." Kurt spoke equally quietly, and now he stared at the coal-black animal that a cowboy led across the corral. "Oh, wow."

"Like the pretty horsey?" The cowboy holding the animal's reins couldn't possibly have gotten any more scorn into his voice. Given the flashy blue-and-red-yoked shirt he sported, I didn't think he should be addressing anyone in tones of derision.

"Oooh. Very pretty." Oh, damn. Kurt was doing that twee little voice he used, just before something really awful happened. Make that, just before he made something really awful happen. I should have thrown him over my shoulder and hauled him out of here—we were outnumbered, unwelcome, and I didn't know enough to risk trying to defuse the situation.

"This ain't just a pretty horsey, dude." From this man, that wouldn't be surfer talk, just an assessment of Kurt's abilities. "This is Midnight Kid, by Midnight Madness out of Bonnie Belle, and he'll be at the National Western Stock Show Rodeo in January." The horse shook its head, making its mane fly. "One of Tredgard Roughstock's finest."

"Should I say 'wow' again?" If Kurt was batting his eyes when he said that, I'd kick his ass myself. If we survived to get out of here with any ass left worth kicking.

"You should, pretty boy. This is one fine bronco. Finest bucking lines in the business. Only a few riders have ever stayed on him the entire eight seconds." The cowboy spat brown juice between his boots and grinned. I wouldn't throw the first punch for him calling Kurt names, though I wanted to, and Kurt didn't look irritated. No, Kurt put on that air of innocence that often presaged a very large transfer of funds from someone else's pocket to his. He'd make that cowboy pay, though I couldn't imagine how. Right now, I just wanted to see the evening out of two eyes that weren't black and swollen.

"Eight seconds." Kurt sounded breathless. "That doesn't sound very long." Oh, fuck, he was picking a fight.

"Bet you couldn't do it, pretty boy." The cowboy led the black horse to the fence and tied it. Behind us, the chute opened and the bronco now bucked out in the arena. A man, clearly older than most of the cowboys and dressed in a much less battered grade of hat and jeans, came to stand near us, but didn't say anything, good or bad.

"Bet I can, asshole," Kurt shot back, still using that oh so dangerous flamer's voice.

Now, I've seen Kurt do amazing things, whether it was walking on a sprained ankle with thirty pounds of gear without a complaint to skiing mountains that looked too near vertical to risk, and he still had all limbs and vertebrae intact. I'd like to keep it that way, but he challenged that cowboy, and it was all I could do to stand there like it was meant to happen. I wanted to clap a hand over his mouth and drag him to the other side of that barricade that we never should have crossed. So there I stood, looking as calm and rocklike as I could manage, and listened to him taunt that cowboy. To run now would bring on the pack, because a lot of people had turned to stare at us.

One way or another, Kurt and I had been in situations I didn't think we would survive, but never on purpose, and I couldn't imagine what had gotten into him now. If the cowboys didn't kill us, that horse would. Except they wouldn't let him ride. Random people didn't get to come back with the bucking stock, let alone ride it just because they wanted to. I breathed just a bit easier about the future state of Kurt's spine.

"You can't do shit." The cowboy threw a saddle over the black horse and reached under to get the girths and buckle them.

"You got some money to back that up?" Kurt spoke archly.

"Don't need it. You ain't getting on any of Tredgard's broncos."

"I've got two hundred bucks that says I can do it." Kurt dropped the swish voice and went to all business.

Where I grew up, announcing that would be an invitation to a mugging, but apparently Kurt wasn't worried. Wish I could say that. I could only hope he'd planned this all the way through, because we'd just fought about money two nights ago.

Jorey had walked into his losses face-first because he didn't see past the obvious when Kurt made their wagers, but did Kurt have the same kind of handle on this situation?

"Then you should have entered the rodeo." The cowboy spat into the dirt again.

"Well, if you aren't interested…." Kurt turned slowly, the first move he'd made toward out of here, and he should have gone faster.

"Oh, I'd love to see you land on your ass, but this is the pros, bucko." The cowboy laughed nastily, and several others joined him. "Tell him, Mr. Tredgard."

"Oh, I don't know." The older man spoke for the first time. "It might be kind of entertaining. An exhibition." He looked Kurt up and down, as if he was measuring the worth of the man. "We could let him have a chance, once the riders have competed. You'll have to sign a release, young man. I won't be responsible for your foolishness."

"Not a problem," Kurt replied. "Of course, there's gotta be something in it for me besides the thrill." He looked around at the cowboys, who varied from grinning to poleaxed at this greenhorn who had been invited to invade their territory. "Two hundred bucks says I can stick eight seconds."

"Not on Midnight Kid, you can't." The cowboy clipped a long thick rein to the horse's halter. "Any other horse, maybe, but he gets one buck-out today and that's mine."

"Hmmm." Mr. Tredgard looked at the horse, looked at Kurt, and decided. "A second time out, once in his career, probably won't make a difference. It should be fair, shouldn't it, Lenny?"

The cowboy boggled at what had to be a reversal of procedure; this Mr. Tredgard was clearly not to be argued with. "Yeah, uh, right. It's your horse...." The cowboy dug into his pocket and brought out some bills. "I only got a hundred on me. Hey, Jim!" he called to a friend. "You want in on this?" Another cowboy shoved his hand in his pocket, and then another dozen clamored to get in on the action. Guess they thought any little chunk of Kurt's stake was easy pickings—they put up more cash than I thought they'd be carrying.

"Mr. Tredgard, will you hold the bets? I'd hate for these guys' mouths to make promises their wallets can't keep." Kurt appealed to the stockowner, who took his two hundred dollars and all the money the others chipped in as well. I hoped there would be enough to pay any doctor's bills that might result from this little adventure.

"You have tack or does Lenny here have to lend you his?" Mr. Tredgard looked a question at our new nemesis.

"If it's good enough for Lenny, it's good enough for me." Kurt spoke past the cowboy to the stockman. There wouldn't be a question of better tack that way, though Kurt certainly didn't have a saddle hidden in a hip pocket.

"Then leave him saddled. We'll call you after the last rider. Go sign your release and hit the rails until it's time." Mr. Tredgard shooed us away. "You're underfoot here."

The horses and riders hadn't stopped their competition for our byplay, and yet another cowboy came back to the corral with dirt on his butt. I decided I liked the chaps look. It was something to keep my mind off my lover's imminent demise.

"Are you out of your mind, Kurt?" I hissed. "You don't have to do this. Just leave the money and let's get out of here."

"I'm perfectly sane." He grinned, and his bright Colorado-sky-blue eyes promised me method to his madness. "And yes, I do have to do this, for a lot of reasons."

"Should I ask?" A cold knot of fear twisted itself in my gut —I didn't want to be the cause of Kurt getting carried out of the arena on a stretcher, but what else was driving him?

Another cowboy grabbed the pickup rider's hand to get carried away from his bronco after the buzzer went off. The announcer declared a score of seventy-eight.

"This guy might just win it. That's the best so far." Kurt managed to pay attention to everything—I hadn't registered any results since the second rider. "And no. Later."

Later. I had to tell myself about a thousand times that Kurt knew what he was doing. I still wasn't convinced.

"Watch now, this is Midnight Kid coming up." Kurt dragged my attention back to the chutes, which we could see through the thicket of people to our left. The muscular black horse came out of the chute, kicking and twisting.

"He's an honest bucker." That assessment, from the man on my left, put a smile on Kurt's face.

"Counterclockwise," Kurt determined. Midnight Kid sent a shower of dirt toward us with his rear feet. "He might—nope, didn't make it." Lenny tipped sideways off the horse and couldn't recover, ending flat in the dirt. The horse bucked again; the cowboy rolled sideways before those murderous hooves could put a dent in his skull. "Close, though, about seven seconds. He's gonna be pissed."

"I hope he tired the horse out for you." I wanted that horse exhausted, with his ribcage heaving, sweat dripping from his flanks, and Kurt having to thump his sides hard to make him move at all. Not happening, though. It took the pickup riders a minute or two to catch him.

"Should be a good ride." Kurt shaded his eyes to see the chutes better. Another few riders came out, a seventy-six, a sixty-eight, and another goose egg, sailing right off the back end of his horse. "Hah! Out the back door!"

"What?" I quit yapping after the cowboy on Kurt's other side agreed with him.

"That particular dismount, Jake." He had a sly grin on his face all the same. "I think we'd better head back. I'm up in two."

The few steps back to the corral and chutes were moments to be treasured: Kurt was still whole and healthy, and so was I. We spotted Mr. Tredgard by the pristine condition of his hat and joined him.

"Oh ho, going to do it after all?" Our opponent in blue and red looked a little worse for the wear; Kurt and I had cheered a bit when he'd fallen. If he was hoping Kurt would come to his senses and leave two hundred dollars behind as the price of shooting off his mouth, he was much mistaken.

"Can't do any worse than you," Kurt replied easily, and stole the hat off his head. "Hold this, Jake. I have to look like a cowboy for a couple of minutes." He tossed his ranger hat to me and clapped the disreputable Stetson on. "I'll try not to land on it." This comforted the cowboy not at all. He glared fiercely at Kurt's back.

Midnight Kid swung his hindquarters against the chute. This horse knew his business, and his business was to buck. Kurt climbed over the rails and onto the horse. I'd watched him ride this summer and last, sitting his mounts effortlessly over the wildest terrain and never coming off, even when rabbits popped up under his horse's feet. This was leagues different—I had to trust in his self-knowledge, and maybe pray a little. Mr. Tredgard motioned me to follow him to a spot with a good view.

"Ladies and gentlemen, before we announce the winners of tonight's saddle bronc competition, we have an exhibition rider.

He's not competing—Dean Tredgard's given this young man the chance to fall off in style. Please welcome Kurt Carlson, from Meeker, Colorado, on Midnight Kid!"

The crowd probably cheered for the town as much as or more than they did for Kurt—he was practically their hometown boy, Meeker being a mere hour's drive away. I hoped the welcome roar wouldn't turn into one of those mass groans on his account, and I didn't want to hear what they'd do if he had to be carried out of the arena. The gate opened and my heart stopped.

Midnight Kid flung himself out of the chute beneath a Kurt who looked as grimly determined as I'd ever seen him, one hand high in the air and his feet up around the horse's neck. It looked like a good way to come off, but Mr. Tredgard only said, "Marked out. Good." Then Kurt's feet came back down into some way that he might actually stay on, though a bit of daylight showed under his butt every time the horse came back to earth without him. He whipped back and forth with the bronco, and eight seconds stretched out to eighty million years.

And that borrowed hat stayed on.

The eight-second buzzer went off, and now Kurt's big problem was getting off a horse that wouldn't stop bucking. Another cowboy galloped past and put an arm out, which Kurt grabbed, letting the other horseman drag him out of the saddle and out of range. The horseman set him down by the fence, and the crowd roared.

I wanted to collapse for sheer relief, which would sort of undermine the entire macho thing we were doing, so I let go of the rail with the one hand I could spare to pump in the air and scream with the rest of them.

"That was Kurt Carlson of Meeker, folks, and if he'd been competing, that ride would have been good for a fifty-eight."

Any ride he walked away from was a solid million to me, but fifty-eight was more or less in the range that the competitors had been getting, and counted even if the horse wasn't fresh. I high-fived him once he'd clambered over the rails, knowing that hugs and full body presses would have to wait for a less hostile environment.

"Told you." Kurt plopped the battered hat back on Lenny, who glowered and spat sideways. A circle of irritable cowboys gathered around us. I thought only the stock contractor's presence kept them from expressing a few opinions with their fists. "What say you, Mr. Tredgard?"

"You stayed on eight seconds and didn't disqualify. Your score would have been higher with spurs, but you had a score. I say you won your bet." He dug all the folded bills out of his pocket and handed them over. Kurt pocketed them without counting. "And I also say you need to get out of here before we start bringing the bulls in, because you aren't going to talk your way on to one of them."

I would have frog-marched Kurt out of there with a hand over his mouth for sure if he'd even hinted at wanting to ride two thousand pounds of stomping, snorting death.

"I'll walk with you back to the stands, gentlemen." Mr. Tredgard gathered us up with a glance and turned to the gate.

Oh good, an escort. Call me nervous, but if I thought we were likely to get jumped with Kurt shooting off his mouth to the cowboys, it was a near certainty once he'd gone and shown them up. I'd be eternally grateful to Mr. Tredgard, once I got past my anger that he'd abetted getting Kurt onto that horse at all. I kept my mouth shut, which seemed to be my best course of action all day.

The noise from the midway grew, and the people around us went from cowboys to families with small children darting around—a short walk that went from one world to another. The scent of animals and hay merged with, and then was overpowered by, hot kettle corn, funnel cakes, and hotdogs.

"I'll leave you here, gentlemen. Think you can keep out of any further mischief, Kurt?" Mr. Tredgard paused outside the trailer marked "No Unauthorized Personnel." Maybe Kurt wouldn't take this to be another bastion that needed storming.

"I think so. Thanks." Kurt put out his hand for a shake, and so did I, wondering why they sounded so amused. Had they done this sort of thing before?

"Give my regards to your brother-in-law, and of course, to your lovely sister Vanessa. And tell them that I said they should have paddled you about twice as often when you were younger. You, young man"—this was to me—"have your hands full with this one." With a last nod, he finished with, "Good luck. You'll need it." He went into the trailer, and I was left staring at Kurt.

"Now are you going to explain?" Some things were a trifle more obvious, but some big dots had yet to be connected.

"On our way home. Is there anything else you'd like to see or do here? Eat another funnel cake? Risk barfing it up on the Zipper?" That was a huge rotating carnival ride whose threatening clanks suggested that it would unzip itself from a cross look. Kurt had refused to ride it earlier—apparently he only risked his life on things where he had some shred of control.

"Not unless you want to look at tractors or chickens. Or see who won the 4-H competitions." I offered choices I didn't think he'd take because I wanted to get him where I could yell at him without an audience.

"It's fifty-five miles to home—I don't really need to know whose jelly won the blue ribbon. Unless you changed your mind about a stuffed animal—there's more games on the midway."

I shook my head. "Nah. Don't want you blowing your winnings trying to get the giant panda that's probably lumpy anyway." I prodded his shoulder to start us toward the gate. "Let's get out of here before we meet any more cranky cowboys, okay?"

"Sure thing." We headed back to the crudmobile, made a quick detour through the grocery in Glenwood Springs, and I got us back on I-70. Kurt waited until we'd gotten to speed before pulling his winnings out to admire them.

"After deducting the two hundred bucks I put up, let's see…." He sifted twenties onto his lap, chuckling softly, and I had to fight to keep my eyes on the road instead of watching bills fall on his thighs. Kurt's thighs were always nice, though seeing them coated with currency was new. "I think it was about sixty bucks a head, once everyone chipped in, but a hundred off of Lenny wasn't bad. Wish it was more." He gathered up the money and rolled it neatly. "There. That's your pharmacy law class, paid for with a half hour of provocation and ten seconds of riding."

"You risked yourself like that for a class?" Kurt had taken my pharmacy school tuition savings plan to new heights, or depths, this time.

"Just trying to keep the student loans down." Kurt patted the lump it made in his pocket. "Besides, once you're through school, you're going to support me in the manner to which we'd like to become accustomed, aren't you?" I nodded, too stunned to say anything else. "Then see, it's in my best interests."

I lost it. "Kurt, nothing you did today was in our best interests! I thought we were going to get shoved around or worse just for being there, you come off with this twee little gay guy act, and then you rub their noses in the fact that you, who have never ridden a bucking bronco that I know of, can stick a horse better than they can! Are you out of your fricking mind?"

"Now, now, Jake," he soothed. "You give a really good impression of a bronco under certain circumstances...."

"Kurt, I am not a thousand pound stallion with sharp hooves and a bad temper!" I think I may have screamed that. He flinched when I got a bit close to a large tractor-trailer rig, and I calmed down and centered us in the lane in time to make the turnoff to Highway 789.

"Stallion, check; temper, check—"

"Kurt, enough. Obviously you and your family know Dean Tredgard from somewhere, so this smacks of a setup, but...." I took a calming breath. "Just explain, okay? We have half an hour before we hit the dirt roads." We wouldn't be able to talk very well once we came to the dust and washboard single track to the cabin.

Kurt tried pouting before he gave it up as a bad job and laughed, his face the open and honest visage that I loved. "You're right, Jake. Tredgard and my brother-in-law Cliff are friends from way back. Cliff's sold him some stock over the years: 'broncos that would not be broken of dancing,' to quote the poem. He was out at the ranch when I was up there in the spring."

"So you set this up ahead of time?" I carefully didn't comment on Kurt's visit home. He'd asked me to go with him, but I'd begged off, and he hadn't pushed.

"No, he watched me help Cliff break a couple of horses. He knew I could stay on or at least come off without a catastrophe. You know, it's a lot easier when there isn't a penalty for pulling leather." He stretched out as best he could and tipped the seat back. "Touching the saddle horn."

"You had money in your pocket," I reminded him.

"Yeah, well, that part I planned." He rested his hand on my thigh, and I could put mine on top of it since I didn't need to shift gears on the highway. "I should have made the bet just getting on and doing it was enough to win, but Lenny Sartain pisses me off."

"He didn't act like he knew you—you know him?"

"There's a history. He might not remember me, but he got me disqualified from a Little Britches event that I should have won." Kurt squeezed my leg. "Don't look so surprised. I told you this wasn't my first rodeo. Cliff and Vanessa kept me in the summers after Mom died. I did ranch kid stuff. Learned a lot. Rode my first bronco at twelve."

I turned off the secondary highway. We still had a ways to go to our ranger's cabin and wouldn't even stop in Meeker itself. "They didn't teach you a damned thing about not giving your partner heart attacks, did they?"

"Probably not," he admitted cheerfully. "You still love me?"

It was probably the only thing that kept me from wringing his neck. "Yeah, I still love you."

Kurt lay back and didn't say another word, though when we finished rattling down our dirt lane and pulled up next to the tanker, he sat up with a groan. "It's late enough we probably ought to get to bed."

We'd have a full day tomorrow out in the tanker and would be up with the dawn.

"I'm ready for bed too." The adrenaline of the rodeo had drained away, leaving me more tired than I wanted to admit, and it was probably worse for Kurt—he'd actually ridden Midnight Kid. Still, he was alive, intact, and going to be lying naked next to me. I'd heard a squeak last night that could have been a bedspring, but then again....

I put my arms out for Kurt once I was under the comforter

that was so necessary in an unheated cabin in the high country, even with a warm man to cuddle on. He sat down slowly, removed his socks, which ended who knew where, and lay next to me. I found his mouth, started slow, and ratcheted up the tongue until he was quite sure about what was on my mind.

"Wanna ride the stallion?" I was pretty well endowed, but he was the one to call me that earlier. "Or be ridden?"

"Er, not exactly."

I squinted at him; Kurt had been thrusting his tongue into my mouth, rubbing against me, and generally behaving like a rutting stallion himself, and then no?

"Something else, but not that tonight, Jake. I can't."

I squinted at him the other way.

"I've been whacked in the ass with a thirteen-hundred-pound horse what felt like thirty or forty times—I hurt."

Kurt said that with such chagrin that I actually held back teasing him. "Aw, poor cowboy, should I rub some liniment on your butt?" I thought that was holding back, really. I'd noticed he'd thrown a tube into the cart but hadn't questioned it.

"Please. And my back. After we're done with the lovey stuff —I don't want menthol and eucalyptus anywhere tender." He sounded serious. "And be gentle with my nuts—they took a beating too."

"That saddle didn't have much of a horn, probably just enough to crash into, huh."

"Oh, yeah. I'd forgotten how much fun it is after a good ride." He kissed the edge of my jaw. "At least I only did it once —the pros had two go-rounds today. It isn't just my ass; it's all the way up my body. Everything's been jarred loose."

"I'll take care of you." Changing our style of lovemaking wasn't a problem—I genuinely hadn't thought what a beating a successful ride might have given him. More softly and slowly, I started working my way down his body. If there was a place that might hurt, I stroked it, massaged it, kissed and licked it. If it made him feel better, good, and if it drove him crazy, also good. I took a long time to get to his cock, and when I did, I took a long time with it.

If he hadn't been too sore to thrust he would have been meeting my mouth on every stroke, pushing deep down my throat, but now, all he could do was lie flat and let me do my playful best. I teased him a good long time, running the tip of my tongue around the head and flicking at the slit, before settling to the strong rhythm of engulfing him. The hand I put to his balls was only to cradle tonight, gentle touching but no rolling or squeezing, not after his pounding in the saddle. His moans tonight were quiet wheezes and short sharp breaths, not the full-throated yelling I could coax out of him on nights when he could move.

The movement in my hand and his fingers fisting into my short hair told me Kurt's orgasm was close, and then he came, shouting with a breath that had to hurt, pulsing into my mouth. His bitter-salt droplets slid to the back of my throat and went down, and I wished that I could dispose of his aching as easily.

"Mmmm." He'd collapsed against the mattress, and his moan had just a bit of pain in it, to go with the pleasure I knew I'd given him. A year of practice since our first fumbling encounters here in the middle of the wilderness had taught me to please him, and Kurt sure knew how to make me happy.

"Not sure what I can do for you," he mumbled. "Maybe come up here and I can suck on you?"

That sounded good, but once I'd straddled his shoulders and gotten into his mouth, it wasn't the right idea. Kurt had to pull away, gasping. "My neck is too sore to get the angle, Jake. I can't breathe."

I lay back beside him, ready to calm myself down. I didn't need an orgasm badly enough to hurt Kurt to get it, not with two good hands and a fair amount of self-control.

"That's okay, Kurt." Tickling my fingertips across his chest, I reminded myself that sex didn't always need to be exactly fifty-fifty. He could have it all tonight.

"No, it isn't." He turned against me, small grunts explaining that it hurt to do that, and tried to wrap his hand around my cock. I'd gone slightly soft, and he stroked me hard again, but it was costing him.

"Leave be, Kurt. There's tomorrow." I stilled his hand. "Just hold me while I take care of it."

"But that isn't right," he whispered. "I scare the shit out of you, worry you, make you do all the work for me, and then not do anything for you? That isn't right," he repeated.

I brushed my lips over his face, thinking. He was pretty immobile but even more stubborn, and he was going to fret. "Stay put. I have an idea."

Getting up from the bed—the lube was on his side—I padded around, jumping a little when I put my foot on his stray sock. We'd had critters in the cabin before. Once I found the bottle, I sat down on the edge beside him. "Just stay like you are." I squished some onto my cock, my own strokes bringing me back to full stiffness, and then touched his crack. "Just let me do it, okay?"

"Jake, I don't want to say no, but—"

"I know, you're sore. I'm not doing what you think." I greased the skin within his crevice but didn't attempt to lube his hole. "I'm not going in."

I crawled in with him, spooning against his back, with my

cock snugged up to his crack. "I won't bump you around, okay? Just lie quietly, we'll be great." With my arm over his chest and my lips against his short blond hair, I moved my hips against his, sliding my cock in the channel between his cheeks.

I was gentle, moving in a small arc, and my very gentleness added something to my excitement, needing to keep control and yet wanting to lose it. Kurt flexed his ass and pushed back against me, trying to help and yet helpless. He ran his fingertips over my arm, those callused, deft fingertips, and they might as well have been travelling over my cock.

Kurt did find something that he could do—he brought my hand to his mouth and sucked in two fingers, laving and stroking them with his tongue, making me glad I hadn't slathered him with balm yet. Slipping against his hot, intimate flesh made me go slow, with time to feel the texture of his skin everywhere I touched him, from the light prickles of hair on his buttocks against my belly to the smoothness of his shoulder beneath my cheek. Sliding, not thrusting, or I'd jostle him—I had to maintain my control over my body, but I didn't have to guard my tongue.

Some wasn't words—it couldn't have been, his body, his mouth, and his stillness dragged incoherent sounds from me. The few words I could manage told him possibly less. "Kurt... oh... good... mmAhh...!" And if that last wasn't a word, it was meaningful, because my climax hit, making me freeze against him, the shudders and the waves pounding through me. I spurted against his back and my stomach, shaken, emptied, but whole. I panted into his hair when it was done, then nuzzled his neck.

"You okay?" I might have gotten a little wilder there at the end.

"Oh, yeah." He stroked my arm some more. "You?"

"You have to ask?" I groped over the side of the bed for the stray sock; if Kurt wouldn't put them in the basket, I'd recycle them, cleaning us up.

"Not really. But next time I'll buck for you." He rolled over onto his stomach.

I leaned to kiss him again, smelling man and a hint of horse. "I think I can stay on for eight seconds." I reached for the liniment, planning to put balm on his aches.

"Good, because there's a rodeo in Saratoga next week."

SIX

I took one look at Kurt the next morning and didn't say a word about him getting up. I'd drive today, and making the sandwiches for lunch without comment plus loading the water bottles into the tanker for the day's patrolling just kind of got done without him having to lift a finger. The truck was going to smell of eucalyptus—I rubbed another layer of balm on his back and thighs before he got up.

I leaned down to rub my lips against his hair. "A lot of the same cowboys will be in Saratoga next week—your little scam will only work the once."

"I don't know about that," he mused. "How many times did I lighten Jorey's pocket?" He rolled over with a grunt, and lifted his lips to me.

"Lots, but it was a different way every time, and he probably didn't want to punch your face just for being around in the first place." I smooched him lightly and offered a hand to swing him out of bed. To my surprise, he took it.

"You might be surprised." Once on his feet, he stretched—a

truly fine sight, but we were going to have to get on the road sometime this morning.

"We aren't driving up to Saratoga. Got that?"

"Spoilsport." He didn't sound too upset, and I concluded that he'd probably had enough rodeo to last him a while. He'd made his point about the money.

Another gloriously bright day under a vivid blue sky streaked with high white wisps greeted us. I almost wished to be part of a horseback team, just so we wouldn't break the quiet of the wilderness with a diesel engine. The winds murmured in the pines, the jays screeched and the meadowlarks trilled, and the grumbling truck drowned it all out unless we stopped to hike to some vantage point to scan for fire or trouble.

I didn't mind that we weren't finding it, especially since today we were scouting in last year's burn area. The forest still looked like hell: charred trunks thrust out blackened branches with ashy stubs of needles, and the springy layer of duff on the ground was gone. The fallen pine and spruce needles made easy tinder, something we brushed and shoveled out of a fire's path before it ignited, but last year's fire had spread on the ground almost more than it had through the timber. The trees that provided the duff had turned to crisp ghosts with nothing left to fall.

Bits of green rose from the ground, promising a recovery one day. Mostly grasses and the occasional wildflower, but spindly evergreens dotted the ground here and there. I knelt by a seedling, barely ankle high. The bare ground around it would leave tan smears of itself on my knees, but I wanted to know what eager adventurer had come to green up the wasteland.

Trying to remember details for telling one evergreen from another, I ran my hand over the needles. Maybe my knowledge of what order the growth returned to a burn area would help more.

"What's that?" Kurt asked from a dozen yards away.

Put on the spot, I guessed. "Lodgepole pine?"

He came to see. "And how do you know?"

I still wasn't sure if I'd guessed right, so I took another look. "Hmm, needles in twos, slightly twisted, and it's coming up on a burn site."

He came to inspect my seedling, kicking a cone my way. "Right, right, and right."

I picked up the cone, its scales flared wide and the seeds scattered. The prickly tip was the only familiar thing about it, but if I imagined the scales lying smoothly closed, it looked like the cones that lay on unburned forest floor or clung to lodge-pole branches.

"You don't see these coming up all over the forest, just here." He knelt to examine my baby tree.

"Because...." I looked at the pinecone, trying to remember the technical word for staying glued shut and settled for "because the cones can't open until the resin melts in a fire." Losing that word was going to bug me until I remembered it.

"Right again. All these little guys could be brothers, come from that one cone." Kurt motioned at the ankle-height brushes of green around us. "Or from several, that would be better genetic diversity, but hey, considering what you go through to get a new lodgepole pine, you take what you can get."

"Yeah. You can't get the new growth until you have the fire." I threw the cone overhand at one of the burned trunks. It bounced off and landed near one of the sprouts Kurt had been examining. "What about those?" It was clearly different, bluish and more conical than straight upright, even at ankle height.

"You tell me." He led me to the other seedlings, clustered under some of the burned pines.

Struggling with details, I told him what I saw. "Um, short single needles, dusty grayish…."

"Glaucous, right." Kurt supplied another missing technical term. "And coming up in a relatively shady spot. What are they?"

"Uh, some kind of spruce?" I hazarded. If I'd known there'd be a test, I would have studied.

"Engelmann spruce, right. They need shade when they're seedlings, or they fry. When they're grown they'll take over this area, be eighty or ninety feet tall." Kurt's words made me see this forest full of gray-green giants.

"How long do they live?" Ninety feet was about eighty-nine and a half feet from now.

"As long as four hundred years." Kurt knelt to brush his hand over the needles. "A hundred fifty years from now it might make a good guitar."

I tried to imagine this infant grown enough to be crafted into anything as wide as a musical instrument. "Doesn't seem possible."

"Absolutely is," Kurt assured me. "And you know what that means, don't you?"

"That I have that long to learn to play?" I'd probably need every minute of the time too.

"No, dodo." He came close enough to cuddle the harsh words away, the scent of his eucalyptus balm mixing with the evergreen resins. "It means that tree will still be here when you finish school."

I was still chewing over Kurt's parable of the trees when our normally reliable tanker developed a nasty hiccup. Something under the hood shrieked in a range that rivaled a dog whistle, and the power steering failed. The truck had been alive and responsive in my hands, but now every little rock in the road required a massive haul on the wheel. I wrestled the tanker over into the brush, crushing a sage and a dozen purple spikes of elephanthead, though it seemed unlikely anyone would need to go around us way out here.

"What was that?" I cut the engine, which mercifully silenced the screaming under the hood, although the screaming in my head got suddenly loud. Town was forty-five miles of bad roads away, and a tow truck at least an hour from reaching us. I reached for the radio.

"Just let the Chief know we have a problem, Jake." Kurt's door snagged on some mountain mahogany, but he slithered out the narrow opening. "And we'll call back when we have a better idea of what's the matter."

We'd lose the daylight in another hour and a half, and dinner wasn't going to cook itself. The sandwiches at lunch were a dim memory. The tow truck couldn't very well misplace us on a single-track road when we knew where we were, but dinner receded another hour at the thought of us mucking around in there first. I popped the hood.

My elderly Toyota was a simple beast, dating from before cars developed masses of spaghetti under the hood—one of the reasons I'd bought it. Barely more than four wheels, heater, and keys, that car had little to go wrong, and nothing so far had happened to it that I couldn't fix myself. Aside from Kurt's theft of a couple of spark plug wires when we'd first met. Even then, if I'd had a chance to look, I might have figured it out, but he'd spirited me away on the back of his motorcycle for an eighty-mile round-trip to the movies in Rifle, and then repaired the damage before I came back in the morning. I didn't think he'd performed any hanky-panky with the truck in the wilderness, and a good thing, because the engine looked like a bowl of ramen with wires and hoses going everywhere. I might be able to find the problem before dark. Tomorrow.

He stood on the bumper, surveying the troublesome mechanicals, then bent down to investigate further.

"We lost the power steering," I told the highly reactive but nonverbal part of him sticking out of the engine compartment.

"The alternator pulley's really loose. The belt jumped the track," emanated from the depths. "But I think we can take care of it ourselves. Grab the tool kit."

We carried a lot more than shovels, axes, and fire gear with us, although some items, like the stretcher that needed two people to carry, weren't as useful as they could be for two rangers alone. I fished the tools out of one of the side compartments on the utility box, wondering what attached to what in there that the alternator made the power steering go out. The same blue pickup we'd seen a few days ago went around us.

"Where do you suppose he's going?" I shaded my eyes to peer after the truck. We'd follow them to wherever they were camped—if we could move. We'd seen this truck now and again for the last two weeks, and if the drivers hadn't moved the campsite in fourteen days, we'd have to roust them. They could camp any twenty-eight days out of sixty, but not all in the same place.

"Long flathead screwdriver and the small adjustable wrench." He stuck his hand out at me without rising, like a surgeon expecting a scalpel to be slapped into his palm. I could only imagine what he was doing in there once I handed the tools over.

"Need a hand?" I asked, not because I expected to be terribly helpful, but I could be a wrench or a clamp.

"In a minute. Need a medium Phillips head with a short shank. It's a little tight." *Skreak skreak* covered his statement. I could see small movements of his arms, and a good yank that nearly flung him off the bumper. "Okay, come hold this."

I hopped up beside him, requested tool in hand, to peer into the depths of the engine. Nothing was obviously wrong to my eyes. Kurt guided my hands to some pulleys.

"Don't let the belt come off while I tension it." He attacked with the short screwdriver, stopping to check the flex in the belt a couple of times. He elbowed me lightly—I jumped down. "We can limp into town like this if the belt's damaged, but I didn't feel any chunks missing."

"So how the heck did you learn to fix trucks and all this other stuff?" I knew how he'd learned to ski, growing up in Jackson within rock-throwing distance of the resort. Some of his other skills baffled me. He hadn't mentioned a secret career as a diesel mechanic. Kurt didn't mention a lot of things unless there was a direct need to know.

"My brother-in-law Cliff ranches, remember?" He blindly handed the screwdriver back to me, trusting me to take it.

"Yeah, and...?" How could I forget? The association between Cliff and Dean Tredgard had to have taken a good five years off my life yesterday.

"I spent my vacations with him and Vanessa every year after Mom died." His voice, already muffled in the bowels of the engine, went softer. One of his confidences back during the fire was that Larry and Vanessa, his much older brother and sister, and later their spouses Polly and Cliff, had helped raise him.

"You'd said." I looked at the western horizon; the sun was approaching it fast.

"Think about it. A rancher can't make a living if he can't do most everything himself." Kurt got his upper body out of the engine. "Try starting it now."

I jumped into the driver's seat and twisted the key. The big diesel growled to life, its usual ferocious rumble was back without any demented soprano additions. Kurt slammed the hood and jumped down, wincing and pretending he wasn't. He joined me in the cab. I pulled into the road without a fight, the steering lively in my hands. We'd be home for dinner soon.

"A rancher has to repair vehicles and equipment, do veterinary work, train animals, manage finances, gauge markets, and about a hundred other things. The more you have to hire done, the less money is left at the end of the year, and that amount can be awfully near zero anyway. So you learn to do it, just to stay above water." Kurt smiled ruefully, his face decorated with a greasy smudge across his nose.

"When I was young enough to have a serious case of hero worship, I followed Cliff around, trying to learn everything to be like him." Kurt laughed. "And then when I got older and developed a bad case of teenaged smart-mouth, he'd give me some tools and make me figure it out."

So that was where he got the hypercompetence. I steered us up the single lane of dirt track that was our road home. "He didn't make you figure it out on the animals, did he?"

"No, he didn't. He coached me or did it with me. Gentling and training the horses was a lot more pleasant than calving season or round-up." A red rag that had been lurking under the seat waved in the corner of my eye; Kurt was cleaning his hands.

"I can imagine." I hoped that when I did meet his family, those last two weren't on the agenda.

"You'll like Cliff. Vanessa too. The kids, well, they're a rowdy bunch, but polite. We'll have to find a long weekend to get up there. Maybe Thanksgiving. They've been waiting for me to bring someone home for a couple of years."

My insides tumbled at the thought of meeting his family, of coming home for the holidays with Kurt, openly and as his partner. And if I didn't—the tumbling turned to gut wrench. "That's a busy weekend for a ski resort. We didn't eat 'til eight o'clock last year."

"Not a problem, it's just a long drive from Denver." He turned to give me the full weight of "this year it's different" with his stare.

But why would it be? We'd still need winter jobs, and Wapiti Creek was right where we'd left it. I didn't want round five, or was it round six of this fight. "There's a smudge on your nose."

He scrubbed at his face. "Did I get it?"

I glanced over, enjoying the sight of blue eyes in his tanned face, but not the storm clouds on his brow. I sort of returned to the topic. "Mostly. Hey—" Given our interesting reception in the bucking chutes yesterday, I wanted to know. "You said he knows you're gay, but—how did he take the news?"

"I was twenty-three when I told them. Cliff was kind of stunned, but he came outside later, just sat with me in the barn. I was mending tack—I needed something to do with my hands that kept me away from everyone for a while." Kurt looked lost in the past. I kept quiet, needing to know how this turned out, not wanting to influence his story in any way.

"Then Cliff threaded a needle for me, and he said, 'You know your father, your brother, and I have tried to teach you everything we can about being a man.' I was braced to hear how badly he thought I'd failed—"

Kurt stopped, and the red rag was back by his face; I didn't think he was trying to get the last of the smudge. "But Cliff just handed me the needle and said, 'I think we did all right.'"

"I think they did a hell of a job," I said softly, taking my hand away from the gearshift to rest it on his knee. He slipped his fingers into mine for the thirty seconds before I needed to gear up.

"They'll like you," Kurt told me, and left it to my imagination about what it would be like to meet my "in-laws."

Kurt's assurances aside, not having to cope with families was one highly attractive aspect of being out in the wilderness. I hadn't even suggested taking him back to meet my family. They'd like Kurt—it was hard not to like Kurt—and maybe they'd adore him right up until they figured out we were sleeping together. I hadn't come out to them yet.

Kurt dragged the nonperishables back to the bear box after dinner, while I assigned myself returning the milk to our "wilderness fridge," which to the untrained eye looked like a large, perforated, plastic carton on a rope. I'd hauled the fridge from its submerged position in the lake before dinner, knowing that Kurt probably could manage a forty-pound weight with the block and tackle we'd rigged, but not seeing why he should have to. I'd made him cook, just so he wouldn't think I was babying him.

When nothing but the ropes to the pulley in the cotton-wood tree and the rock remained visible to show where we stashed the chilled things, I sat down on the grassy bank to look over the water and enjoy the night.

Pines threw their silhouettes against a sky of pinks and yellows fading to aqua where the sun no longer touched. The water lay nearly still, making pink reflections broken into rings where a trout surfaced to take an unwary insect from the surface. Frogs ribbited "I haven't gotten laid yet" from the shore, breaking the light susurrus of the wind moving the tops of the trees. The night would get chilly in the mountains, even in July, but now in the twilight, it was perfect.

The aqua had moved down to brush the horizon, leaving indigo in its stead by the time Kurt came down the path to join me. He said nothing, lowering himself slowly to the ground beside me. I rested my hand on his thigh, content for the contact and the quiet companionship. The frogs complained about their celibacy, which I would heed before Kurt started croaking, but for now it was enough to sit together near the places where I'd offered him every part of myself for the first time, a little over a year ago.

"How can I leave this wilderness one minute before winter drives us away, Kurt?" I spoke to the dancing reflection of the moon in the water.

"By keeping your eye on the larger prize." Kurt rested his hand on mine. "Unless your dreams have changed."

"No, but… I don't want to go yet."

"It gets harder to go back the longer you've been away from it. Trust me, I know."

"How?" I knew he'd gone to the University of Colorado in Boulder. We'd even overlapped a couple of years, although he was an upperclassman then and we'd never met.

"I graduated high school early because I got the offer to join the ski team. My dad tried to talk me out of it, because I had a ski scholarship offer. I could do both, he said—ski competitively and get my education. But Boise State U versus going to Norway and Austria and skiing against the Hermanator and Jorey Taylor? Not much of a contest."

"No, not even close."

"So I joined the team, seventeen years old and thinking I was hot shit, and maybe I was for a while, although I never won a thing, never even stood on the podium." Kurt paused, curling his fingers between mine, squeezing from the top. "And then I had that stupid, stupid unicycle accident."

I refrained from saying that unicycle accidents couldn't sound like anything but stupid, but he'd told me this part—balance training with Jorey. He'd come off a parking barrier wrong.

"No place on the team, no education, no prospects, just a bum ankle and enough money saved to get the education and the prospects. But I'd been away for a couple of years, I'd be older than the other freshmen, I'd this, I'd that…. I tried every argument in the book. Cliff got so tired of it that he threatened to drown me in the stock tank just so he wouldn't have to hear it again."

"How close did you get to the cow-spit water?" I'd been pushing Kurt's limits the last few days, and there was a lake right in front of me.

"I didn't actually get wet, but the whole family finally ganged up on me. They sat at the kitchen table with me in relays until I filled out applications, and made me rewrite essays until they were satisfied to the last comma." He snorted softly. "I would really hate to have to subject you to Cliff, Vanessa, Larry, Polly, and my dad all giving you the beady eye about your education, but I have been trained by the best."

"We aren't going to Wyoming just to let your family

harangue me." Just the thought of meeting my lover's family, let alone his family with an agenda, disturbed the peace of the evening.

"You aren't going to make that necessary, Jake. I want them to feed you turkey and pumpkin pie and see that you can stay on a horse." He must have felt me freeze, because he added, "Someday."

"I'm going back, Kurt, but—"

"No buts." Everything in his demeanor changed—his soft storytelling became contempt between the capital and the period of what he said next. "If your dreams have changed, Jake, say so, but I think you're afraid of the competition."

Kurt had *never* sneered at me like that. Laughed at me, sure, laughed with me, more times than I could count, but he'd never sneered, even when I'd confessed my only experience on horseback had been at summer camp. So taken aback that I couldn't come up with anything to reply, even nonsense, I spluttered, all dignity gone.

"Yup, instead of you being the smartest guy in the room, you're gonna be sitting with a hundred other people who are all used to being the smartest ones in the room. Maybe even smarter than you."

I found my voice, finally. "I am *not* afraid of the competition!"

"Then your ass is gonna be in class in September, and I'll be there when fire season's over."

I wasn't so pissed that I didn't recognize the trap he'd just sprung on me. "I'm going, Kurt, but I'll be even older and smarter next year."

"You'll be one year further from the discipline of the classroom, a year more used to living out in the world, and the young ones who haven't had two years to forget all their organic chemistry are gonna eat your lunch."

I jumped to my feet, trying to leave this idea behind. "No, they won't!" I stood at the edge of the water, secure in my belief that Kurt wasn't moving fast enough yet to dunk me.

"Because you aren't going to fart around an extra year." Kurt spoke from right behind me.

The jolt made me easy prey—one strong hand at the small of my back launched me forward. The water slapped me, sucking me down. Thrashing to find the surface, I inhaled a snootful of lake, choking even after I found the air. I glowered at the Kurt-shaped blank in the night sky.

"Not as gross as the stock tank, but it will do," he observed from above me. "Although I wasn't trying to drown you." He put his hand down to extract me.

I was so mad I wouldn't take his hand. I tread water, hacking and furious. "This fight is not over, Kurt."

"Sure it is. Nothing to fight over. You go back to school, just like you planned, I amble in when the weather turns, and we're all cozy." He disappeared, leaving me to find my own way out of the lake. I wrung out my shirt to dry my hair and face, grimacing into the dark after a man who wasn't there anymore.

Kurt had dripped onto the grass like this when I'd shoved him in the water last year. Of course, he was blatting on and on about us, how I was about to leave him because I couldn't stand that we'd had sex.

I'd been trying to make him shut up and listen to reason.

Kurt would say the same.

I squished back to the cabin, feeling my way in the dark, and took a quick trip through the camp shower. It was still moderately warm from the sun, so he hadn't refilled the cistern from the well, else the water would have been freezing. I'd have to take care of it in the morning, although the hike to the wellhead would have let me put off going into the cabin for a few more minutes. I wasn't so sure I wanted to talk to Kurt again just yet.

The cabin was dark—he'd already gone to bed. Slipping quietly in next to him, I didn't reach for him. He lay on his back, hands beneath his head. Maybe he was asleep. Maybe he was pretending. Maybe I'd pretend for him, and we could start over in the morning with kisses for a new day, and he'd stop leaning on me about school. I stared up into the darkness of the rafters, where something rustled.

"It's not really the city or the money, is it, Jake." Kurt spoke softly into the silence a moment after I'd concluded I was safe from further conflict. "It's not the competition; it's not that your dreams have changed. You're just shoving everything into the future."

I didn't know how to answer questions that weren't really questions, so I grunted something not quite a word.

"But something is still making you hold back. And the only other thing I can think of is that it's me. Us. Well, how you feel about us."

"I love you, Kurt." That was true, now and forever, even if I was angry with him. My wrath was chilling into fear now, and the love might be the only thing to give me a warm core.

"I know you do. I love you too. But letting the world know about that really, really freaks you out." His soft voice in the dark made it just a fact, not an accusation, but....

"I was okay with it in Wapiti Creek." "Okay" was stretching the truth to fit; the end of the season was a lot different than the beginning. I had kissed him under the mistletoe at Christmas dinner.

The brittle chuckle said Kurt remembered the progression of events as well as I did. "You were, sort of, but that was among people we might only know for a few months, people we might never see again unless we made a point of it. Not colleagues that you had to spend four years with."

Not family, I finished in my head.

"I can't make you change how you feel—you have to work that out." The mattress dipped—he was rolling beside me. I imagined he was leaning on his elbow, staring at me in the dark. "I was hoping you'd gotten used to the idea of people knowing about us, but I don't think you have, not really."

Once again he'd found the bull's-eye.

"I saw how you reacted to the idea of Thanksgiving dinner with my family. You didn't even suggest meeting yours. I'm not happy about it, but I understand."

Probably better than most—he'd broken up with someone whose family he'd resisted meeting, about four years before we'd met. I reached over to hug Kurt close to my chest, because words were untrustworthy things right now. He spoke into my neck, kissing me lightly first. My pulse throbbed against his lips.

"But school won't wait. Your whole past built to that, and your future hinges on going. I won't let you throw it away for me. I'm a broken-down old ski racer with a dusty degree in business administration, and I'm not worth that."

"I don't care about that, Kurt."

"I care. If being with me and your future are impossible together, we get rid of one, and it won't be your future."

"You aren't going anywhere!" I squeezed him so hard in my surprise that he squeaked.

"Not kidding. If an embarrassing boyfriend is the only

thing standing between you and your plans, we get rid of embarrassing boyfriend."

"Oh no. No." I did not want to envision a life without Kurt. Years of studying took on a new hatefulness if I had to do them alone.

"I don't like that either, Jake, but if I'm hanging around trying to look like a roommate, sooner or later we're going to slip. Maybe if we dated girls casually or something, or if we didn't live together, but I don't see how else to do this." He held me a little tighter.

"You're breaking up with me over school?" Just saying the words gave them a horrible reality.

"I'd come crawling back around Halloween, see if you felt any differently then, but… yeah. I think I am." He tried to get up, but I wasn't letting go.

"No. This is the stupidest plan I ever heard."

He poked my side, expecting I would guard and let him escape, but this discussion made even ticklish sides sober up. I didn't do more than twitch, and he quit struggling. "Worse than your idea about more and more delay?"

Nope. Probably not.

"Jake, you're trying to hang on to three things: your future, your fear, and me. You can have any two of the three. I only have control of one of those choices, but I will not let you dump your future without a fight." He reached up to run callused fingertips across my cheek. "Please choose wisely."

He said no more, but he didn't fall asleep for a long time. He was probably thinking of the same things I was—of what life would be like if I let go of my career plans. Or if I let go of him because I was afraid of showing my real self to the world. But I still didn't know how to let go of my fear.

There's times I really hate when Kurt's right.

SEVEN

Our first kisses of the morning turned into vigorous sex—I kept Kurt pinned with his legs over my shoulders to demonstrate how much he wasn't getting away from me. Not that he was struggling now, even if I was smacking into his ass harder than Midnight Kid.

Knowing that people would look at us and imagine us doing exactly this crossed my mind at the wrong moment. My building orgasm dispersed like a puff of smoke, but I wouldn't say a thing to Kurt—I slid down his body to take him in my mouth, letting him finish with his happy noises in my ears. I said nothing about my own spoiled moment. It wasn't his fault. I didn't deserve to feel good.

"We'll take the Thistle Creek road today, okay?" Kurt threw water bottles and his flat brimmed hat with the blue jay feather into the tanker. "Maybe we can find that blue pickup or their campsite."

It bothered me that we hadn't located our long-term guests in our regular patrolling. The forest was big but not that big. I slid into the passenger seat, parking his hat in my lap. In some circles, a blue feather in a hatband had a very specific meaning. Not that I expected to find a chapter of the Society for Creative Anachronism around here, but that feather said quite clearly, to those who knew, that Kurt was gay. Did Kurt know the symbolism?

Kurt always knew where he was and what he was doing. After three years in Boulder, it was unlikely that he thought the jay feather was merely a pretty ornament. He didn't make a big deal out of it; he just quietly lived as he wanted. Why couldn't I do that?

Heading up the narrow single track, I tried to keep my mind and my eyes on our surroundings. Nothing seemed out of place on the road up to the highway, although we got out of the tanker three or four times to scan the distance, enjoy the view, and kiss each other at the tops of the ridges. Nothing seemed to be on fire today.

"We're headed toward Rendezvous Lake Lodge," I pointed out, right after my stomach grumbled. The sandwiches would keep until dinner, and our buddy Max might have some of his smoky, tangy ribs ready for lunch. As a matter of fact, I thought Max, whose role in this area was "news bureau," might have some information to share about our mystery truck. Quite as important as the ribs.

"So we are," Kurt agreed, and the family camping with two kids was a temporary hindrance. We stopped to chat—best to know who was running lose in our woods doing what.

Their campsite was far enough away from the stream that the couple had to have read the forest rules; we didn't have to measure to know the tent was at least 120 feet back. No horses to worry about, and nothing wheeled like an all-terrain vehicle either, to grind tracks into turf that was more fragile than it looked. The parents were friendly, but the kids....

The little monsters thought it was great fun to try to play "stump the ranger," although if they didn't know the answers, they wouldn't know if I was spinning a little BS. "What's this?" the freckle-faced boy wanted to know, pointing at a thistle, and "What's that?" from the slightly smaller girl made me think. I wanted to call the plants weird names like "lady's fans" and "speckled hogwort," but Kurt, who had a little more patience and a lot more knowledge, identified half the meadow for them before calling it quits.

"There isn't one here, but we saw it while we were hiking farther up the valley," the mother told us. "What local flowers are red? We saw quite a lot of them."

"What shape were they?" I asked, trying to look useful here. That was always the first question Kurt asked me when I needed information. "Spiky is probably paintbrush."

"These were more cups," she said, wrinkling her brow. "They almost looked like they should be in a garden."

"Copper mallow?" I guessed. Kurt nodded—always good when his first thought matched mine.

"Thanks. That gives me a place to start looking when I find the field guide." The look she gave the tent said the zipped hatch concealed chaos. I wished her luck finding the guide, the bug spray, and the sunscreen.

Max, proprietor of Rendezvous Lake Lodge, our friend, and the maker of the best ribs in Colorado, had information to go with the platters of meat. He sat at the table with us for a few minutes, enjoying the way we tucked into his good cooking. If we hadn't had an audience, I'd have made love to that rib with my mouth, just for the pleasure of making Kurt crazy, but diners at other tables shouldn't be privy to that. Max, either. Just because he'd caught Kurt and me in a semibareassed situation when he'd come to rescue us after the fire last year didn't mean he needed a more graphic statement of what we were to one another.

I often wondered what Max had thought when he and the horses had come along about the time Kurt went to the mouth of the cave without a stitch on. I'd scrambled into my clothing before coming out to greet our rescuer. Max had never said a word about it. For the man who was "information central," this was either incredible restraint or total obliviousness, but either way, I was grateful that he hadn't spread his suspicions around —that I knew of.

Just because I wasn't being deliberately provocative with a long, hard, delicious bone in my mouth didn't keep me from closing my eyes to better savor the rich meat with the crisp edges and piquant sauce. If this was his last meal, then the condemned man would die happy. Sex on a plate, that's what Max served us. A little moan escaped me. Right in the middle of Kurt's question.

"Have you seen a medium-blue pickup around?" Kurt paused with a rib hovering before his lips. "Dodge, looks like midnineties, with a big scratch on the driver's side?"

"Sure." Max handed me a napkin. "They've been in a couple times. Two guys, wanted to fill a propane tank and eat. Except… nah. Two men. They didn't make trouble, paid cash, got some sundries at the shop. Just campers, I thought."

"Could be. We've just been seeing them around a lot and don't know where they're camping." I didn't rush the bite of pork down. "They always seem to come by when we're in the middle of something else."

"I'll tell Carlene to flirt with them a little, ask some questions, if they stop in again." Max only seemed to be everywhere at his lodge; Carlene ran the gift shop, cleaned rooms, and had an underactive tact gland. She'd driven Kurt and me to a fire site, making rude cracks about us all the way, until Kurt shut her down with a pointed observation.

Kurt must have been remembering that too, because he looked up from his plate with alarm. "If she can be a little less heavy-handed than usual, sure."

"I'll see what we can find out." Max stood and pushed his chair against the table.

We finished that meal in reverent silence punctuated by the sighs and *mmms* that tender barbecue and crisp coleslaw deserved. Maybe I could talk Max out of a pint of sauce that Kurt and I could enjoy in private. We waddled out of the dining room with full bellies and peaceful hearts, ready to top off the tank at the lake's edge.

While the tanker fed from the lake, I trailed my fingers up and down Kurt's back, too sated to do more than lick a streak of barbecue sauce off his cheek. A canoe *whished* by, propelled by a man and a woman who understood paddling—they went in a straight line at steady speed, dipping their paddles first on one side and then the other. I pulled my hand away from Kurt's back, wondering if they'd seen the licking.

"They don't know us, we don't know them. It's not a big deal, Jake." Kurt's shoulders stiffened, and he froze with his head turned slightly. Guess he'd wanted to turn that lick into a kiss. So did I, but all I did was stroke one more length of his spine. He relaxed under my hand, and then we broke to shut off the pump and stow the intake hose. We climbed back into the tanker and set off into the wilderness.

Kurt drove fairly slowly, letting us scan the horizon line for smoke and the forest for anything odd. An entire afternoon went by, with chirring of locusts and the calling of the ravens and jays following us every time we got out of the truck to hike to a vantage point. We didn't see anything unusual until we decided to make one last pass down a fire road headed into the Flat Tops.

"That path looks fresh." I pointed out a track into the brush where the grass bent down. "Think the elk found a new route to water?"

"Let's check." Kurt stopped the tanker as far to one side of the road as he could, which didn't leave a whole lane open. Anyone who came by would have to either wait until we returned or risk their paint. "Grab the shovels."

Just in case. I would have felt better with a .44 caliber weapon. That trail could have been made by a bear.

We picked our way up the path through juniper and gambel oak higher than our heads. The elk hadn't been doing their job of keeping the gambel oak nibbled down—why did they shun a stand of luxuriant growth? "Um, Kurt…?"

The path widened into a clearing, blazing with flowers. Reaching past our knees, bobbing in the light breeze, the field of blooms stretched a quarter mile to distant evergreens. The land might have been painted with blood, splatters of red atop the ground, undulating as if the earth breathed.

"Weird. Wonder if this is what those campers saw? They certainly aren't copper mallows." I leaned to feel the silky petals. "So many."

"Flanders fields," Kurt murmured.

I cocked an eyebrow at him. "What?"

He looked at me as if I'd grown a second head. "I thought you were an educated man, Jake." His voice went lower and came out with a catch.

In Flanders Fields the poppies blow
Between the crosses, row on row
That mark our place; and in the sky

The larks, still bravely singing, fly
Scarce heard amid the guns below.

We could hear larks' song from somewhere in the poppy field—the hairs on the back of my neck rose with his words.

We are the Dead. Short days ago
We lived, felt dawn, saw sunset glow,
Loved and were loved, and now we lie,
In Flanders Fields.
Take up our quarrel with the foe
To you from failing hands we throw
The torch; be yours to hold it high.
If ye break faith with us who die
We shall not sleep, though poppies grow
In Flanders Fields.

He stroked the red petals on the thigh-high plants and dashed a hand across his face. "I never could recite that without choking up."

"I don't think I could either. What is that?" I came to rest my hand on his shoulder. He hunched to hug it between his cheek and his shoulder but straightened again, his hands full of the scarlet cups. A bee flew toward one of his flowers, and he released it, making no impression on the insect, which dived into the wreath of stamens. The poppies swarmed with bees, making a faint moving cloud over the flowers. Bee heaven. I wondered if the pollen narcotized them at all. Was poppy honey a controlled substance?

"Did you never see the old soldiers wearing poppies on Veterans' Day?"

I shook my head, but his eyes were on the flowers—he couldn't see. "I don't think so."

"The World War I veterans are all gone now. When I was in grade school, we'd do programs with tottery old men as guests of honor, recite this poem. You never did?"

"No."

"Must be a small-town thing then, where the American Legion and the Veterans of Foreign Wars sponsor half the activities. I never knew why poppies grew on the battlefields and in the graveyards."

"*Papaver somniferum*, it grows well in disturbed ground and in many soils. The sap yields not less than 9.5 percent opium, which is a Class II controlled substance. Same for poppy straw, which is all parts of the plant aside from the seeds, which are useful as a food source." It was my turn to recite.

Kurt snapped to attention. "Where the hell did *that* come from?"

Given our recent fights, I didn't really want to admit what I'd been reading, but this was Kurt asking. "Um, *Remington's Pharmaceutical Sciences.*"

Kurt turned around to smile approval. "So you have been studying. Good. You'll need that somewhere in the next few years."

Two thousand tissue-thin pages had more information than my head could contain—I had been reading, skipping from topic to topic, worrying about committing the monstrous thing to memory. A reference book meant you could refer to it, I hoped. "Battlefields and burial grounds qualify as disturbed land, I'd think."

"Oh, yeah." Kurt frowned at the bobbing blossoms. "Prickly poppies aren't *papaver* species. *Argenome, Argemone,* something like that. They're white, and the foliage is different, not so long and stringy. California poppies are ankle height and yellow. Jake, I think we have an invasion here."

I cleared my throat to get the words out. "We have a bigger problem than that. The damned things are blooming. We're going to have sappy seed pods from here to the tree line in a month, and there's only one reason anybody wants this many poppies...."

My shovel might as well be made of toilet paper for all the use it would be as a weapon. I'd rather meet up with a bear right now instead of the people who planted their enormous cash crop in my wilderness. "Kurt, let's get out of here."

EIGHT

Kurt didn't waste breath agreeing with me—he took three steps back up the path and then left it, motioning me to follow. He stepped carefully, crushing as few plants as possible with each step. I followed suit, trying not to create a trail that anyone could follow. With every sense prickling, I picked my way between the gambel oaks, mentally cursing the elk that hadn't reduced the brush to manageable heights. On the other hand, my head wasn't sticking up above the vegetation like a target.

The bees seemed to move along with us—I had to steel myself not to swat at them. They didn't seem interested, so if I refrained from aggravating them, they'd probably refrain from stabbing me. Kurt puffed one away that flew too close to his face, but didn't react to our escort otherwise.

A couple of deep woofs from somewhere behind us made us both look around and pick up the pace. Any dog that went with a bark that deep had to be the size of a moose. If it had a human with it, I didn't want to meet the guy. And if it didn't....

No wonder the elk didn't forage here with the Hound of the

Baskervilles guarding the farm. I hefted the shovel like a base-ball bat, wondering when the beast was going to come through the undergrowth. With one eye over my shoulder, I followed Kurt on a route I thought ran parallel with the road and toward the cabin.

"Are we going to hoof it all the way back to camp and come back for the tanker with a squad of DEA agents?" I named the group I thought most likely to have jurisdiction.

"We could." Kurt ducked sideways, away from another bee. "But if nobody's lurking, I think we could just drive it away, and we've never seen a thing."

"Could we maybe move two shrubs closer to the road and get out of the bee highway?" The damned things were even thicker here than at the poppy field. I wanted a netting to hang off the brim of my Aussie bush hat.

"Hive's probably close." Kurt edged between two gambel oaks.

I peered around, trying to see where the hive might be. Kurt backed into me while I had my back to him. We both grunted, trying to keep the surprise from getting any louder, although my heart played kettledrum in my chest.

"Found the hive." Kurt backed up another few steps. "So did the bear."

Perfect. Hazards on two sides, possibly three. The fourth side opened to a long way to anywhere. Maybe we could use it to go around. Except we might not be past the poppy field. Choking the grip on my shovel, I whispered, "I don't hear the dog."

The bear was probably too involved with dinner to bother us if we didn't look like competition or a second course. If honey and grubs could keep it in one place, we'd go around and everyone stayed happy. Around meant find a break in the trees, but the way we'd come hadn't had a lot of openings. It did hide us from the road, though, and even if the brush was scragglier, ranger-green clothing would blend in until we moved. I led us back through the narrow path we'd come, all of four steps.

The dog blended in pretty well, too, until it growled. I stopped short.

"Kurt." I couldn't take my eyes off the tan-and-white beast that seemed to be all teeth. "Dog."

"Shit."

Holding my shovel blade forward, I peered beyond the dog, ready to slice if it moved. I couldn't see anyone following it, but I hadn't seen the dog either until I was much too close. It growled again, swelling to about twice its seventy or so pounds.

"What do we do?" I didn't have enough room to swing at it, and would have to advance another four feet to reach. Sounded like a terrible idea to me. The dog and I regarded each other balefully. I thought alpha thoughts for domination and wished I could run.

"Sit."

The dog didn't sit.

"Sit." I tried putting more authority into my voice. Maybe it hadn't been trained in English. "*Siéntete.*" I tried the one other language I knew. The dog either didn't know the word, or wouldn't take an order from me.

"Back up." Kurt put his hand on my shoulder, guiding me. "Don't swing yet. There's a break where I can get to the side."

With every step backward, the dog marched forward an equal amount, lifting its lip with every warning grumble. It didn't close the distance—it would probably do that in a rush. Maybe it wouldn't. Yeah, maybe it would forget all about us and snap at bees instead.

I wish.

The monster advanced on us as we crept backward. The break in the brush felt about a mile away—with every sneer and growl that dog taunted me with the knowledge that it could rush me at any moment. The sweat ran down between my shoulder blades; another trickle dripped beside my nose. I wouldn't wipe it away. I would do nothing that took my eye off that damned dog. Too many muscles on that mutt, and too many teeth, and too big a sense of my vulnerability. Only Kurt's hand on my shoulder, guiding me, kept me from breaking the tension with a yell and a swing. Another bee flew past my face.

"Almost there, Jake." Kurt's shovel blade swung into position above my head. "Pull to the right, make it go past you. Ready?"

Ready to scream, yeah. "Ready." I took a firmer grip on my weapon and challenged the dog. Shaking my shovel, bellowing, "Yeehaw!" I hurled myself sideways into the branches. The dog leaped at me, jaws wide. I smashed my shovel into its side. Kurt slammed his shovel down in an arc. He struck the dog's back end. The monster ran past us, snarling and slavering.

It wanted to turn and savage us, but a shaggy brown arm flashed out. Scimitars at the end ripped tracks into the dog's side; blood flew. A dreadful ululation filled the air, with yelps and squeals from our attacker.

We didn't stay to see the end of that unequal fight—the bear and the dog could hash it out. We ran.

Through the brush, toward the road, Kurt one step ahead of me. The noise stopped abruptly. I didn't want to imagine why; I was just glad that it wasn't me or Kurt lying slashed or chewed, leaking our lives into the ground.

Kurt halted us a few oaks shy of the road, putting his finger to his lips. I tried panting quietly, enough adrenaline coursing through my system to fly me jet-pack style back to the cabin.

We froze, trusting to ranger green and immobility to hide us. The crunching of tires on the road made me want to throw myself flat to the ground, but Kurt remained still. I struggled to do the same.

The oaks weren't so thick as to keep us from seeing the road from our hideout. The blue pickup we'd sought earlier went past, backward this time, with only one man visible through the open window. With one elbow hanging out the window, his head out and bent around to see his road, the driver didn't seem to notice us in any way. Perfect. Where this guy might go was a separate problem—maybe he'd back up until he hit a turnaround or a side road, although if what he really wanted lay farther up this way, he'd be back. Maybe he thought he'd find an opening in the high brush and come around us, blazing his own new trail. We could write him a citation for that, get his info, and pretend we knew nothing else about him. Then we could turn it over to the Chief and the feds, and let the folks with the big guns take care of the larger problem.

Or we could find one of those wide turnarounds ourselves, and go patrol some other section of forest while the Drug Enforcement Agency mobilized. That sounded really good. We'd MacGyvered a solution to the attack dog, but I had no illusions about being able to take on the sort of folks who'd leave that beast to defend the fields. Six acres of poppies was more than enough reasons to put snoopy rangers in the ground.

The truck receded into the distance, the sound growing fainter. I dared move, putting one arm around Kurt's shoulder. "Still intact—that's good." I felt a little wobbly and was content to stand for a moment, treasuring the absence of large animals and angry men. "Took us a little close to that bear, huh." It could have reached out and clawed Kurt—he had to have gauged our distance to the micrometer, or considered the bear the lesser threat.

"Had to." Kurt slipped his arm around my waist. "It was busy with the hive and wouldn't have looked up if we hadn't practically thrown the dog at it." We leaned against each other, too wrung out to move for a moment.

"You and bears." I shook my head. Last summer Kurt had tried to drive away a bear intent on raiding our supplies. That bear, possibly the same one, had been completely unimpressed with Kurt's cussing and rock throwing, though it hadn't cared for me rushing it from the safety of the tanker, honking madly. Nor had it liked getting soaked with the high-pressure hose. We had all the same weaponry now, up the road and out of reach.

"Think the coast is clear?" I eyed the sky, still blue but with a front of storm clouds to the northwest.

"Let's stick to cover and be sure." Kurt started us up with a brief kiss and a little swat on my butt.

We picked our way single file through the tall brush, ready to freeze at any noise. Once I thought I heard a sound, but it was only the squawk of a jay. We picked our way out of the thicket into the road behind the tanker, rather than proceeding all the way to the path that had attracted our attention to begin with. I was just as glad—that path might have been booby-trapped, something we'd had no reason to suspect an hour ago.

"Think he did anything to the truck?" That horrible idea put a lump of ice in my gut.

"No way to know if it's not obvious." Kurt shrugged. "We don't even know for sure if the pickup is involved."

"Hard to imagine it isn't."

The tanker looked untouched, no compartments open, the water tank as full as we'd left it. No handprints in the fine beige road dust covering the forest-green hood. No sense in fighting the undergrowth on the passenger side door—Kurt and I would both swing in the driver's side. I pulled open the door, ready to slide past the floor mounted gearshift, with Kurt right behind me.

A gun barrel pointed directly at my nose. "Stop. Don't give me an excuse to shoot."

NINE

The muzzle looked about three feet across at close range. The man half lay on the seat, half crouched on the floor, pointing sure death at my face. I froze—Kurt froze. I wished he'd run. I'd take my chances with the guy's reflexes if Kurt would run. Around the truck, melt into the woods. Use the time before the guy could disentangle from the gearshift.

I was never going to leave the tanker unlocked again. It might not matter. Kurt didn't run.

The man hauled himself up from the floorboard, the cannon in his hand pointed steadily at us. "Get in. We have places to go."

I couldn't move. I couldn't come closer to him, to the death he carried.

"The less you piss me off, the longer you live." He motioned with his free hand. "Get in, both of you."

Kurt broke my indecision with a pat on the back. My arms and legs were made of wood, but I hauled into the truck. Not good. We shouldn't do this. Kurt should run. I was toast, and too close to the gun, but Kurt could run.

Kurt wouldn't leave me. He swung into the driver's seat. "Bit extreme, don't you think?"

"Maybe." The man, dressed in camo pants and a gray athletic T-shirt, turned slightly, enough to point his pistol at my ribs. "Maybe not. What had you so interested out there, ranger?"

"A bear." Kurt spoke the half-truth without a hitch. I couldn't have done it—most of my brain was focused on the pistol, inches away from my skin.

"What about the bear?" the man asked.

"It found a hive of wild bees. It'll stick around 'til it's cleaned out the goodies. We try to keep track of the superpredators in the forest." Kurt spoke straight ahead.

The superpredator I worried about most sat next to me. He didn't seem reassured by Kurt's story.

"Took you long enough."

"You try following a trail of scat and broken branches backwards."

"What else did you see, ranger?"

"Not a lot. The gambel oak's pretty tall around here. Lost the road for a while."

"You found it now, pal."

"Last thing we told the Chief was where we'd stopped and why. We need to call in, or he'll think the bear got us." Would the threat of reinforcements make any difference here? I had to try.

As a bluff it was both reasonable and weak. The handset to the radio didn't cling to its hook on the dash.

"Too bad. Drive." The gun's barrel didn't waver from my chest.

Kurt started the engine and eased the truck into first. I could practically hear him thinking about knocking the gun away from me when he reached for the gearshift. Our captor did too.

"Don't even think about it."

The first fear passed, leaving me a little shaky and with a growing rage. Could I disarm him without one of us taking a large-caliber bullet in a vital spot? And nowhere he'd take us would be safer than where we were right now.

The road had enough ruts that Kurt wouldn't have tried to accelerate past twenty-five miles an hour anyway, but he crept just fast enough to hit every rut with a bone-jarring thump. None of us were buckled in, and the gunman's aim wavered with every jerk. I tried not to look at him or his weapon but still track which way it pointed. Kurt had to be jolting us around on purpose—my kidneys might come loose before our captor ever fired a shot.

Kurt took one deep rutted section at an angle that put the medium-duty truck at least two inches into the air with three tires. I saw my chance.

Lunging, I slapped the gunman's arm forward. He fired—a huge spiderweb crazed the windshield. Crackles mixed with the gun's report. He fired again, struggling to bring his firearm in line with us. Kurt hit the pedal, making the truck leap forward, twisting us back and forth, hurling me against first the gunman and then Kurt. I wrestled with our assailant's arm, throwing an elbow into his face. His nose yielded—I hoped it hurt like hell.

I forgot danger came in both hands. The guy rabbit-punched me, taking a kidney shot when the tanker flung us toward the dash.

My spine bowed, flinging my head up with the pain. I lost hold of his arm. The gun flashed toward my face, a murderous blue-gray blur. Agony exploded through my eye and nose, and then again through my temple.

"Stop!" he roared.

I could do little through the haze of red throbbing through my head. Kurt hit the brakes, grabbing at me to keep me from flopping into the dash. The truck settled back, taking me with it.

"Get this through your thick skulls—I can drive this rig myself. I don't *need* either one of you alive. One of you will do for now. Dropping both of you would probably save me some problems."

Through the eye not rapidly swelling shut, I could see his gun pointing at Kurt. Not for the world would I provoke this man into shooting Kurt.

"So drive, and drive like you actually know how." He felt at his nose with his free hand. "Can't blame you for trying, but don't do it again, because now I'm pissed."

We didn't dare say anything on the endless journey up the single track. When we got to a curve around the base of a flat-topped peak, a turn we'd taken a hundred times in the last two summers, he stopped us, pointed straight into the brush.

"You"—he flipped the muzzle of his gun toward Kurt—"get out and get that tree out of the way. Hero here will pull the truck forward, then you put it back and get in."

Run, Kurt! I wanted to say in his pause, but he lifted the gun to my face.

"And if you don't, Hero here loses some teeth."

Doing exactly as he was told, but keeping one anxious eye on the truck, Kurt found one gambel oak that wasn't anchored to the ground. It didn't look dead; it had plenty of green and was as crisp as its neighbors. If it had been cut more than three hours ago, it should be wilted, if not shriveled, but no, it looked exactly like the rest of the shrubs.

The gunman slapped my shoulder—*get over.* The pistol

followed me the eighteen inches across the bench seat and behind the wheel. I didn't know if he planned to hit me with the gun again or use a bullet if I disobeyed—if I knew where we were going, I'd ram forward as fast as I could, leaving Kurt to fade into the bushes. A dead man's foot held down an accelerator as well as a live man's, if you jammed it properly.

Kurt would either get home or last as long as it took a second guard dog to find him. Or come after me like the cavalry. I pulled the tanker through the break in the trees.

"Pretty good disguise." Kurt eyed our captor warily, as if he'd hit me again while Kurt's back was turned.

"We know a thing or two about camouflage. Get in."

Less than a few hundred feet past the barricade lay a campsite so established that my first instinct was to roust them for having stayed more than two weeks in one spot and too close to water to boot. A stream ran beside the four tents, each large enough to hold four. They were pitched around a fire circle that held a propane stove. That partially explained why we hadn't found the site or the men just from the traces of smoke, although the well-cloaked path had done its job. Brush gave way to tall spindly pines growing too close together to bush out. Stumps cut flush with the ground showed where the campers had modified the landscape in another unauthorized way. Somehow I didn't think we'd ever take them to task for these particular alterations to the forest.

Kurt pulled the tanker beside a tent, aiming between trees.

The growling engine drew two more men, both armed, one with a handgun just as large as the cannon now pointed at my face, the other with a small semiautomatic rifle. The clip looked too long for the gun.

"Get out, and don't do anything stupid. Drop the keys on the floor."

Too late—we should have abandoned the tanker and walked back to the lodge, so anything stupid was now entirely a relative thing. We'd known two men went with the pickup and had seen one drive away. The other two were a truly unwelcome surprise, although Max had sounded doubtful about his head-count. Maybe because they were dressed like our captor, in utilities and T-shirts, and had hair clipped nearly as short.

The keys jingled behind me. "Hands up."

We slid out the driver's door, into the forest of weapons. Kurt looked calm—I tried to, but my new understanding of "shitting yourself with fear" probably showed. I clenched my ass and told my guts to calm down—either we'd be dead soon or we wouldn't, but humiliating ourselves in an animal reaction wasn't on the schedule. Our captor prodded me in the spine with the gun's muzzle. I didn't need the reminder.

"What did you catch, Sarge?" The man with the handgun grinned unpleasantly.

"They find something that don't belong to them?" Semiautomatic seemed to be estimating the scatter of his bullets at short range. My hope he'd take out his pal if he decided to shoot evaporated immediately—our captor slid out of the general line of fire, leaving me and Kurt pinned against the tanker.

"Think so, but they ain't saying. They've seen me and that's already too much."

"We only saw you because you were lurking in our truck." Could I get them to fight amongst themselves? Anything to improve the odds, which were rapidly going down. The hitch in my voice probably didn't help.

"Shut up. What are we gonna do with 'em, Sarge?"

Sarge looked up at the sky and found too little daylight left for whatever nefarious plan he'd been hatching. "Tie 'em to a tree. We'll deal with them in the morning when Buck gets back."

"Go get some rope, Tubbs." Semiautomatic told his buddy.

"Go pick a tree, Jonesy. Not too far, but not too close—I don't want to smell it when the ranger boys shit themselves." Tubbs went to fetch, sniffing, "Rangers. Hah."

If I could use my fear as a weapon, I would, but now I was getting mad. Hard to do anything about it with my hands above my head and a platoon's worth of firepower pointed at me.

"And don't hurt them doing it. We aren't animals." Sarge's words weren't exactly comforting.

"What are they, POWs?" Jonesy grumped, motioning us away from the tents.

"I thought we were noncombatants," Kurt countered. "We don't have ranks or serial numbers."

"You're around here and can make trouble—you're combatants as far as I'm concerned." Sarge helped herd us along.

"Since the worst we can do is tell you you're camped less than a hundred feet from running water and give you a ticket for it, how dangerous can we be?" Kurt persisted. "We'd even help you move camp if you didn't know the rules."

"Fuck the rules." The unpleasant snicker behind us promised trouble. "And we ain't moving."

"Hope you've got your latrines well away from the creek, or you're going to contaminate about a third of the watershed in the forest. That tends to bring more rangers tracking upstream, looking for the cause." Kurt's persistence in quoting forest rules sounded completely stupid to my ears, but... Kurt always had reasons for what he did. Maybe making us look rule-bound and not too bright was a survival strategy. Because rangers armed with water sampling kits did not sound like the imminent arrival of the cavalry to me.

"This looks good enough. We can hear 'em if they try anything." Jonesy stopped us. "Hey, Tubbs!" he yelled back at the camp. "Where's the damned rope?"

A few minutes later, Tubbs turned up, cussing under his breath. "All the rope's still in the damned truck. All we got is bungee cords."

"That ain't gonna work, dumbass." Jonesy snarled at him. "What are we gonna do, rubber band 'em together and hope they stay?"

"We could just shoot them. They won't run away if they're dead."

I really hated Tubbs right then, but if the option was to make them shoot us in the back while we ran as opposed to facing them when they fired, I was all for running. They didn't give me the idea that they'd miss.

"Then you'd have to move us, because if you don't, that bear we found is gonna amble right into camp in search of our bodies." Kurt bought us a bit of time with that image, I hoped. "Coyotes, too. Maybe wolves. A mountain lion ranges through here. They all like carrion just fine."

The silence behind us could have been cut with a knife.

"Bootlaces," Sarge said calmly. "Take theirs and tie 'em up. Guess I gotta do all your thinking for you."

"Hey, I want those boots!" Tubbs complained. "The soles on mine are getting worn."

"Blondie here looks like his feet are about the same size as mine," Jonesy said speculatively. "Think we can get the laces back after."

After what, I did not want to speculate, but was afraid I knew. Kurt and I knelt to remove our boots. Amazing what you'll do when large caliber firearms prod you from behind. Pulling the laces out felt a lot like being asked to dig our own graves.

"Sit down, backs to the tree," Sarge directed us, apparently not willing to let his companions do any more of their own thinking. Maybe he was all that stood between us and immediate death, because Jonesy sounded willing to take some risks.

"We don't have to outrun the bear, ya know. Being dead and all, you won't be running too fast, will ya?"

"How good is your camp hygiene? I'm surprised you haven't had visitors already." Fuck. Shouldn't have said that. Now they'd be jumpy, maybe even set watches if they hadn't been already. Ex-military probably did, and these guys reeked of military background. Though when Uncle Sam asked for a few good men, he should have kept looking. Fuck anyway. The watch would probably feel duty bound to stay awake now.

"Shut up!" Tubbs jerked the bootlace tighter around Kurt's and my wrists. "Told ya there were bears in these woods, Jonesy!"

"They're messing with your mind, jerk-off."

Sarge tied another lace to our last free wrists, binding the lodgepole pine between us. The bark scraped my back. "Get their ankles too, Tubbs." To us: "You should be able to lie down to sleep, if you work at it."

We were helpless, but so far, we were still breathing. This might be our only chance to talk them into anything. "You planning to starve the prisoners?" I didn't think they'd hand feed us. Food was the last thing I wanted, but a free hand was much further up the list.

"Waste of good supplies." Jonesy relaxed his stance with the firearm.

"Our lunch is still in the truck," Kurt chimed in. "Nothing out of your supplies."

"We have water in there too," I pointed out.

"How nice of you to bring us dinner, pal." Tubbs licked his lips. "Let's go see what else is in there. Betcha got lots of goodies we can use."

The first aid kit was probably a goner, not that there were any narcotics in there. The locusts would probably strip the truck of everything from the maps to the tin of wintergreen candies Kurt bought me.

"Leave it all," Sarge commanded. "Don't touch it. Don't leave fingerprints. If everything's intact, the authorities will have to work four times as hard to figure out what became of these two."

Tubbs cast Sarge a dirty look. "Send the paladin around the hill so you can loot the bodies," he grumbled, and I still thought the truck would get stripped clean.

"You gonna police us, or make us sit here in puddles?" Kurt made the appeal likeliest to get them to treat us prisoners humanely.

"I ain't fishing your prick out of your pants." Tubbs shot that down.

Jonesy followed quickly with "Me either."

Sarge, who at least had argued against killing us right away, glared at his cohorts. "We'll have something figured out by the time you yell for help."

"Just don't yell real soon." Jonesy shouldered his weapon, handling it much too casually for my tastes. Shooting us on purpose was one thing, but shooting us too soon by accident was another entirely. I wanted to breathe for all of my remaining time.

"Jonesy, you can guard the prisoners." Sarge's military ideas were going to get us killed yet.

"Hell, no. I ain't sticking around to smell his feet." Jonesy aimed a kick at Kurt. I could feel him twist to avoid the blow. "Gonna take all evening to figure out how to decontaminate those boots."

"*Don't* abuse the prisoners!" Sarge barked in a "no possibility of disobeying" voice.

"We ain't in the Army no more, Sarge. You think we still gotta obey the Geneva Conventions?" Jonesy sauntered back toward the tents with the gun pointing over his shoulder, Kurt's boots in his other hand.

Maybe Sarge could only make his restrictions stick so far, but at least Jonesy wasn't hanging around to argue the point. Neither was Tubbs, who marched off with my boots, whistling a tune.

"I suppose you aren't really going anywhere." Sarge flipped the safety on his pistol. "Being as you're a little tied up. And your feet do stink, ranger." He jammed the weapon into his waistband. I could hope he'd blow his balls off, except that would leave us at the mercy of his savage companions. He left us, using the last of the daylight to get back to the tents, where a glow from the propane stove made the beginnings of shadows.

When he was well out of earshot, I whispered, "I had hoped to die in your arms, but not for some decades yet." I looped my pinkies into Kurt's and squeezed. He squeezed back.

"I'm not going to believe we're done until I'm actually on the ground bleeding out." Kurt squeezed again.

"Max's barbecue makes a pretty good last meal." I'd have asked for it if I was condemned. The irony of having gotten it accidentally wasn't lost on me, but seemed inconsequential in the face of reality. My previous thoughts of a condemned man dying happy mocked me.

"Hey." He squeezed my pinkies hard. "Things could be worse."

"Mmm, not sure how. I have a raging headache and can't see out of one eye. We're tied up, barefoot, have about twelve hours to live, and can't spend any of it making love." At least I could touch Kurt and hear his voice.

"The mountain is not on fire, the bears haven't wandered by, you still have all your teeth, and best of all…." Kurt paused dramatically, which I used to contemplate the joys of full dentition and inability to bite the sons of bitches who tied us up.

"Best of all," I prompted him, before frustration took me over completely.

"They didn't search us."

A small bitter laugh was the best I could manage. "Why would they? If we had anything to fight back with, we would have used it while we still had hands."

"We still have hands, Jake. Stuck together, but we have more movement than you might think." He wiggled his fingers against mine. "Once it's fully dark, we're going to see if all those bedroom gymnastics have made us limber enough to get into my pocket. Or maybe yours."

"Mine?" I tried to think of anything I had on me that would improve our situation one bit. No explosives, no guns, no radio, no cell phone, not that there was any reception up here—that was for fancy areas like Wapiti Creek. Nothing but a packet of lube, because we might get the urge over any handy boulder, and a few other pocket things, none of which would take down three armed men.

"Depends on which pocket you keep your buck knife in."

Damn but he sounded smug. Except—"I don't have a buck knife."

The tree shook slightly with the impact of his head against the tree trunk. "That is exactly why you're going to become a pharmacist, Jake. You'll survive a whole lot better in the city."

"Thanks a fucking lot. My Swiss Army knife is in my thigh pocket." I wasn't such a dillrod that I went totally unprepared in the wilderness.

"I should have known you'd be terribly literal about the brand. It's okay." He stroked my fingers. "I'm a little on edge, sorry."

He was still thinking better than me—I was hovering at the edge of the screaming meemies when the anger didn't clear my mind. I didn't want to be angry with him. "It's okay. I'll back off on the literal."

At least he still had enough faith in us getting out of this situation to make a crack like that. I wasn't sure I did.

I had a growing problem too. "Think I need to pee." And of course, once I thought about it, I *really* needed to pee. I couldn't recall how long it had been—hours and hours at any rate. Of course, once I thought about draining the lizard, I was thirsty too.

"Yeah. Let's see if we can get one set of hands around."

We had enough slack to twist our wrists against each other, and with enough writhing, bending, and leaning, we got his right hand to his fly. If that tree had been any wider, we wouldn't have managed. But—

"Stop."

"What?"

"After the big deal we made earlier, we can't do this ourselves. Someone's going to come by to check; they'll be able to smell the pee, and if we aren't wet, they're going to suspect something. Maybe tie us tighter or search us. Or we try for the knife first and wait to pee."

"I take it back about your survival instincts." He sighed, whether from the fullness of his bladder or the prospect of yelling for help we didn't need. "At least they'll check on us when there's nothing to see. I can't wait much longer."

"He might untie one set of hands to let us unzip and then we could overpower him." I didn't have a lot of faith in that scenario, but it was a ray of hope.

"By drowning him?"

"Don't make me laugh, or I will piss myself," I muttered, but it was the first ghost of humor since we'd found the trail to the poppies. Maybe we would get out of this.

We could see the outlines of tents in the light of the lanterns hanging from branches in the camp, and the men moving around. Voices weren't carrying this far against the whisper of the wind in the pines, creaking the tall trunks. An owl hooted softly nearby, reminding me that other predators roamed. We were about to call one of them to us.

"Hey, Sarge!" Kurt yelled. One of the figures in the camp looked up. "We need a hand here!"

"And some water!" I called. If we didn't ask, we wouldn't get.

The laughter bubbling up from Tubbs and Jonesy certainly carried—they hooted at Sarge's errand. "Bet they're gonna love it!" and "Can't piss when you're hard, ranger boys! What's he gonna have to do first?" followed the bobbing flashlight that eventually came toward us.

"I brought water," Sarge growled. "Why the hell can't you do this yourselves?"

"Should have picked a smaller tree," I countered. "We can't reach."

"Well fuck." He aimed a sports bottle at my face, directing the stream of water into my mouth. I swallowed, not too dismayed by the splashing—it felt good. He shared the water with Kurt. I was glad he had the decency to do this much.

"Gotta pee," Kurt announced after his drink.

"Me too." Maybe I could use his buddies' words against him. "You going to fish our dicks out for us?"

"Try not to enjoy it too much." Kurt took a chance with that remark, I thought. "But do it before I piss myself."

"Keep talking, smartass, and I'll let you do it in your pants." The flashlight beam bobbed randomly around us, and then swept the trees more deliberately. "Or we'll find out if you can do it hard."

"Like you're going to make me hard," Kurt gibed.

Since Kurt himself couldn't make me hard right about now, I just snorted.

"I'm going to untie one hand, and you're going to take care of it yourself," Sarge decided. "You can hop over to a different tree and hop back, and if you make even one move to untying yourselves, I will knock you over and kick the shit out of you. Roger that?"

"Roger," Kurt answered for both of us. So much for overpowering him. Not that I could have done much. The world was still wobbly.

I could live with the threat if it meant he wasn't going to handle my junk. A successful attack while we were pointed away from him, bathed in the powerful beam, wasn't going to happen, but just being able to take a whizz was a tiny good thing. Kurt and I hosed down a lodgepole pine. Happiness could be made of very small crumbs in a sea of shit, I decided, shaking off and tucking myself away.

We'd already tested the knots, too securely tied to be

undone in one yank. It wouldn't be a matter of absorbing necessary damage for long enough to get free if we rushed him now—he could have our heads stove in before we'd gotten even one bootlace untied. Hopping back to that tree was the most horrible thing I'd ever done. Every bounce sent swords lancing through the goose-egg on my head, but the true pain was feeling Kurt jumping back into the frying pan with me.

"Sit down," Sarge commanded. "Stick your hands up." He tried juggling the flashlight while he tied and ended up dropping it on my thigh.

"Fuck, man!" A five battery Maglite was no marshmallow.

"Shut up." He whipped the ends around tying, the flashlight on the ground at his feet.

What little resistance I could manage by clenching my fist might buy me an extra millimeter of slack—the lace was snug but not biting when he finished. I had to hold to that millimeter, because I'd just allowed myself to be bound again. Should have taken a dump while my utilities were undone.

"Good night, boys." Sarge retrieved his flashlight to inspect us. "Yell if you see any bears."

I followed him back to the camp with my eyes, the cone of light ahead of him marking a path back to the tents. "Have fun with 'em?" someone called out, but the joke must have grown stale enough that they didn't make any more cracks. One by one the lanterns winked out, leaving the camp dark and silent, except for the groaning of the pines.

"Net gain, I think." Kurt wiggled his freshly retied wrist. "They don't seem to have posted a watch, and we aren't tied so tight."

Unclenched, my wrist had enough slack to move freely within the lace.

"We'll let them fall asleep, and then we blow this pop stand."

The night's soft sounds bathed us—insects hummed in the leftover heat of the day, and small rustlings in the low junipers could have been the deer mice the owl wanted so badly. It hooted again, mournfully announcing its intention to hunt. I peered up at the sky, wanting to see the stars, but the crowns of the trees waved against the constellations. My one good eye watered—I blinked the blur away.

"I love you, Kurt." I wanted to say it now, before we set out on what could be a death march.

"Love you too, Jake." Tiny finger strokes on my pinky were as good as kisses right now.

"Would you really break up with me if I don't go back to school?" We might not have much time left for honesty or anything else.

"That's an argument for another day, Hot Stuff." He patted my knuckle with a fingertip. "First we survive."

"I want to know, Kurt." The ground under my butt turned to cement while I waited for his answer.

"I will do whatever it takes to give you a future." He shifted uneasily against the tree. "Today and whenever."

A night bird cried out somewhere above our heads. "Including running if I get picked off?"

"I'd have to come back for you."

"Don't. I mean, don't do it right then. You keep running, get help, get weapons, and then come back for me. Don't stick your head back into a trap just because I got... well." I patted him. "You keep running. Promise."

"Don't imagine failure, Jake." He swatted my hand, annoyance in his voice.

"Just telling you. Kurt, I don't have binocular vision right now, the world is swimmy, I'm nauseous, my legs are shaky. He hit me a pretty good one in the truck. I think I'm concussed, and if I run into a tree in the dark...."

"Gotcha. But don't. I want us both out of here." He stroked me now, comforting me. "Think the tanker keys are still on the floor?"

I shook my head reflexively, regretting it immediately when my stomach rolled. "No, think Sarge picked them up. Heard it."

"Then we can't just drive out. Damn, I wouldn't have minded flattening a tent or two on the way." He twisted around. "My knife's in my front pocket. Probably easier to get, no flap."

We contorted, scraping against the tree trunk, finding out which direction my elbows didn't bend. With some huffing, corkscrewing, a couple of muttered curses, and a good scrape across the back of my arm, Kurt got his hand into his pocket.

"Got it!" His triumphant cry was 100 decibels softer than the achievement deserved. "Now to open it."

I tried grabbing the casing, rotating it in my hand until the blade side faced Kurt. "Can you get your nail into the slot?"

We scrabbled a bit, fighting the knife with one hand each—it fell on the ground, a sharp *snick* saying we'd been close to success. "Where'd it go?" We patted frantically in the pine duff, leaning to find the precious tool. It had flipped a good foot beyond our reach—we had to scoot until the tree trunk threatened to break our bound wrists when we leaned.

"I have a better idea—just go with me." Kurt lifted our hands above his head. I had to reach back to let him work, both hands behind the tree trunk. I felt like a marionette, but the greasy click of the opening knife and the hushed scraping of blade against bootlace made the lack of control just fine. "I bet all their prisoners escaped."

"If they could undo the knots, yeah." They'd looked tight and secure to me. My right hand suddenly fell free.

Swiveling around on his knees, Kurt made swifter work of the second side. Enough starlight filtered through the trees for me to see a dark stain on his forearm. "How bad did you slice yourself?"

"That's the least of my problems," Kurt muttered, sawing between my ankles. "Now get mine."

The bootlace parted quickly under the blade. "You want to keep this out?" Running with knives seemed marginally safer than running without knives tonight.

"Mm, yeah."

Kurt helped me to my feet. I swayed in place, finding my feet, and suddenly doubled over, vomiting against the tree. Helluva a way to revisit my lunchtime ribs. "Damned head injury. I gotta go slow, Kurt." And hang on to him. Every pine needle, pebble and twig jabbed my feet, some sticking to the socks that were all I had on. Rescuing our boots—not happening. I threaded my arm through Kurt's, a mockery of the wedding procession we'd never have, just to stay upright. A "staying alive" procession worked for me.

We'd taken three steps when warning grunts told us we were going the wrong way.

TEN

"I don't see it." Kurt's low and frightened words put ice into my belly. If he didn't see the bear, which way could we run?

The bear grunted again. Maybe because of my head injury, or maybe because of my fear, the noise came from every direction at once. "It probably didn't come through camp."

"Right." Kurt pulled me backward, one slow step at a time. "Maybe it won't follow."

I didn't have much hope for that, but maybe it would stop to investigate the nice stationary supplies I suspected our captors kept near the tents. Weak knees had to keep supporting me. I stepped back with Kurt, trying to find our pursuer. The grunts got a little louder, and if they sounded more curious than threatening, they were still coming from between sharp three-inch teeth.

The Milky Way cast enough light that we weren't walking totally blind. The moon cast shadows with the high brushes of pine tops, making every dark spot a potential bear. With one eye swollen shut, I hadn't the depth perception to tell animal from shadow—a thousand hunters filled the night.

Kurt pulled me around a tree trunk. "We're almost at camp."

"We have to warn them."

"The bear might leave them alone."

Maybe, if it was full enough of dog, grubs, and honey, but the bear was following us. It *huffed* again, sounding closer. "It might not leave us alone. They have guns." The bear and the men could fight it out while we ran. If I could run. But we could be a long untraceable way into the forest by the time the dust settled.

"Okay. We yell and run." Kurt was really putting a lot of faith into my ability to run.

Run and yell suited me better. The bear sounded about twelve feet away. A tent loomed pale to my right. We gave it wide berth. I gathered breath, and never used it.

I tripped over a tent-rope, pegged ridiculously far out. My yell became *whump*, face down in the pine duff.

Served me right for scaring him earlier—the man in the tent yelled for me. "Bear! Bear!" Sounds of thrashing, metallic *snicking,* and he burst out of the tent. Only to trip headlong over me. My ribs took the blow—my gasp sucked old dead pine needles down my windpipe. Struggling to breathe, struggling to stand—Kurt hauled at my arm.

The camp came alive around us—Kurt got me to my feet, dragging more than lifting. One shot, a second, a flashlight beam swept around, more yelling. "Bear!" A burst of bullets peppered the night.

I staggered after Kurt, leaning on him, choking. The choking churned into nausea—I turned my head, not wanting to spatter Kurt with my weakness. Heaving, bending double, I could barely keep to my feet. "Leave me." I gasped.

"No!" Kurt wrapped my arm around his neck. "Keep going."

Armageddon broke out around us—gunfire crackled on all sides. The bear's grunts became the wail of aggression, maybe pain, its rising shriek high against the muzzle crack. One of those bullets might find us. A man screamed.

"Can't" became a flood of bile. I fell to my knees, nearly taking Kurt down with me. *Go* I gestured, finally finding some air to say the word. "Go, you gotta go." But he was tugging my arm.

"Go!" Another round of puking threatened. "You promised."

But he dragged me to my feet again. "Come on!"

I staggered—he threw his shoulder against my middle, trying for a fireman's carry. Oh Lord, I'd die, drowning in acid, if he made it. I outweighed Kurt by twenty pounds—he knew it —he hoisted anyway. He couldn't run with me—we'd both die. I thumped his back. He straightened and took my arm.

I tried to run—Kurt pulled me away from the noise. We reached the last tent. Empty. No screaming, shooting man defended it. Past it. And one last piece of pine crap came off my lip to sail down my gullet. I fell to my knees, choking, spewing. Kurt yanked my arm. I pulled away.

"Go," I hacked out.

"No!" Kurt spat back. "Get up!"

The yelling came our way—I'd run if the world would stop spinning. I toppled. "If you love me, go."

I could feel his indecision—he had no time to dither. I held my breath, wanting him to believe it was my last—anything to make him leave, to save him.

"I love you, Jake." Then he was gone—I could feel his absence like pressure relieved.

I wanted Kurt to melt into the woods—no matter what happened to me, he'd be impossible to catch. I'd die tonight so he wouldn't die tomorrow. A few hours exchanged for many years. A fair trade.

One I was about to make.

"Here he is!" Someone kicked me in the ribs, driving the air out again. It'd be tedious if it didn't hurt so much.

"Where's the other one?" Another blow caught my thigh.

"Knock it off!"

Did he mean my head? Another foot crashed into my shoulder. A bullet sounded better than getting stomped to death.

"Stop it, dammit!" Sarge. Had to be.

"He led that damned bear into camp. Couldn't even escape quiet!" I could hear the men circling around me. Looking for the best place to kick. My shin. Fuck. World blazed red. Wouldn't kill me, just hurt like hell.

"You run away from bears, asshole. Even him!"

Not now, not with my leg on fire. Not curled in the fetal position, trying to protect my head.

The argument raged over me. Every word was one more breath, one more moment with the pine duff coarse against my cheek. One more moment of agony that meant I still lived. One more moment for Kurt to put distance between himself and this hellhole.

"Don't abuse the prisoner!"

Too late. Someone nailed me from behind. My balls went nova, pain blinding me.

"Just kill him now!"

"Back off, Tubbs!" A shot rang out.

No new agony bloomed. The bullet hadn't gone into me. The pain would stop if it did, right? My gut would quit heaving?

"Do it, dammit!"

"He was trying to escape!"

Jonesy or Tubbs would have just killed me. Maybe Sarge was the only one left with ammo.

"It's his duty to escape and you know it. You know what duty is, Tubbs."

I risked opening my one good eye. Someone loomed over me, his feet bare inches from my nose. I might get my last few hours.

"Fuck duty. Fuck the Geneva Conventions. Shoot the asshole and get it over with."

Maybe not. Maybe just a last few minutes not getting kicked to death.

"No. I'm not going to shoot him just because you're pissed off." The feet shifted in front of me. "Ranger boy ain't going nowhere tonight, and he'll move himself in the morning. Pick him up."

Rough hands grabbed me, hoisting me to my feet and keeping me there. Jonesy, or maybe it was Tubbs, didn't have to squeeze my armpit so damned hard. Didn't take my mind off my balls. I heaved again. Someone grumbled that I'd be less trouble dead. I'd heave on him if I could turn my head that far.

"His buddy'll come back."

"His buddy's long gone."

Lord, I hoped so.

They partially marched me, partially dragged me back amid the tents. The bear lay on its side, fur torn, dark pools soaking the pine duff. Poor bear. It saved us once. It saved Kurt. I loved that bear like a brother.

I would be its brother in death.

"Looks like you'll get your wish, ranger. We'll have to move camp now." One of my captors spat at the carcass.

"We'll throw it in the pickup when Buck gets back. Dump it with him." Sarge disappeared into his tent. A lantern illuminated it from the inside; his shadow rummaged around in a box or trunk. He returned a moment later with something that went *szzzzz* when he tugged. "Hold out your hands."

He wrapped my forearms and wrists with duct tape and shoved me toward his tent. "You stay in here with me." I hit the tent floor with an *oof.* He wrapped my lower legs equally efficiently. "Try and bite your way out and I'll tape your mouth."

My nose was clogged from all the vomiting—I didn't want to suffocate. "Don't think I could."

He tossed the tape back at the trunk. "I didn't think you and your buddy would get loose either." He left, and I was glad of it, because I heard words like "Should just fucking kill him now" coming through the Gore-Tex walls.

I could hear them outside, discussing my fate. Just to be sure, I tried getting my wrist to my mouth. Might be able to get the first loop or two chewed apart, but the wraps closer to my elbows, not happening. I looked around for something I could saw on once Sarge fell asleep. Cot legs, nope, he'd wake. Trunk edge, maybe, but it was behind me. Maybe I could roll over to it. Cardboard box, probably not, and there was stuff on top to wobble and fall.

I still had my Swiss army knife in my cargo pocket, making a dent in my thigh. With my forearms taped, I hadn't a prayer of reaching it.

"Get Jonesy patched up and then get some sleep, men," sounded like a forlorn hope after all the adrenaline of the fight. Sarge returned to the tent. Dimming the lantern until it shed just enough glow to see his face, he reminded me of my helplessness. "You ain't going anywhere tonight." He stuffed a wadded up jacket under my head. "Can't blame you for trying. Can't even really blame you for the bear."

"We did kind of think we could outrun you." Being doomed already let me speak—telling the truth wouldn't stop my breathing earlier than scheduled if he hadn't already put a bullet through me when emotions were running higher.

"So you brought it our way on purpose?" His voice went hard.

"No, just this was the only direction we were sure wasn't toward it." I remembered the predator's noises surrounding us. "We could hear it, but we couldn't see it."

"That's one bear that won't shit in the woods no more." Sarge sat down heavily on the cot, making it creak. He leaned his head into his hands, his elbows resting on his knees. "You did warn us it was around."

"Must have finished off the hive." I wondered what the surviving bees would do. Rebuild in some handy snag or dead tree, probably, and visit the poppies again. I could have used a little poppy myself at that point—everything from my hair to my ankles ached, roiled, or throbbed. I hoped Jonesy needed a hell of a lot of tape. I'd let Doc Schneider know to look out for slash wounds, maybe gone septic, when I went in to get patched up. Well, no, guess I wouldn't. Nice thought though.

"Stupid fucking bees." He shook his head. If I did that, mine would fall off.

"What's wrong with bees?" Sarge had a little too much disgust for honey-making bugs. They'd flown around us yesterday—was it really only yesterday?—without bothering us.

He snorted at me. "I like honey as much as the next guy, but I don't like bees. I'm allergic."

You never have a bee around when you really need one. Except if Sarge was swelling up, Tubbs and Jonesy would finish me off as if I stung him myself. "How bad?" Now I began to hope we wouldn't meet any bees in the daylight. Sarge would kill me fast. The other two would probably kneecap me first.

"Need an EpiPen to keep breathing." He stretched out on top of his cot, giving a wary look at the single insect fluttering around the lantern. In nothing but a T-shirt and some boxer shorts, he had a lot of exposed skin, but the moth wouldn't care. It wanted the light, batting against the lantern again and again.

"That's too bad. There's a lot of bees in this section." In the future I was supposed to have, I'd be standing up behind a counter wearing a white dispensing jacket, counseling him on proper use of the epinephrine injectors and about keeping an eye on the expiration dates. Sarge was keeping my death from being too soon or too messy, at least from his point of view, but it didn't make me any more inclined to mention the two EpiPens in the tanker's big first aid kit. Jonesy and Tubbs would strip the tanker tomorrow no matter what Sarge said; they'd recall sooner or later that they really weren't in the army.

He tucked his hands behind his head, watching the moth. "I know. If it weren't for the fucking bees, Buck and I wouldn't need Jonesy and Tubbs."

"Can't get near the fields, huh." Dead man talking. I should shut up. Kurt might pull off something yet. With twenty miles in the dark, barefoot, and no radio. He might get to Rendezvous Lake Lodge instead—that was only another fifteen miles in the dark, cross country, over terrain I couldn't recall.

Max at the Lodge had a small arsenal and phones—except he'd probably talk Kurt into mounting a two-man assault before dawn instead of calling Sheriff Dodd. Max was the practical sort; he'd figure removing these three and hiding the bodies in the woods would save all sorts of taxpayer dollars. Then we could explain, "Gee, Mr. Drug Enforcement Agency Man, sir, we found this here field of poppies growing all unattended…."

That'd be a lovely problem to have. Delirium was setting in.

"Thought you saw the poppies. Your buddy almost had me convinced you didn't." He left off watching the moth to stare at me.

"I'm dead anyway," I pointed out. "Might as well have an honest conversation."

Kind of too bad I had such a short life expectancy—the nausea was subsiding, my leg was down to a dull ache, my balls still throbbed from the kick but might feel okay by morning, and lots of people got around with vision in one eye. I'd see out of the swollen one again in three or four days, if—I shouldn't dwell on it.

"Death does have a way of stripping away the crap, don't it?" He rolled to his side. "I saw too much death in Afghanistan. Saw too many buddies buy the farm. Or get half blown apart. But death got to be an old friend over there."

There was not one single thing I could say to this.

"We learned ways to cope that don't show up in the handbooks. Made friends with some of the people, doing some good while we were there, and the farmers showed us how to brew poppy tea from the leaves. Could feel good for a while, forget a little, not be too zoned out.

"They didn't grow a lot of opium over there before the US Army came, you know. Just a little, for medicinal use at home. No big fucking fields of opium by the acre. And then we showed up. We had orders not to wreck the land, not to destroy the crops, and they used that to grow drugs under our noses. But some of them shared."

He trailed off dreamily. I wondered if he brewed a little tea even now, if he braved the bees to harvest a few hours of peace.

"Poppies follow war, I think." He knuckled one eye.

"In Flanders Fields the poppies blow / Between the crosses, row on row…." I remembered a few lines aloud.

"You know that."

Even with one eye, I could see he was interested. I remembered another line: "We are the Dead." That wasn't one I wanted to focus on. "Yeah, a little. My partner knew the whole poem."

"Did he now?" Sarge slid down to the ground beside me, making the conversation seem hideously intimate. "Did he say the line about 'If ye break faith with us who die / We shall not sleep, though poppies grow / In Flanders Fields'?"

"Yeah, he said the whole thing. He was thinking about the veterans." I would share that much of Kurt aloud.

"I think we've had faith broken. For the dead. For the living. We're getting fed into a war and for what?" He leaned back against his cot, tipping his head back. "There's no grand idea to fight for in Afghanistan—it's the land where empires go to die. England, the USSR. Now the United States."

Way too abstract for me. "So you learned a few things about farming and came back to the United States ready to share the happy juice?"

He toed me more than kicked me, but prodded his sock foot into my thigh. "Don't see why everyone else should make some bucks and not me. Poppies grow just fine in this country. You just need some out of the way place to raise a lot of them."

Nothing I could say at this point would undo the damage, but he ought to know what he'd done. "Suppose what happens to the people who use the heroin doesn't bother you, but you've really fucked over the ecosystem around here. The forest is going to be wall-to-wall poppies, crowding out the native species. Billions of teeny tiny seeds—those suckers are invasive."

"Oh boo hoo," he mocked me. He patted my shoulder, the derision leaking out of him. "Like I'm going to leave any seed heads around. Too valuable."

"You're putting a lot of faith in Tubbs and Jonesy for that, aren't you?" I shrugged his hand away, reawakening the throbbing in my head with the motion. "They don't seem like the sharpest tools in the shed."

"By the time the seed heads form, there's nothing to interest the bees." He smiled down on me. "Don't worry about your precious ecosystems."

Bees visited the native white prickly poppies too. Could the two breed? Next year the meadows might look splashed with blood.

"I'm not going to grub up my poppies just to please you, but you could make a last request or two." Sarge regarded me curiously, as if he hoped I'd ask for something he wanted to give.

"Untape me and hand back the keys to the tanker?" Maybe he didn't really want to go through with this. Maybe I could miss the trees even without binocular vision.

He laughed quietly. "Nice try, ranger. Has to be something you can enjoy all taped up on the floor. Water? Sandwich? Cigarette?"

"Water." The others were too revolting to consider.

He got up to find a water bottle, which he put into my hands. I didn't try to sit, afraid of stirring the whirlpool in my guts, but squeezed the fluid into my mouth at my own pace, savoring the wetness and clearing out the foul taste. I felt a lot better after half a bottle. I could feel human again. Just in time to feel angelic, probably. But it was a small pleasure I could still savor.

Until I thought about Kurt, barefoot and waterless out in

the night. He'd hike to safety, I hoped, oh I hoped, and maybe any rescue he could mount would be in time. Sheriff Dodd would have his men out in a heartbeat, but did he need to wait for the Feds to mobilize? The national forest might be their jurisdiction. Suddenly I liked the thought of Max, Kurt, and a couple of hunting rifles a whole lot better.

Except I'd never seen Kurt fire a gun of any kind. But Kurt had grown up like a ranch kid. Surely he'd be a good shot. Maybe he had been a good shot once, good enough to overcome a year or more without practice. Getting me back would be an incentive. He'd promised.

Sarge set the water bottle aside after I held it out, unable to drink any more. "Good thing you didn't ask for a woman. They're in seriously short supply out here."

I held on to the water with an effort. The Meeker girls wouldn't have a clue about these guys—I had an awful vision of Lindy at the grocery store offering to sing karaoke at the Flattops Lounge with Tubbs, or Tanya taking Jonesy bowling the way they asked us every time we came into town on our days off. Nothing good could come of that. They pursued me and Kurt more out of habit than a history of success, but they'd be interested in new men come to town. I didn't want them mixed up in any way with this bunch. And they'd flirt, I knew they would. My grimace gave me away.

"Oh ho, ranger, you don't like the girls?" Sarge drew the right wrong conclusion.

I wouldn't give him the satisfaction. He did not need to know one single thing about my life. He did not need a clue of how precious Kurt was to me, or of what lengths Kurt might go to in order to get me back. He hadn't even asked my name. Might make me too human. Might make me harder to kill. Fuck him.

"Sarge, how about I clobber you in the head with a pistol two or three times, kick the shit out of you, and then suggest a woman?" I really liked the shit-kicking part right now. "Your pal racked me pretty good."

"Jonesy is a bit of a hothead," he reflected. "But he kept you from asking for the impossible."

I refused to believe that dying without another glimpse of Kurt was impossible, only impossible for Sarge to provide safely. I wouldn't ask.

He surveyed me, from the crust of grime on my face and the swollen-shut eye, moving down my torso, arriving at my sock-clad feet after about three times as long as Kurt usually took. I didn't like the surveillance, but I might need that last request for something even less pleasant. What the fuck was he thinking? Maybe only wondering how hard it would be to lift my dead body, but there was too much speculation in his face, even if I could only see it in 2-D.

"Bet you're pretty popular with the ladies, being such a long, strong fella. They love the wide shoulders and the muscles."

I got the shoulders swinging an axe. I'd like to swing an axe at him.

"Kind of handsome, under all that dirt. Or you were, before—"

"Before you pistol-whipped me." Let's bring this into the here and now. I jerked back to give him a Cyclops-glare.

"Well, yeah, but you were trying to escape. First duty and all, but we couldn't have that. I could have just shot you then."

Yeah, he could have. I was lying on my side, my bound hands and knees toward him, and the small movement of my head let the bunched jacket unfold a bit. I had less pillow than before, letting my head tip down to the floor. With two-handed awkwardness, I tried to bunch it up again into a semblance of comfort.

Sarge took the jacket away to crush it back into a cushion and replaced it beneath my head. What was the etiquette of this? Should I thank him for making me less miserable than he could? I decided to say nothing. If he really wanted to be kind, he'd give me a lift back to the cabin—he had my keys.

"The options are kind of limited, but is there anything on your bucket list we might be able to scratch off tonight?" Sarge cocked his head at me. "I ain't heartless."

No, he wasn't, but his heart was in a damned strange place. "Can't think of anything that looks possible. Still haven't been scuba diving in Vanuatu."

That's what I'd told Kurt, back when we'd played a variation of this last summer. But Kurt and I were on the same side—our death was burning toward us, the flames licking up the gambel oak and mountain mahogany on its way to our cave. He'd grieved for making decisions that we feared would kill us; I wasn't expecting to die at Kurt's hand. We'd eaten sushi together, just once because it's three times as expensive in a ski resort, which was another thing I'd told him. And we'd had sex, because we both wanted it. And kept wanting it, and wanting each other. I prayed Kurt was safe now.

"Not a chance. But hey, I could show you the secret behind three-card monte or the shell game." He reached up for something on the cardboard box. "Won't take long."

Probably not. I'd let him show off without mentioning that Kurt used three cards to take a hundred and twenty bucks off an Olympic medalist last winter, before the skier gave up in disgust. I didn't listen or watch Sarge's hands so much as think about what Kurt would do with all the wads of cash he'd generated for the "scholarship fund." I could just see him cramming it into some startled student's pocket, saying, "This is your first semester, in memory of Jake."

"Think you could do it now?" Sarge interrupted my train of thought.

Of course I could. I could have done it before. Kurt had taught me, one of the many skills he'd shared. "Not with my hands tied."

"Guess we just wasted ten minutes, then." Sarge put the cards back on the box. "Come up with any other stuff for your bucket list?"

"Dying of old age?" I suggested wearily.

"Oh, ranger." Sarge patted my hip. "You do keep trying." He left his hand on me. I tried to throw it off with a twist. He lifted it away. "Don't tell me you've never thought about it. Never wondered what a man could do for you."

None of his damned business what I'd thought about—I hadn't thought about it with him.

"That has to be on your bucket list, ranger. Finding out what another's man's cock is like."

I could say this honestly. "That is so not on my bucket list, Sarge." Once, but not now. I knew Kurt's body as well as I knew my own. Knew what he liked and how to do it for him. And maybe—one day—eventually—after I was gone a while—Kurt would find someone else who'd love him like I did.

"Sure it is." He licked his lips. "Your last chance. Nobody to know."

"I'd know. That's enough." Maybe I was unbelievably stupid to say this to a man who could make my death quick and painless, or long and agonizing, but it was just the truth. I'd rather go out with Kurt as my one and only.

Sarge reached for my hip again, and this time he didn't back off when I bucked his hand away. "I'd make it good for you."

"Make the sex good, or make my death good?" I'd make him look at it.

"Either. Both." He didn't flinch from the idea—my blood ran a little colder. "I'll give you a good death no matter what, ranger. I said I ain't heartless."

It might not be him doling out my ending. If he didn't back off, I'd yell and make Jonesy and Tubbs come running. How long Sarge's authority would last after that would probably be measured in seconds. They might have two bodies to dump next to the bear's.

Logic before screaming, no matter how dry my throat got. "Damned hard to get it up for a man who plans to kill me."

"See how little you know, ranger?" Sarge reached for my fly. "You don't have to get it up at all."

Oh shit! No! *No!* I pulled my knees up hard, twisting away, the nausea rising again and nothing to do with my concussion. "My last grantable request is that you don't do this." My voice rose a little, and that may have jogged Sarge's memory about other men in the camp, running on as much adrenaline as we were.

He hooked his fingers into my waistband. "You don't know what you're missing. I get my dick in there, bash a little pleasure spot on every stroke, you'll be wishing you did this every night."

"Don't care what you think I'm missing." I scooted backward, away from him, my utilities tenting out where he'd snagged me. "I'm not missing a thing."

"That's because you get some every night?" His eyes went narrow, calculating. "Your partner takes care of you that way, huh?" He pulled at me, making the twill dig into my waist.

"He's my partner," I snarled. "Don't talk about him like that." I writhed, trying to dislodge Sarge's hand from my clothing, and if it made my gut roil, puking on him would cool him down fast. I began to hope all that water would come back.

"Oh, so you're a big old homophobe? Is that it?" Sarge released my waistband with a theatrical lift of his hand.

"Don't talk about my partner," I repeated, not sure I'd won the battle.

"Maybe 'cause he *is* your partner?" Sarge smiled without mirth or seduction. "Your ranger partner and your bed partner?"

"He's my partner," I insisted. Blame the head injury for the lack of originality, but I wasn't going to tell him anything more than I already had.

"Some partner." Sarge dropped his hand in his lap. "You're here. He's not. He left you."

"I told him to go." I'd begged him to go. I'd played dead, though probably not enough to fool him, so he'd go. One of us should survive.

"He left you behind. Hell of a partner."

Kurt would think of something. Kurt always thought of something—he always had reasons for what he did. If he did something awful on the face of it, like going to a love nest for a sex party—or leaving me behind—there was a good reason for it, and he'd make it good. My eyes prickled anyway. He had left me. I'd all but commanded him to go—but he did. I turned my face slightly, letting the one tear slide into the jacket. Sarge didn't get to see that.

"He did what I told him. He's a great partner." Kurt would be back. He had to come back. I didn't know what kind of artillery he'd bring, but if Kurt brought it, it would be enough. He always made it be enough. One reason out of a thousand why I loved the man.

Sarge patted my shoulder this time. "Sure, sure. He's a great partner. Left you behind, that's just peachy." He didn't let go, his grip firm and unyielding. "You know, ranger, you're not in such a great position to object to anything."

I might lose, but I'd be loud in losing, even if he decided to tape my mouth. All the stuff on the cardboard box would fall if I kicked it; the cot would crash. He'd yell if I kicked him—I could flail around. Jonesy and Tubbs would come running, guns blazing, sure they'd find another bear eating us. They'd take it from there if my pants were down. Last resort. Try second to last.

"Sarge, you've shown you're an honorable man. Right from the moment you caught us. You haven't abused the prisoners, you haven't let the others do it. You haven't forgotten what honor is." I tried the last approach before screaming. "Don't throw that away. Not over me, not over something as temporary as an orgasm."

He froze—I had to hope my words found their mark. "Honor. You say the damnedest things, ranger." He removed his hand, cautiously, as if it might do something else he didn't authorize it to do. "Should have gagged you before you started making sense."

He got up slowly, as if he'd aged a hundred years down on the ground with me. He found a blanket to throw over me and doused the lantern. The cot creaked in the dark.

He said not another word, and I had nothing left to say, robbed of words by relief. I wouldn't have believed it possible, but after listening to him move in the dark for a while, I fell asleep and dreamed of Kurt.

ELEVEN

We woke the next morning to dawn light and the sound of a gasoline engine. Sarge was up and shucking into his camos before the engine cut. He left me on the floor, stepping over me on the way out. He didn't speak to me—I suppose I was just so much obstacle now.

Trussed up and stiff from a night on the ground in a fetal position, I seemed to be made of aching concrete. I tried stretching, but working the kinks out works better if you can unfold the kinks. I felt better from the shoulders down, and worked to roll to my knees.

"Hey, Buck," I heard through the tent walls.

"What the fuck happened here, Sarge?" a new voice demanded. "The place is a fucking war zone."

"That's about what happened. I caught the rangers, but one of 'em got away, and not before leading a goddamned bear through camp."

"Shit. We gotta move that."

I hoped they enjoyed the task. A brown bear could weigh three or four hundred pounds. I reached a position approximating all fours, butt in the air. Better straighten to kneeling before Sarge got a look and changed his mind about leaving me unmolested. My head wasn't entirely clear, but better than last night. Not that I wanted to share that bit of news.

"What did you catch?"

That was Sarge's cue to come back and hoist me to my unsteady feet. I wobbled once standing, but more from not moving than from the head injury. He steadied me, and I didn't enlighten him about how much clearer my head was. Wobbling a little more than necessary convinced him I'd collapse if he tried to march me outside with the baby steps the duct tape made mandatory.

"Getting tired of picking you up off the ground, ranger." Sarge opened a knife large enough to make me suspect masculinity issues. Two quick swipes with the blade freed my legs. He let me stretch as much as I could with my forearms still secured, and led me out into the cool morning.

"Little worse for the wear, ain't he?" The stranger, who had to be Buck, inspected me like so much meat. "He won't be a lick of help getting that bear into the truck."

Sarge nodded. "Useless."

I swayed in place, anxious to reinforce that claim. "War zone" sounded right—the bear lay on its side, rivers of blood matting its coat in a dozen places, its belly chewed to hamburger by the hail of bullets. Gobbets of flesh and fur spattered the ground; reddish brown trails streaked the side of one of the tents. For all I appreciated the bear's sacrifice, I didn't want to touch it.

"Well, hell." Buck shoved me aside, bouncing me off the trunk of a pine. "Stay out of the way. Sarge, go get the troops." He stomped back to the pickup.

Sarge didn't take his eye off me, yelling instead for Tubbs

and Jonesy. You bet I would have run. Staggered. To anywhere I could find a broken branch or sharp rock to slice the tape on my arms, and maybe all I could have fought back with was that rock, but I'd go down fighting if I couldn't stay hidden. I just didn't have enough of a possible head start to risk it, and Buck could run me down without too much problem right now. He pulled the truck up by the bear, maneuvering to bring the tailgate square with the carcass.

The men emerged from their tents, rubbing their faces and muttering at Buck, who grumbled back at them.

"Sit down," Sarge growled at me—he had to be certain I wasn't getting back up unassisted, at least not with any speed. I plopped down cross-legged and prepared to enjoy the show. This might be the best part of the entire adventure.

Third best. Best was Kurt getting away. Second best was talking my way out of a rape. But watching those four shitheads struggle with a heavy, leaky, very dead bear was pretty damned good. Laughing out loud could cost me some teeth, but maintaining a straight face while they heaved, hauled, and cussed was likely to strain something internally.

At one point they had the bear's front end on the tailgate, and Jonesy trying to get far enough underneath it (at Sarge's order) to lift it on his back. Bet now he wished he hadn't put so many holes into the animal. The bear hadn't gone entirely stiff with rigor—the body flexed although the leg joints had gone rigid, and the irregular flopping made their job that much harder. Buck struggled to keep the front end from slipping off, losing the battle inch by inch. Until he lost the whole war, and the bear slipped off, squashing Jonesy flat. He struggled out from under the animal, streaked and globbed with its juices, cussing harder and louder than I'd heard in some time. Kind of inventive too—I'd have taken notes if I thought I'd have a chance to use some of those pungent phrases.

Be a pity to explain about a block and tackle now. One rope and three or four pulleys, or something rigged as pulleys, and one man could have lifted the bear by himself, with another driving the pickup beneath it. I settled in for round two.

They finally got smart and used a rope to winch the bear into the truck bed, a few inches at a time. The whole operation took about an hour, and by the end, all four of them looked like the bear had mauled them. Couldn't happen to a nicer bunch.

"Fuck!" Jonesy pulled his shirt off, trying not to wipe it over his face. "That sucks."

"You can stay and clean up. Getting that bear out won't be so hard." Sarge looked from Buck, who was smeared from groin to eyebrows, to Tubbs—no contest who was cleaner. "Tubbs and I can dump the bodies."

Meaning me. Giggle time was definitely over.

"You can get a clean shirt, Tubbs—don't want to attract attention we don't have to." Sarge was relatively clean, aside from his hands, but Tubbs bolted for his tent, shucking out of his shirt on the way.

I had to attract some attention, and now. "Uh, Sarge. Got a problem."

"What now, ranger?"

"Same one I had last night." And not a damned thing I could do about it with my arms sticking up from my chest like a dull silver erection, my clasped hands making a flesh-colored glans. I wiggled my hands slightly desperately—I'd waited for over an hour to be policed.

"Oh, come on." Sarge grabbed my arm, dragging me uphill and away from the water at least. A few trees farther on he scowled at me. "If I'm gonna do this, I gotta touch you, 'cause

I ain't cutting you loose. You gonna call me out on honor for it?"

I shook my head. "Just do what's necessary." I braced myself to be handled, and he didn't make a production out of it, just fishing my dick out of my clothing. I had to stand there for some time, while he turned away and pretended to be unaware, whistling some tuneless notes. He tucked me away unshaken. Can't hardly get good help these days. At least my bladder was empty.

"Come on, ranger." Sarge led me back to the tanker. Tubbs waited at the wheel of the pickup, idling behind the tanker. "Get in. We got a ways to go."

"No last meal for the condemned?" Not that I wanted food just then, but I thought he owed me, even after the policing.

"A quick rap in the teeth will take your mind off your belly. Get in." He held the door for me and snapped the seatbelt around me, pinning me with bonds I couldn't undo.

I'd go down fighting, I promised myself, hating that I was going along with his orders so meekly. But first I needed an opening, and preferably my hands. Something sharp in the tanker would do it, or I could wrench the wheel sideways at an opportune spot. But something, anything, so that Sarge didn't plug me without a fight.

Buck opened the camouflaged gate for us, and we were back on the single-track road, Tubbs following in the pickup. Dimly, I wondered how many times Kurt and I had driven right by the hideout this summer. Not that it would matter now.

Sarge drove my tanker competently, not grinding the gears or revving the engine. Somehow the small kindness to the truck felt like a horrible contrast to what he planned to do to me.

"What are you going to do with the tanker?" Was the GPS still on? Could the Chief be tracking us even now? A forlorn hope stirred that he'd noticed something wrong last night and might even now be joining forces with Kurt and Sheriff D— best not get too excited.

"Gonna hide it in plain sight." Sarge smiled grimly at me. "They find that tanker sittin' in the grocery store parking lot in Meeker, they're gonna think you and your partner are off chasin' women, neglecting your duty. They won't think to look for you where you'll be."

"Where's that?" If I knew, I might be able to take advantage of some natural feature. Something had to be to my advantage, even without being able to run.

"We'll leave you and your buddy Smoky in the White River ravine off the service road. Gotta be able to dump that damned bear direct from the truck bed. Or we'd just plant you for fertilizer." Sarge geared up, coming around the bend to where Kurt and I had first noticed that fateful trail to the poppy fields.

Another fragment of the poem Kurt recited came back to me.

Short days ago
We lived, felt dawn, saw sunset glow,
Loved and were loved, and now we lie,
In Flanders Fields.

Kurt would not break faith with me, but I was fast running out of opportunities here. Was he lurking by the flowers, expecting that's where they'd take me? Sarge didn't pause at the poppies—the plants would keep blooming without his supervision, although a lot of very tiddly elk might be grazing there now that the Hound of the Baskervilles wouldn't chase them off.

Sarge squealed the truck to a halt, flinging me forward—

only the seatbelt kept me out of the windshield. "Goddammit all to fucking hell!" He dragged the gearshift into neutral. "What asshole left this piece of shit here?"

A dirt-colored Toyota blocked the single track through the head-high brush, its hood and trunk up to signal distress. My Toyota.

Kurt.

TWELVE

Caught between the crudmobile, which I would bet good money wouldn't start even if we had keys, and the blue pickup driven by Tubbs, the tanker wasn't going anywhere just yet. Not even the medium-duty diesel could power through the gambel oak on either side of the track. The tall, sturdy bushes would hamper Kurt's ambush, but we'd be there until he sprang it.

Staying the hell out of his way seemed like my best bet, helpless as I was. Besides, once Sarge went slamming out to see how to move the car, I could start sawing the duct tape apart. The hook where the radio handset once hung might be sharp enough, or something amongst the junk behind the seat.... The seatbelt would be no restraint at all once I had my hands back.

"Get out." Sarge unclipped the seatbelt. "Can't leave you in here—fuck knows what you have stashed." Had he heard my thoughts? "Come out this way." He paused with the door half open.

I didn't budge.

"Come on!"

I didn't respond to his urging, but I did when he reached for his pocket.

"I can just shoot you now and it won't matter."

It would matter to me. I scooted out the driver's door and followed him to the Toyota. I could see exactly what was wrong —Kurt had pulled one end of a spark plug wire out of the distributor cap, a trick he'd used once before to immobilize my wheels. I wasn't about to offer any helpful insights—I wouldn't even admit to recognizing, let alone owning, this car. Any hope that showed on my face they could attribute to my extra time spent breathing.

Tubbs marched up to the engine compartment. "What the fuck is wrong with this piece of shit?"

Sarge leaned over the engine, prodding. "Shit. Bet the dumbass is miles away, and I just fixed his damned car. Tubbs, see if he left the keys."

Getting in my car, Tubbs didn't seal himself away, since the windows were down. He disappeared, checking the floorboards, and Sarge went around to the back of the car. He'd have to shut the trunk to be able to back the vehicle up and out of the way, if it would start. I feared for my grill and radiator if they decided to use the tanker to push with the Toyota in neutral if it didn't. I checked from side to side, looking for a good direction to fade into the dense vegetation. Running was still beyond me, and if they just shot me and left my body to lie where it fell, I'd have done half their work for them. Where was Kurt?

"Fuck! Shit!" Sarge flailed wildly. An insect whizzed by, and another. Black and yellow, kind of fuzzy.

"What?" Tubbs popped upright.

"Fuck!" Sarge clanged the trunk shut, still thrashing at the air. He staggered alongside the car, starting to buckle. More insects hovered around him.

"What did you do to him?" Tubbs scrambled out of the car, leaping at me.

"Nothing!" I tried to fend off his blows with my bound hands. His fists crashed against my forearms, missing my face. "Bees!"

"Fuck the bees!" Tubbs swung at me again. "What did you do?"

I knew what the bees did—deprived of their hive by the bear, they'd gone looking for a suitable place to rebuild, and my open trunk must have looked like a safe haven.

"He's allergic!" I dodged again and swung back with my bound arms. The man might die before I could convince Tubbs.

"Bullshit!" He cocked his fist to punch me again. Something sharper and faster slammed into my shoulder.

I fell backward into the brush. Too shocked to hurt—yet—I stared at eighteen inches of arrow with pink feathers at the end.

"Dammit!" Tubbs screamed. He fell beside me, partly on me.

A matching arrow poked through him.

"Jake! Jake!" Kurt crashed out of the brush. "Are you okay?"

"Not." I couldn't get my hands to the entry wound.

Kurt whipped out his buck knife to slit the duct tape. All that silver stuck to each arm was the least of my problems—I had hands again. I touched where the arrow went in. Cotton, damp with my blood.

"Don't pull!" Kurt yanked my hand away. "God, Jake, I'm sorry."

Wouldn't pull. Didn't want to bleed to death. Knew the theory—arrow would plug wound. For a while.

Kurt dashed away and was back almost instantly with things from the truck. He clipped the arrow to about six inches from my skin. He whipped open the big first aid kit. "Gotta stabilize the arrow." He froze, staring in horror at my groin. "Jake, what did they do to you?"

"Nothin'. EpiPen." I could think what else was in there. "Stick Sarge. First." I wouldn't die—yet. Sarge might have stopped breathing.

"Fuck Sarge." Kurt lifted me to sitting. "After what he did to you."

"He'll die." Didn't want that. Sarge had been decent to me. "Stick him. Please."

With a grunt, Kurt yanked out one of the EpiPens and cocked it. He sprang to Sarge, jabbed the needle right through the denim into Sarge's thigh and was back to me in seconds.

"I'll wrap this so it stays." His hands were deft, twisting a long bandage around the arrow and then around my chest, over one shoulder and across my back. "Let's get you in the car."

"Sarge too." I took his hands, but he had to lift me with one hand in my armpit—I shook too much to assist. "Throw him in back."

"Why? Not after what he did to you!" Kurt helped me wobble to the car door.

"Don't wanna lose my first patient." I could hear Sarge rattling, struggling to drag oxygen through a swollen throat.

"Oh all *right!*" Kurt wrestled him to his feet and pretty much dropped Sarge through the car door, pushing his feet in enough to close it. "Him too?"

Tubbs chanted, "Fuck fuck fuck," in a tiny voice, his hand wrapped around the arrow's shaft.

"Him too." I would have helped if I could move.

Kurt practically vibrated with urgency to get going, but he dragged Tubbs to the car as well. "Don't touch that!" he screamed when Tubbs tried again to pluck at the arrow. "It's keeping you alive!" He clipped the arrow short and shoved the man into the car practically on top of Sarge. "In, Jake, please now. We gotta go, now."

I fell more than sat in the Toyota's front seat where he steered me, twisting slightly to keep the arrow away from the seat. I didn't want to dislodge the plug that kept most of my blood inside where it belonged.

Kurt flung the first aid kit in my lap and leaped into the driver's seat, started the engine, and threw us into reverse. "Don't die, Jake, don't die, I'm sorry, I'm sorry!" His chanting seemed to help his skill in driving in reverse, or maybe the smaller vehicle made enough difference, but we scooted backward a long way before he found a place wide enough to turn around. Once he could go forward, he pushed my little rattletrap as fast as he could without shaking me right off the seat. "I'm sorry, I'm sorry, we'll be on pavement soon, I promise, Jake... just don't die." Enough dust floated through the open window that I hoped soon was really soon.

"Don't feel like dying yet." Did feel like wolverines with poisoned teeth were chewing on me, but mentioning it didn't sound productive, not when Kurt kept glancing fearfully at me and mumbling "Sorry, sorry, don't die. Don't let him die." Maybe it was a prayer. He drove with the whitest knuckles ever seen on tanned hands.

"Glad you came for me." If I didn't move much, I was kind of okay. Putting one hand on his thigh steadied us both.

"Told you I would." He took one hand off the wheel to pat me.

"Tired." I meant me, but he looked it too, pale and drawn, his eyes flicking between me and the road.

"You're shocky. I should have laid the seat back."

He didn't stop to adjust the seat, and it would have put me on top of Sarge and Tubbs if he had. They lay tangled in the back, in crappy condition, but both still with us. Didn't know anyone could breathe that loud and not be in a death rattle, but he kept going. One EpiPen for how many bee stings? I wondered muzzily. We had a trunk full of bees getting jounced around. Probably scared and angry bees.

Time passed—how much, I don't know, but the bouncing stopped. Pavement. "Don't die!" Kurt begged me again. "Don't touch the arrow!" he screamed into the rearview mirror.

"How'd you...." I couldn't finish the thought.

"Followed the road," Kurt told me, but I missed the rest, my eyes closing in spite of myself.

Crashing from the back seat roused me—Tubbs and Sarge thrashed. I lifted my head to the sound of Sarge croaking, "Get it off me! Get it off me!"

He threw himself away from the seat back, and a few little shapes hovered in the air. "Bees," I mumbled, watching one get sucked out the open window. Never thought about the crudmobile's trunk being bee-tight. Another bee flew out from behind Tubbs's head—he yelled and swatted at it.

"Might wanna drive faster," I suggested to Kurt, forgetting for a moment about the squirrel-on-a-treadmill horsepower that was all the Toyota could generate.

"Trying." Kurt ducked his head as a bee hovered near his nose—the draft from the open window whisked it out. The next one he puffed away, but the third made him swerve all over the road, to the sound of Sarge's moans and Tubb's swearing.

"Fuck!" Sarge slapped at his neck—a brownish smear marked his skin. "Got... me...."

Um, right, didn't want Sarge to die.... I fumbled at the first aid kit. Should be able to... to... cock it, yeah. I got the outer tube open and dropped the injector in my lap. Couldn't use my right hand to pat for it—that woke the wolverines. Took me a second or forever to find it. Had to pull the safety seal off with my left hand and my teeth. Now what?

Yeah, stick Sarge. He looked kind of blue. I had to lean way over Kurt to jab at his thigh. Missed once, and caught the arrow against Kurt's arm. A hundred angry weasels joined the wolverines. I gasped at them and swung blindly at Sarge's leg. Something connected, and I left the injector flapping from his skin when I couldn't hold it there anymore.

"You're fucking killing him!" Tubbs roared, but Sarge started breathing again, sounding like a thousand pounds of chains in a washing machine. "And you're killing me!" He started pawing at the arrow again.

Hah, I thought. *Like you weren't planning to kill me?* "Don't touch...," I grunted.

"Don't pull the arrow!" Kurt screamed for me.

A spray of blood shot across the car, spattering Kurt's arm, my face, the dash. Fine mist reddened the windshield. I couldn't twist around enough to see, and couldn't reach to do a thing about it anyway.

"Fuck! 'm dyin'!" Tubbs bellowed. Might have been right— the cursing got quieter and soon stopped.

"Sweet Jesus." Kurt hadn't even slowed. I cranked my eyeballs up enough to look at his face. A tanned track dripped down through the red. "I told him not to do that."

I patted his thigh with my left hand, the only bit that worked. "You tol' 'im."

"Don't die, Jake!" he implored me again. "We're almost there."

Almost—tricky concept on fifty miles of dirt track and two-lane country road. I nodded off again. Couldn't help Sarge if more bees stung him—only had two EpiPens. Tubbs—not a damned thing I could do for Tubbs. Not a damned thing I could do for me. And Kurt—all I could do for Kurt was to stay alive. Wanted that. Wanted that a lot. 'F I was asleep, I couldn't pull....

Shouting and tugging roused me—Kurt's voice, yelling my name, instructions. Floppy, can't move m'self. Lying flat, blue going to white, faces over me. Kurt. Where's Kurt? Wolverines gnawing again.

"BP on this one's stable!" Tha's nice. Wonder who. Wanna go back to sleep. More shouting. All these busy people keeping me awake. Touching me. Don't want 'em. Want Kurt.

I woke to a twilit room and a squeezing on my arm. Tight, then loosening, a hiss. Warm fingers on my wrist. Hey, I still had enough vital signs to detect. I was reclined at an angle, not lying flat. Weird. I flexed, wanting to fix that.

"Shhhh, don't move yet, Jake," a woman's voice cautioned me. Who? "Are you with us enough to talk?"

I grunted something meant to be *yes*, but my mouth tasted like they'd dumped the dead bear in it. Trying to work up enough spit to talk wasn't working; the woman held a straw to my lips. Cool water rewarded my feeble effort to suck. Strengthened by the sip, I took another pull, and another, the ursine flavor dwindling, though nothing but a half a tube of toothpaste would really make it go away. "More?" I croaked.

"You need it." She gave me another sweet cup. Never tasted anything better.

I blinked up at her, one eyelid flapping, the other twitching.

Inventory time. Chest, something sticking out of it. Not an arrow. Arrow, no longer sticking out of me. Kurt, not around to explain that one. Swollen eye, still swollen. Wolverines, nibbling, not rending. Hands, free, but something sticking to the back of one. Probably attached to that hanging bag. Clothing, gone. Well, mostly. Side of head, throbbing. Entire body, stiff, sore, able to stretch a little, which let me find all the spots that hurt, which was most of me.

Thought processes, muzzy. I had questions and couldn't remember any beyond "Where's Kurt?" I couldn't even get that much out, not enough air. "Kurt?"

"Still down in the emergency room." At my grunt, she clarified. "We had to triage you guys—with two puncture wounds and one anaphylactic shock to deal with, picking stickers out of feet had to come last."

Nothing worse for Kurt. Good. We'd get back on patrol pretty quick. Wonder how the wolverines would like chopping trees. Bet they'd growl.

"Sarge?"

"Which one is he?" The nurse, she had to be a nurse, adjusted something on the tubing attached to the bag. Um, IV bag. Yeah. More words were coming back.

"Bees."

"Still with us. Full of epinephrine, steroids, and antihistamines, but still with us. Good job from whoever stuck him with the EpiPens—that bought him some time." She reached for something at the side of the bed. "Would you like me to wash your face with a cool cloth?"

"Please."

The nurse stepped to the sink at the other side of the room to dampen a cloth. I looked around, not wanting to move anything but my eyeballs.

Hospital room, not a lot of fancy equipment, woman in a chair sitting quietly. Mrs. Chief. Bless her, she'd answer questions, if I could just get them out.

"'Kay. Cuff him." I ran out of air at "him."

She chuckled. "So your partner said, although he's not much of a flight risk yet."

"Tubbs?" I braced to hear polite evasions or bad news.

"He needed every pint of blood in the hospital, but he's a lucky man. He might even keep his arm." She came back to sponge my face.

Sagging into the mattress, I let her wipe me down. I was so sure Tubbs had bled out in my car. So sure the silence meant a corpse rode behind me. And not a damned thing I could have done to stop it. Not even sure I wanted to. He'd made a good start on kicking me to death—my nuts still ached from his boot. But still…. Didn't want to think about it now. "Cuff him too." I wanted to add "He's a bastard," but the thousand-pound grizzly sitting on the right side of my chest wouldn't let my lungs work.

"He's probably not going anywhere, but I'll mention it to the deputy." The cool cloth felt good.

"Me?" I hissed as she swabbed my eye, but her hands were gentle, and I could open it to a slit when she finished.

"You're going to have a spectacular collection of bruises and some interesting scars. Nothing as bad as what your partner thought." She wet the cloth again and came back for round two.

"Wha'?"

She shook her head, refusing to say more than, "Be glad he was wrong."

Kurt wasn't wrong all that often. I'd make him cough up his

suspicions, just as soon as I got my hands on him. "Head?" *I need that brain.*

"We think you have a concussion. Let's do some checks." She tortured me with a penlight, shining it into one eye at a time, twitching it away and making the purple/orange spots dance. She had to pry open my injured eye, but her satisfied nod had to mean it was doing what it was supposed to. "Pupils equal and reactive to light, always good. Are you nauseous?"

"Not now." My stomach wasn't making evil suggestions about the water. "Was last night." Was it last night? Was a little shaky on that.

"We'll know more once you're able to sit up. You won't be playing football for a while, with or without a helmet." She made a note in a chart. "Or reenacting Custer's Last Stand." She regarded me curiously, as if she wanted to ask for details. Didn't think I was supposed to tell her. Didn't matter, because I couldn't make that many words.

The nurse motioned to my visitor. "Do you know who this is?"

Turning my head enough to look her full on brought a groan—everything hurt, and now I was aware of the pressure of dressings against my shoulder and upper chest and wrapped around my back. I finished the motion with my eyes. "Mrs. Chief." My other mother.

Her strained but hopeful face brightened with a half smile. Lifting my hand was hard work, but I raised it enough that she took it in her own, squeezing me tight. "I'm glad you're still with us, dear."

Finger pressure had to answer—words weren't going to force past the lump in my throat. If not for Kurt, I would be lying at the bottom of a ravine under a bear, never to be seen again. I squeezed again, suddenly grateful to all the aches for reminding me I was still alive.

"I'll stay with you, Jake." Mrs. Chief leaned down to brush my forehead with her lips, making her feel even more momlike. For the third time since I'd come to the mountains, my own mother had avoided getting me back in a box.

I didn't know who I wanted more right now, Kurt or my mother, but if I couldn't have either one of them, Mrs. Chief was next best. Rangers didn't get adopted officially until after their third season, she'd told us last summer. Kurt had asked her once if she'd be his mother. He was eligible now—this was his fourth. I think we might both need her. Who was staying with him?

She added her other hand to our knot of fingers. "You and Kurt are both my boys. Harold's with him now."

Who was Harold? Oh, yeah. Chief. "Good."

"I'll be here until it's time to get your mother from the airport." The simple pressure of her hands would be gone for hours. I held tight for now. Maybe she could send someone else? Four and a half hours each way to Denver—would leave me nine hours holding Kurt's hands. If he'd show up. "Where's Kurt?" Maybe I asked that once.

The nurse pulled the chair closer to the bed. Mrs. Chief sat down without releasing my hand. "Still in the ER, sweetie. Special Agent Souder needs to interview him, and you. But not yet."

Sleep was sucking me down, and Kurt—he couldn't have slept since yesterday morning. "Kurt's 'xausted."

"You too, I think." Mrs. Chief stroked my hair. "You should rest."

"Sleep is a good idea," the nurse agreed. "Take the opportunity now." She dimmed the light, leaving only what filtered in through the window blinds.

"Tell Kurt…," I called to her on her way out the door.

"I will," she said, and on my descent back into slumber, I didn't question what she'd say.

I woke up thinking that whatever zowie-juice they'd put in my IV had worn off, though I was back to square one on soreness. Flexing everything told me quickly that I wouldn't be back to work again in the morning—I had a tube sticking out of my chest, and I couldn't lift my right arm off the mattress. And I hurt like hell!

"Kurt?" was my first question, even before "Toothbrush?" Speaking in single words made me feel brain-damaged, but the less I breathed, the better I felt. Rolling around in broken glass pretty much described what my inhalations felt like.

The nurse helped me sit by ratcheting the head of the bed up, watching me critically. "He left with the Chief, the sheriff, and enough deputies and Forest Service enforcement officers to mount a small war." She waited expectantly, as if I should fill her in on the details of the conflict.

No, not offering details. I'd save my breath for someone in authority.

I stayed upright unassisted long enough to convince her to wheel the little table over, give me a glass of water and a kidney basin, and permit me the joys of a minty fresh mouth. Accomplished left-handed, and with only a few dribbles down my chin. My yummy clear-liquid breakfast disappeared with a few similar mishaps.

The nurse came by with a round white pill she swore would sedate the wolverines that were starting to nip at my shoulder again. When she and the doctor poked, prodded, and exclaimed over the color of the fluid dripping from the drain coming out from under my arm, every wolverine in the forest came to take another bite. I was glad the wounds were bandaged up, out of sight if not out of mind, and certainly not out of perception. I asked for another pill.

Such few activities succeeded in exhausting me beyond reason. Worry for Kurt took more out of me—but he was just the navigator, right? He wouldn't be going in after Jonesy and Buck—his army would, right? We weren't authorized to carry weapons; we were the grunts with shovels. I'd shake all the details out of him first thing. If we could get some privacy around here, I'd kiss the details out.

With my head on my pillow once again, it occurred to me to call my folks, let them know I was battered but alive. Later. After this nap I so desperately needed. I could see Mrs. Chief poking her head in the door through my fluttering eyelids—huh, they both worked, sort of—and I threw her a smile before letting them slam shut.

That pain pill probably started out as a poppy. Ponder that later....

I woke up irritable—couldn't people let an injured fellow sleep? This was a hospital—they should be quiet, let a guy recover.

Angry voices—no—one angry voice, one pleading voice—in the hallway outside my door resolved into words. I tried to sit up to listen, a process that required several intermediate steps. But I recognized that voice.

"Please—he's my partner! I have to see him!"

Why weren't they letting Kurt in? Didn't they know I wanted to see him more than anyone in the world? I couldn't get up, but maybe with a power assist? I found the button to the bed. Slowly, slowly, it pushed me where I couldn't lift myself. A mess of tubing hung off my hand and my face. I brushed the tubing away from my nose, letting it fall where it would. Wouldn't tackle the hand yet. Or the thing sticking out of my chest.

"I'm sorry, sir, but you aren't family and you aren't on the Forest Service list." That wasn't my nice nurse—I'd go have a word with the bitch. If I didn't fall. If I hit the dirt, it would be all their fault for not letting Kurt in. I swung my feet over the side of the bed to the sounds of more fruitless pleading. The floor was a good ten inches away from my feet. Tried yelling that it was okay for him to come in—uh, no. The deep breath stopped before it started—the wolverines woke up angry. They were sitting on my chest, growling, and when I tried to breathe, they tore out large chunks. I couldn't get enough air.

Sliding down to find solid floor with my toes revealed I was wearing a hospital johnny, open in the back and sliding up, and not a damned thing else. I balanced myself, one hand on the bed and wishing I dared put my head down to clear the spinning, but the wolverines didn't like the posture change. I wobbled, demanding the world stop whirling. All that air going by, and I couldn't suck enough in.

Another voice—uh, wha'? "What is the problem here, Kurt? Of course. You come with me. Thank you, nurse; we'll go see Jake now."

I had two seconds to get that gown down around my thighs before the door opened to admit the one person I'd be embarrassed to get caught bareassed by and the one person who could catch me bareassed any time but this. I gasped with the move-ment—that brought the saber-toothed wolverines.

"Why are you up, Jake? I brought your friend."

I had to say something before Kurt lunged at me for the big hug I so desperately needed, although it might just look like he was keeping me from falling off my suddenly extra-shaky legs. And when he caught me, it was gonna hurt like a son-of-a-bitch. The arrow didn't hurt this much—and I absolutely had to have enough air to say something. Now. I could rasp out enough to warn him.

"Hi, Mom."

THIRTEEN

Kurt did lunge, but only because my knees failed completely.

He nabbed me before I went all the way to the floor, his arms like steel around my chest, caught under my own arms. I couldn't help it—I screamed. The scream hurt worse than the capture. One side of my chest refused to inflate. All the teeth stuck in it kept me from the air, except I had to take another breath. Dying sounded really good right now.

Quiet whimpers hurt less. I clung to him one-handed. Not using my right arm hurt a little less. Like saying bailing made the *Titanic* sink a little slower. "Bed. Down," I mouthed more than said.

Kurt tried to be gentle, I know he did, but damn.... I yelped again before he got my butt on the bed. Maybe he thought I was a wussy, but I hadn't imagined I could hurt like this. A bear joined the wolverines to rip at my shoulder.

"I bet you're dizzy, dude. They've been pumping you full of the good stuff."

The "good stuff" right now was any drug that let me forget that the two people I'd be gladdest to see in all the world—*if* I'd had a few minutes to prepare them both—had gotten together at least once without me. And maybe it would stop the agony too.

Kurt jolted every hole, rip, and stitch from my armpits up; I squeaked with pain only because I refused to breathe enough to yell again. Every predator in the forest gnawed on my shoulder. Another thin squeal escaped between my clenched teeth. "Set me down."

Just moving me pulled at the wound—sweat popped out on my forehead and lip, and the world went swimmy again. Pain lanced through every muscle from my nipple line up on that side. Another twenty wolverines came to feast. Falling into Kurt signaled lunchtime.

Pain or no, his arms around me were welcome—I sucked strength through Kurt's skin just knowing that once again he'd been there to catch me. He hoisted me closer to upright, a position I wasn't holding with my knees gone wobbly, and turned me enough to slide my butt onto the bed. My cheek rasped across his chest, my stubble catching at the jersey of his ranger-green T-shirt. If my mother hadn't been standing there watching with a certain amount of horror, I'd have clung on, and maybe shaken with relief. But she was watching.

I hoped that expression was because of my near-collision with the tiled floor.

Kurt helped me shift over, every motion wringing another squeak through my clenched teeth. I had to be scaring him. He lifted my legs with one hand under my knees, as impersonally as any nurse, and flipped the light waffle-weave blanket across my lap. Maybe my junk hadn't just waved hello across the room. A constellation of boot-print bruises on my thighs certainly did. He settled me back against the pillow. I couldn't help it—the pain leaked out my eye and down my cheek. Fuck. I shouldn't have gotten up.

My mother gave the equipment the once over, finally reaching out to depress a little button on the side rail near my hand. She took my hand in hers, squeezing tightly, only letting go to stab the call button again. Twice. When the nurse poked her head in the door, my mother gave her a steelier glare than I could manage, saying, "He's in pain."

The minute 'til the nurse came back with relief in a syringe lasted a year. She pushed the contents into the IV tubing, and held my wrist. I could have told her how fast my heart was beating—that's how fast the damned predators were gnawing. Too fast. I wanted to calm down, just to reduce the throbbing. And I wanted to breathe in enough air that I might not have to do it again for a while.

The nurse checked the tube coming out of my chest, following it down to a box on the floor. "You didn't pull the tubing out of the canister, good. That would have let a lot more air back into your pleural space, and then you'd really feel awful. We're trying to get the air out of there." She put more tubing back on my face, sticking little prongs into my nose. "Leave it, Jake. You need the oxygen, and then you won't have to breathe in quite so deeply."

Okay, I was on board with that, even if the tubing was one more irritant. I used to like to breathe. Wish Kurt would get that terrified look off his face. Was scaring me.

Just getting the med inside made me feel better, even if it was hope rather than drug that worked first. Soon the wolverines would back off. They'd have to. Nothing could chew forever, right? Mom held my hand, letting me squeeze hard enough to break until I could hope the ones with the biggest fangs might go to sleep. Kurt stuck his hand in mine, tacitly giving me permission to squeeze, but it was my right hand, and I wasn't testing how the muscles connected on that side. I still held on—he probably needed it as badly as I did. He probably didn't need me squeezing the knife wound he'd given himself when we escaped—I could feel the edge of a dressing on his wrist.

It took long enough that a doctor wandered in, the first I recalled seeing since we screeched into the emergency room this morning. An older man in a white coat, he checked the tube coming out of my armpit. When he asked me for my pain on a scale of one to ten, I told him, "Five. Was nine, got med."

"I ordered two to four milligrams of morphine every four hours as needed. I believe you just got four, so give it another few minutes. Jake, you might not be tracking well enough to register the details, so I'll explain to all of you. If it's all right that he knows." The doctor cast Kurt a significant look.

"Is." I would use that much air to make it clear where Kurt stood. "Everything." I hoped that would be clear enough. I couldn't fight this battle every time. Why did it have to be a battle at all?

"The arrow caught the top of your lung, but missed the cephalic vein and the brachial artery, lucky you. So you've got about a thirty percent pneumo/hemothorax. That's how much of the lung is collapsed. It will reinflate as we get the air and blood out, but you're going to feel like hell for the next couple of days. Any pink foam you cough up is blood, and in this case, better out than in."

Dear Lord, I hoped to not cough at all. It might kill me.

"We're limited in what we can give you for pain, because of your concussion, and I'm sorry about that, but raising your intracranial pressure might knock you right off your perch.

You're alert and oriented enough at the moment, but you might not stay that way. So we're being cautious."

Fuck cautious. I'd like another four milligrams.

"We will premedicate you for your pulmonary hygiene, which is a fancy way of saying 'supervised coughing.' We want you to get the air out of your chest cavity, which will go out this chest tube."

That explained the thing sticking out of me, but it also sounded like an invitation to hell. "Supervised coughing." That meant deep breaths. Maybe with meds on board first, I'd live through it.

"You aren't getting out of that bed for any reason until at least tomorrow, and possibly the day after. Breathing will hurt. Talking will hurt. Coughing will really hurt. Falling will make you wish you'd died already, so don't get up."

Somebody could have mentioned that earlier. "Already tried."

He shook his head, one corner of his mouth pulled back. "Ranger, I believe you're a tough guy after what you've already been through. Leave the macho alone for a couple of days. Now let's see about your face."

He pressed fingertips against my cheekbone, moving around my eye socket. Nothing seemed to crunch unpleasantly, though it hurt. "We took an X-ray, and nothing's broken, but this is a pretty spectacular crush injury. There may be scarring. What did you get hit with?"

"The flat side of a pistol," Kurt answered for me. Lord, I loved that man. "Same for the concussion."

My mother let out a dismayed squeak and squeezed my hand even harder. I squeezed back, trying to reassure her. Probably wasn't helping.

"No wonder you look like you went three rounds with

Manny Pacquiao. How's the vision out of that eye?" He pulled an ophthalmoscope out of his pocket and flicked the light on.

Whoa! Hadn't even thought of that one! I tried cranking the eye open even farther, and realized it hadn't occurred to me because it hadn't been a problem, aside from the swelling. "Okay."

"Good." He peered inside to verify that nothing was floating around loose. "We'll keep checking as the swelling goes down." Pocketing his instrument, he gave me even better news. "We'll advance your diet as you can tolerate it, keep you resting at this angle, or higher, and you stay in that bed until we give the official word you're supposed to get up. Aside from torture every few hours with coughing, you're going to mostly lie here and heal for a couple of days. You're young, healthy, and you'll mend pretty fast. Not fast enough to plan on fighting fires any time soon."

When speaking a sentence at full volume without wanting to cry was my current greatest aspiration, going back to work didn't even hit my want list. Might be different tomorrow.

"Sheriff Dodd wants to talk with you, Special Agent Souder wants to talk to you, and I've given orders that they leave you alone until tomorrow at the earliest." I could only nod thanks at that one—talking at all, especially with the authorities, could wait. "I'll see you again in the morning."

Kurt had edged down by my feet, leaving the doctor room to work, and Kurt drew the man's attention now. "Good job with the first aid, Kurt. Some reason you didn't call for an airlift though? We'd have had a chopper out." He put a hand out to Kurt, who took it after a slight hesitation, and accepted the shake.

"Wish I could have. Would have been a lot faster." Kurt

glanced me an apology. "Our tanker's radio was disabled. I did what I could."

"You got everyone here alive." The doc let go of Kurt and came round the bed to take my mother's hand. "Mrs. Landon, don't worry too much. Barring anything unforeseen, he'll be good as new."

With that pronouncement, he left us to our relief. The morphine and the good news combined to leave me limp and weary—I was glad to know I'd mend, even if I felt like something the bear wouldn't eat right now. Kurt came closer. I wiggled my fingers at him, which he interpreted correctly. He took my hand, and Mom held my good left hand in both of hers, and I was willing to lie there like that until the rest of the wolverines went back to their dens.

I wasn't up to making official introductions, but Mom knew who Kurt was—she'd sent him a Christmas present and listened to my last year of phone calls, where he'd figured prominently —and Mrs. Landon couldn't really be anyone else. And of course Mom would know the right thing to do too.

After we'd all soaked in my good prognosis a while, she came around the foot of the bed to Kurt, and did her mom thing. She hugged him, and if she only came up to his nose and objected to the way he smelled, of woods and sweat, she said nothing, but pulled him close. "Thank you, Kurt, for bringing my boy back in." She didn't let go. "Thank you so much."

Kurt nearly wrapped his arms around her but hesitated, his hands shaking in indecision before he finally pressed them flat to her back. Mom hugs, aside from Mrs. Chief's teasing, just weren't part of his life. He'd been ten, he said. Ten years old the last time his own mother hugged him, and now she had to be looking down from some blessed afterlife and hoping my mom would be kind. If ghostly Mrs. Carlson had been paying attention, she'd know my mom wouldn't be anything but.

"Had to," Kurt finally gruffed out. "He's a pretty good partner. I expect to get years of wear out of him." The tendons in his forearms sprang into relief under his skin—he glanced up at me, his eyes full of *is this all right?*

Better than all right—I nodded and mimed a tiny kiss while her face was buried in his chest. He puckered back over her head.

"Don't misplace him," my mother admonished Kurt, pulling back. "And you—" She turned to me, leaning carefully to rest her lips against my forehead, her hand on my good shoulder. Every inch of her vibrated with the need to hold me close, but she had a clue about the irritable wildlife just itching to chew on me again, and kept the contact small but intense. I was happy to let her stay there just as long as she liked. If I could touch Kurt too, everything would be perfect.

He pulled on my toes, just enough to let me know he was there. Not enough to scream aloud to my parent that he wanted to crawl in that bed with me. I wiggled my toes at him and got tweaked again. It wasn't a hug, and it wasn't a kiss, and it would have to do for now.

But the two people who loved me best in all the world were with me, and maybe, just maybe, some of my appreciation dripped down my cheek.

Mom pulled back to look into my face, making sure I was really still in there behind my eyes. "Okay, enough of the soppy stuff," she declared, a tear running across the sharp plane of her cheekbone to plop onto the blanket. "Somebody explain in detail what's going on here."

I was kind of interested in that myself. Maybe Kurt had some answers, although what I wanted to know started right about the time I'd faceplanted into the pine duff beside a tent in the enemies' camp.

"Uhhhh." Kurt filled the thinking time. "Special Agent Souder and his officers are burning a lot of contraband vegetation. You know, I had to let them bring motorized vehicles into the forest without a ticket? They've been mowing all afternoon—"

"Kurt, dear." That tone of voice had wrung many a confession out of me. "I'm interested in the part that resulted in my only son lying in a hospital bed. Start there."

Okay, the short story. I could do that especially since the pain was receding and thought returning. "Got caught, hit, kicked, caught again…." I ran out of air and had to struggle for more. This next was where my mother would rescind any hope of "other son" status for Kurt. "Got rescued. And a little shot."

"Who was shooting?" She did that "angry vulture" thing with her eyebrows that made the wise but guilty flee. Unfortunately, I wasn't able to get up and run, and Kurt had a death grip on the bed's railing.

"Uh, that would be me, ma'am," he admitted, his eyes fixed firmly downward.

"You shot my son." Her voice was flat, deadly. Funny how a short, blonde, fiftyish woman who looked one step off a golf course could turn into the scariest thing in the Rockies.

"I was aiming at the man who was trying to kill him, ma'am. They were dancing around pretty lively." He looked up, begging her for understanding.

"Accident, Mom!" I could think of several things much harder to heal from that could have gone down. If I could use more than two words per sentence, maybe I could defuse the coming explosion. Superheated gambel oak didn't have a thing on my mother. "Accident!"

"No shit," Kurt mumbled, and flinched for the language.

She gave him a quick "mind your mouth" with her eyes, but didn't drop the subject. "Please tell me the other guy looks worse."

"He was still alive when I went out to the poppy fields." Kurt definitely sounded of two minds about that.

"Only until I get my hands on him!" my mother declared. "But still…."

Kurt flinched again. Probably the utter sincerity in her voice.

If I could talk more, I'd explain they were planning to take me to the White River and drop a dead bear on me. I looked up at her, willing her to process this enough to keep accepting Kurt as my friend. From the concrete set of her frown, it wasn't working. "Kurt rescued me."

That many words brought on a coughing fit. Ghostly bears jammed their claws in deep, and I had to spit fluid. Someone held a blue basin before my face. I horked foam. Pink. Great. Better out than in. I spat again, and fell back against the pillow. Kurt brought a wet washcloth and wiped my face.

I wasn't done convincing Mom. "Ambush. With bees." That was almost one word too many, but I didn't start coughing again.

Got her. She went from livid to scared to bewildered in two point four seconds.

"Will someone please start at the beginning?" She glanced back and forth at us. "Is there a beginning?"

I squeezed her hand, because I didn't like how the beginning happened. "Kurt?" I'd help explain as nonverbally as I could.

"We discovered a poppy field and got caught by the scum who planted it. Jake got clobbered when we got caught, and when we got away, he didn't get all the way away. I did. I didn't want to leave him." The look of utter helplessness on his face should have made Mom understand exactly how hard that was for him to do.

"I made him." There, three words, no cough, and her face lost some of its gathering wrath.

Kurt talked to the waffle weave blanket more than to either of us. "Jake couldn't run, I couldn't carry him, so I hiked back to the cabin, grabbed my bow and arrows and the Toyota, and blocked the road. They got out to mess with the car. I did a little shooting and dragged everyone to the hospital. Um, Jake, I have to replace the headlight, I hit a post outside the emergency room. Sorry." He met my eyes.

As a distraction, the headlight didn't keep me from filling some of the sizable blanks in that story. I knew pretty nearly where the camp was compared to our cabin; he'd glossed over a fifteen-mile hike in the dark, barefoot. Closer to twenty miles if he'd kept to the road. Maybe his celestial navigation was good enough to take the straight line, but there were two creeks, a peak, and a ravine with a river in the way. I tried not to suck in the deep breath for the "No shit!" that feat deserved, but Mom was standing there—she didn't need to know.

Nor did she need to know what happened in that huge gap between Kurt's recital and mine. I didn't want to tell Kurt. Nothing had happened, and I didn't want him marching downstairs to punch Sarge hard in his swollen throat.

Kurt swayed a little, his knuckles whitening against the silvery bedrails. "And I have no idea how to get the bees out of the trunk."

Something he didn't know, huh. Someone around Meeker probably did, and would, before the swarm died of the heat.

"I'm not sure that even makes sense. When did you sleep

last, Kurt?" Mom asked, and it was a question I was afraid I could answer—he'd been running for weapons.

"Don't recall." He tried smiling, but his rictus was more the look he'd had when he'd fled a forest fire on a sprained ankle.

"Sit." I poked at the big chair I'd last seen Mrs. Chief in, using my one liftable hand.

He shook his head. "If I sit down, I may not get up for hours."

"If I'm hearing this right, you've been up since yesterday morning? Jake, is he always this stubborn?" Mom looked ready to shove Kurt into that chair. I wished her luck, although he was swaying a little—maybe I should just wish him a soft landing.

"Always." One of his best qualities. And probably the only reason I was around to discuss his muleheadedness, not that I wanted to share my thoughts on barefoot, midnight forced marches with her.

A knock on the door interrupted my thoughts. Mrs. Chief poked her head in. "Hello, Jake. Am I interrupting?" She glanced at my other guests.

Kurt read my face and answered for me. "Hi. Mrs. Landon, this is Mrs. Chief, our ranger mom. She feeds us brownies when we come into town."

"And deals with the paperwork if they land in the hospital." She waggled the papers at me. "We've met, dear—I collected Diane at the airport."

"Wha'?" Had I missed a day completely?

"It's about 7:00 p.m., Jake. We got to the hospital this morning." Kurt anchored me in time.

"How'd you...?" I wouldn't be the least surprised if she'd flapped her arms as the fastest way in from Detroit.

"Mrs. Chief arranged a lift on a slurry bomber coming from

Denver on its way to a fire in Utah." Mom loved adventures like that—she might have enjoyed the excitement except for the reason she'd had it. I tried to look healthier. Hah. "They just set me down at that postage stamp airport on the edge of town, filled the slurry tanks, and took off."

"How big is that fire?" Again Kurt asked what was in my mind. Would the Colorado rangers get called in to help? Not that I was going to be any help at all, but they might want Kurt to go.

"Sixty percent contained and not your problem, Kurt," Mrs. Chief scolded him. "And Jake's problem is the blanks in the paperwork. Worker's comp always has more forms than you'd think."

I groaned. I could not deal with paperwork or questions right now. Mrs. Chief clucked sympathetically. And then I had the best idea. When better to shove something off on your mom than when you're her poor, poor, wounded baby? I thought better of big puppy eyes but did get another groan out for effect. "Mom…? Please?"

"I suppose I can take care of anything that isn't actually a signature." Mom stroked the side of my head, avoiding the bruises. "And maybe someone will tell this story with more details and fewer bees."

"I'm not sure there is a way to get the bees out of the story, but I'll try. Let's go get a cup of coffee and take care of all of this." Mrs. Chief held the door open for my mom, and I silently called down all the blessings of heaven on her for leaving me alone with Kurt.

The door clicked closed behind them. An instant later Kurt had me wrapped in his arms and I didn't care about the fanged things that might object. I held tight with my left arm, finding his mouth. Relief flooded me—he was okay, I was okay, or I would be.

I don't think Kurt cried on me—it was just rain, we'd been saved by rain before, and we'd kissed each other wildly while the water fell from the sky. That had to be it—Kurt crushed his mouth to mine and any sniffing was me cutting off his breath. Yeah, I'd kiss him until I was sure of it.

After the first onslaught, he pulled back a few inches to inspect me. "You look like shit, Hot Stuff." He kissed me again. "But I have never been so glad to see you."

"Same to you." If I mouthed the words with no breath behind them, I didn't wake the pain much.

He did look like hell with a clean face, probably the only bit of self-care he'd done since stumbling into the hospital with us. Bags under his eyes were fully packed, but his drawn look receded a little further when I lifted my mouth to him again.

He rested on his elbows across me, his feet still on the floor. If that door opened he'd be standing again in a heartbeat, but for now we'd get as much use out of a bed as we could, though not as much as we'd like. I'd plaster myself against his skin and sleep for a week. First. Then I'd fuck him into the mattress. But for now I'd hold him tight and rejoice that we were both still breathing.

"So, concussion, black eye, enough boot prints you don't have to tell me they stomped you, an arrow wound, and you have no idea how sorry I am about that, Jake, and what else?" He tried to take inventory without letting go.

I thought about that. "That's all." He sagged against me—I massaged his back with my good hand. Wonder how long it will be before I'm back to work. Something the nurse said floated back into my mind. I used a puff of precious breath to put the words straight in his ear. "What did you think? Had to be bad."

"Never mind. Sometimes it's good to be wrong." He headed off more questions with his lips against my cheek, but I could hold a thought through a kiss. Maybe.

"Tell, Kurt," I insisted when he pulled back to look at me again and could read my lips. "You tried to leave wounded behind. Why?" His first thought would be for me, but abandoning the others, even if they were murdering scum like Tubbs, was so unlike him there had to be a reason.

"When I saw you, you had blood all over your groin. I thought...." He laid his cheek next to mine, the rough scratching of our whiskers a caress of its own. "I'd have finished them off for that alone. Except you wanted me to take them along. So either you didn't have a huge grudge or your heart's way too big."

My stomach tried to do a double gainer. What better reassurance could I give him than touch? I guided his hand under the blanket to my crotch, cupping his fingers around my balls. "Don't think I could have fought, if...."

He played with my nuts, taking my mind places it shouldn't go when that door might open to admit my mother at any moment. Then he brought it back to now by whispering, "You might be surprised. I've castrated a lot of calves. They always get up and run away."

Once again he'd jumped to a really wrong conclusion, but I couldn't be sad about how wrong this one was, and I wouldn't laugh at him for it. I kissed his ear, trying not to think of the other horrible things he might have done on his brother-in-law's ranch. "Not my blood."

"Whose then? And why?" He fretted less with his hand on the evidence.

Did that door lock? A latched door would probably give us away as surely as walking in on us. "Bear's. Sarge policed me with dirty hands."

Kurt growled into my neck. "Still want to punch him for pistol-whipping you." He let go of my balls and went back to rubbing his cheek against mine. "I heard a shot after I left. I was terrified they'd killed you. And I was going to shoot every last one of them and leave the bodies for the scavengers."

"Sarge. Stopped them kicking me. You came back?" I hadn't even considered that Kurt might have come back.

"Close enough to hear them yelling about what to do with you, so I knew you were still alive." He pulled back enough to look into my face—all I could see was blue eyes and tanned skin, the best sight in the world. Having a bed and not enough energy or privacy to use it might just kill me.

"What about you?" I trusted him to know what I wanted.

"Kept to the road. I didn't get cut up too bad." One side of his mouth pulled back. "I owe you a pair of running shoes."

"Huh?" My size eleven shoes would flop right off his size nine-and-a-half feet.

"Didn't bandage well enough, I guess."

"You okay?" The big first aid kit was still in the tanker—he would have had to improvise. He'd had treatment earlier, I knew. The nurse mentioned stickers but not stitches, and he was using his hands like the gash on his wrist was a mere nick.

"I'll live." He came down to kiss me again, softly this time, more brushings of lips than ardent need. "So will you. Good thing."

Noises in the hallway made me glance to the door. Kurt stood up, adjusting his lie with one hand and my blankets with the other. No one came through, so he reached for my hand again.

"After we got here?"

"I called the Chief, he called Sheriff Dodd and Special Agent Souder, they rounded up their posses, and we went out to hunt us some poppy growers. I got to ride in the Humvee 'cause I was the navigator." He grinned. "The citation for camping too close to water and for too long in one spot was my big contribution to the capture, which wasn't all that exciting—they were scrubbing their clothing in the creek, and their hands were so cold they couldn't pick up their guns."

"Bear goop." Poor bear. He'd kept Kurt safe again. I squeezed his hand.

"Blech. I suppose we could cite them for hunting bear out of season and without a license if they didn't face bigger charges." He leaned to place a kiss on my good eye.

"Mmm." I reveled in being alive to accept that caress. "Camping citation?"

"Made it ranger jurisdiction—I didn't have a pocket full of FBI." That brought a chuckle out of him. "We needed probable cause for moving in on them with the biggest guns we had. They didn't exactly have a "We planted these poppies!" sign at their well-disguised front gate. The agents have been mowing since I left—it's almost sad. That much beauty laid waste."

I thought of the palm-sized red cups of bloom atop hip-high stems, the petals ruffling in the breeze, scarlet across the huge meadow. A poisoned beauty, growing where it didn't belong and for reasons that spelled broken lives. Still, imagining swaths of flowers falling to the blade felt like something had been taken out of the world. And yet—

We are the Dead. Short days ago
We lived, felt dawn, saw sunset glow,
Loved and were loved, and now we lie—

"No Flanders Fields."

"No," he agreed softly. Was he recalling the words too? "Then I hitched a ride with Sheriff Dodd and came straight here from the jail. I like the look of those two on the other side of bars." His grin became a grimace. "I suppose there'll be all sorts of official crap we'll have to do for the trials."

"Long time 'til then." Could be years.

"Yeah. I'm just glad I got you back, Jake." He bent to kiss me again. "Since I probably shouldn't *do* what I'm thinking about to prove how glad I am, at least not right here and until you've healed a little more, how about I tell you?" He licked my upper lip and nibbled on it.

I held the back of his neck with my good hand, keeping him close, wishing I had enough air to play this game properly.

"I'd start with peeling off every stitch of your clothing and inspecting you from top to bottom, preferably in bright sunlight, just so I can make sure everything's there. Gotta be certain about these things. And if there's a bruise, I'll kiss it, make it better, and if there isn't a bruise, I'll kiss it anyway just 'cause it could have had a bruise…." He rubbed his lips over my forehead, demonstrating. "You did collect a lot of bruises."

A rapping at the door made us snatch our hands away really fast—Kurt jerked to the upright and innocent position fast enough to make a sonic boom. A few words came through, as if Mom had to finish her conversation, but then she entered.

Maybe if I sprang this on her now, the news about me and Kurt would get lost in the rest of the story. Get all the shocks out of the way at once. We were in a hospital. If she fell over, help was around the corner. I said nothing.

"That's all taken care of," Mom told me. "Nothing like bureaucracy." She came to the bedside again, with a measuring eye on me and one on Kurt. "You're still on your feet only because you're too obstinate to sit down, I think." She touched a lever on the chair, which let out a metallic screech on its way to expanded, but it finally stretched out to something long enough to be slept on.

"We're done with stubbornness, Kurt." With one hand on each of his arms, she guided him backward to the chair. His eyebrows reached toward his hairline, but he didn't object. Mom in force of nature mode was only to be obeyed; she'd have cut off his objections with a *tsk* anyway. The makeshift bed folded his knees out from under him with his last step, dropping Kurt heavily. Mom finally let go and glared him into the prone and semicomfortable position. "I'll find you a pillow and blanket."

Those two items lurked in the closet. She fluffed the pillow but let Kurt put it beneath his head himself, and snapped the blanket out over him, shoes and all.

"You're going to sleep until morning with any luck." She knelt to put a good-night kiss on his forehead. "You did well. Thank you." With a last pat to his shoulder she consigned him to slumber. "You too, Jake. You'll heal faster. I told that Special Agent he couldn't talk to you tonight." I got the same treatment: tucking and a kiss, much like when I'd been a feverish eight-year-old. It made me feel better then, and hadn't lost much of its curative power.

I kissed her cheek when she was still in range and whispered, "Glad you're here."

"I couldn't be anywhere else." She squeezed my hand. "I'll be staying tonight with the Chiefs, if you need me."

She dimmed the light to next to nothing, and the door clicked behind her. I was musing that my mother had just tucked us both into bed when his first light snore rattled from

Kurt's nose. He always snored when he was exhausted, and he'd earned the sound effects, but rats, he was too far away to poke into rolling over.

But it was the sound of him alive, safe, and close. I let Kurt rumble me to sleep.

FOURTEEN

They'd wakened me twice in the night for some morphine and coughing, fortunately in that order. Kurt rose to stand with me, letting me crush his hand while the nurse percussed my back. The pain didn't respect the drug—the predators feasted. The nurse didn't let me put the head of the bed down, saying I'd drain best from the semi-Fowler's position. Maybe so, but it didn't make my sleep any more restful.

We hadn't been awake much past the yawn and stretch stage the next morning when Mrs. Chief solved all questions of Kurt's clean up and breakfast. Not that I stretched much—a few millimeters on my right side and I stopped that in a hurry. But Kurt had both hands splayed into the air, making his ranger-green/dirt-color T-shirt ride up to show me his middle. I enjoyed the pull of muscles vicariously.

"You can leave him be until he's had breakfast, Terry!" Mrs. Chief chased Special Agent Souder through the door he'd opened about one nanosecond after his knock. Kurt's and my stretches collapsed like trailers in a tornado.

"I do need to interview him, Mary Jo, and before they've

179

had a chance to compare notes." Agent Souder gave her a stern glance, which became a full on glare to us, as if we'd colluded all night long. A nurse knocked and came in, a pill cup and a tray in her hands, but she backed out much faster when Agent Souder cleared his throat at her.

Mrs. Chief continued her defense: "Honestly, you can see the poor boys just woke up!" She gave the glare back good as she got. "Kurt, why don't you come back to the house, and I'll find you a pancake and a clean shirt?"

"Thank you, ma'am, and if that generosity stretches to a razor…?" Kurt ran a hand over his two-days-worth of stubble.

"Of course, and I think Jake needs the same. Terry, don't you pester the poor boy!" Mrs. Chief gathered Kurt up and bustled him out. That relieved Agent Souder visibly, though from Kurt's and my inability to spoil his case or from Mrs. Chief's being out of haranguing distance was hard to say.

"You gonna hand me that bottle?" I rasped out, willing to spend the air on making him uncomfortable. Souder'd chased Kurt out before even letting him visit the can.

"Uh, no. I'll get you a nurse." Agent Souder disappeared, and I found I'd bought myself an excellent half hour of getting clean and fed.

Shaving was a challenge, since I had to do it left-handed with the communal electric razor and missed several tracks of coffee-grounds brown whiskers, which the nurse tidied up for me. I wanted my right hand back, and I wanted it now, since I also managed to spill juice down my chin and shoot a piece of toast across the tray while attempting to butter it. I wanted to talk to a doctor a lot more than I wanted to talk to Agent Souder—he'd gotten plenty of information from Kurt, and I needed to know how I was going to rehab this stupid injury. I started with another bout of supervised coughing, which hurt slightly less and brought up less blood. I liked my blood best when it stayed inside and I didn't have to see it.

What I wanted didn't keep me from spending the entire morning rehashing the events of our discoveries, capture, and escape, until Agent Souder was satisfied that he'd wrung every drop of information from me, two and three whispered words at a time. Even my mom poking her head in every half hour on the dot didn't stop him for a moment. I gasped about poppies, guard dogs, bears, and beatings, and he wouldn't tell me a thing about Sarge and the others, except to say they were all alive and in custody. Didn't seem like a fair exchange to me.

"Don't want you going all Stockholm on me," he said, when I asked for the third time about Tubbs.

"Not a chance," I shot back. "Same kind of wound." I tapped near the dressing on my shoulder.

"That's a question for the docs," he temporized, and then relented. "But you were a thirty minute patch job, and he was a two hour patch job. I don't think you were hurt as badly."

Guess Tubbs would pay for every evil thing he'd done in his life when the nurses made him cough. I couldn't feel too bad for him.

Mom finally lost patience and chased Special Agent Souder out when she escorted an apprehensive nurse with a syringe into the room for my latest bout of torture. Maybe it was the needle that spooked him, or perhaps it was the extra-vigorous bubbling in the canister on the floor—air and fluid were exiting my body via that chest tube. I'd have run away from it myself if I could have.

But it really helped to have someone to hang on to when I had to cough.

Mom kept me company while I dripped my lunch down my chest. Oatmeal never tasted so good, and had the virtue of falling out of the spoon slowly. Eating left handed was a skill I hoped to not need for very long. Breathing was a bit easier but my right hand still refused to rise more than a few inches above the mattress. My nurse offered encouragement and antibiotics, and Mom kept up the conversation while I fought with my food.

"Your partner is a very nice young man, Jake," she mused. "I had a chance to talk with him this morning, after I pried him out of the sheriff's clutches. You never mentioned that he skied competitively."

Mom could well have extracted every detail of Kurt's life in twenty minutes flat. Something about her absolute interest in whatever she was being told made people open up. I wondered what Kurt might have spilled without intending to. "He doesn't talk about it much."

"And I had a good long talk with the Chief, and of course, with Mary Jo."

I couldn't imagine who Mary Jo was—oh yeah, Mrs. Chief. Hard to recall they had names outside what we rangers called them.

"They think very highly of you and Kurt. You must have impressed them, both of you." She gave me that fond "of course you're a star" look that had accompanied so many of my achievements. "I'm not sure they impress easily."

What could I say to that? I shrugged with my working shoulder, and recovered another blob of oatmeal from my gown.

"Where is Kurt?" I barely aspirated, and Mom looked puzzled while she figured out what she'd seen me say.

"I think he's cleaning your car." She went quiet, and if she was imagining how the Toyota got stained and how easily it could have been my blood, well, so was I. Removing the spatter would be a good step to getting back to normal, but did Kurt have to be the one doing it? I loved the man for his outsized sense of responsibility, but this seemed like a bit much.

I spent part of my afternoon sleeping, part coughing, and part with Sheriff Dodd, discussing the pros and cons of pressing charges for assault. No, we decided; that would get folded into the charges on a federal level. My bigger worry was that Kurt would face charges for shooting Tubbs and me.

"Not unless Tubbs wants to make the federal prosecutor's case for him," was the sheriff's assessment, and after that I breathed easier.

Both Mrs. Chief and the Chief swung by, one with good wishes and a sandwich for my mom, the other to discuss the goings-on in the forest.

I tensed when I saw the Chief settling into the chair, now folded up, and placing his ankle upon his knee. If he was going to chew on me, though, would he be so relaxed? Mom decided he wasn't going to eat me, so she slipped out the door.

"I'm sorry you got hurt, Jake," the Chief told me. "We don't expect this kind of trouble out here, though now we'll have to be more alert to it, because if one crew tries it, sooner or later someone else gets that same bright idea. It's a much bigger problem back East, though with marijuana, not poppy."

I thought the high, dry meadows of our mountains weren't so different from conditions halfway around the world.

"Back there, more of our rangers are law enforcement officers, and they routinely go armed. They don't have so many rangers at your level, seasonal staff with tankers and shovels. But they're prepared for trouble and often find it. I'm sorry it found you this time."

"We wouldn't have been that much better off if we'd been armed," I whispered. "We got ambushed." Only after I got that out did it occur to me that was the most syllables I'd been able to string together since I got here.

"You'd have been prepared for that possibility." The Chief's bushy eyebrows knitted together in sad reflection of a need for paranoia that we'd never had. "We'll have to step up precautions."

We silently pondered the state of the forests for a few moments before the Chief asked me, "Have you talked with your doctor about your prognosis and rehab?"

Since I hadn't been on my feet since that disastrous attempt to get into the hallway, that was a question much on my mind. "No, sir, but I'd like to."

"I'm sure you do." The Chief got to his feet. "We'll be sending Kurt back up to your section with the tanker and one of the Forest Service law enforcement agents for now. Rest and heal, Jake." He looked like he was about to give me a fatherly shoulder clasp but thought better of it. He stopped, hand poised in midair, and gave the canister on the floor a dubious look. "Take care now."

He left, and I pondered the state of my future. Nobody belonged at that cabin with Kurt except me.

FIFTEEN

Mom tried to keep me occupied with small talk in between visits from medical staff and the naps that I wished were a whole lot longer, just to bring Kurt back for a visit that much sooner. She promised he'd come by that evening, but when he came in, the news wasn't good.

At least we had some privacy for it. Mrs. Chief lured Mom out with the promise of the best pie in the county, which I knew would be found in the diner opposite the Laundromat. We had at least an hour free of parental interference, though nurses were liable to come barging in on the heels of the knock. It kept him on his feet, though not out of my arms. Arm. The right one still wasn't following directions very well. I kissed him until we both gasped.

"You're breathing better," he noted with approval. "And you aren't gurgling like a fountain."

The burbles from the canister on the floor had blended into the background, but now they were loud in their absence. "No, I'm not. And I can get a complete sentence out without feeling like there's a dozen knives in my chest."

"Getting better already." Kurt dove in for another kiss, which was giving me notions unsuitable for beds that folded up in the middle, despite my pain. "When are they going to spring you from this joint?"

"Don't know. Gotta get that chest tube out first."

Kurt lifted my hospital gown to examine the clear plastic that disappeared between my ribs about six inches below my armpit. "The only long tubular thing going into you should be my dick."

I snorted at that, and had to admit, "It still hurts when I laugh." I gave the tube a crusty look. "That must have hurt like a sonofabitch going in, but I don't remember."

"Just as well." He dropped the worn cotton to a level that wouldn't startle stray nurses. "You groaned and passed out." At my grunt of surprise, he elaborated. "It's a small hospital—three emergency patients and they were running out of hands, so they put me to work positioning you. Don't tell the accreditation board."

Remembering how he'd begged me not to die, it might have cost someone some fingers if they'd tried to make him let go, so yeah, they probably made the most of his reactions. I wouldn't ask him how they actually inserted the tube. Might be too much like inserting an arrow.

"Hey, Hot Stuff," Kurt murmured, nuzzling my ear again. "The Chief is sticking me with one of the Forest Service LEOs until you're better. He'll be staying at the cabin until I get you back, so... do you want me to scurry home and rearrange the place before he and I go up in the tanker tomorrow?"

Our cabin didn't look the way it had last year, when we slept in sleeping bags on Army surplus cots. We'd left the cots folded up in the corner and used the queen-sized bed we'd bought for the winter in Wapiti Creek employee housing. Not much mistaking that we slept in it together.

My first reaction was *Hell yes!* but a more measured thought came to the surface. "You're going to have to deal with this guy —will it make a problem for you?"

"Don't know. Not even sure who it's going to be yet. I met four of the officers but didn't really talk to them." I could feel his cheek moving against mine in what had to be a smile—I'd made him happy by controlling the knee-jerk reaction. What small steps I was taking toward my closet door.

"If you don't know, then maybe err on the side of caution?" I didn't want Kurt getting grief from a temporary partner when they had to spend days on end together in the truck or in the cabin.

"Especially since I don't want to share it with him." Kurt let me know, lips to lips, how much he liked sharing it with me. "Mind if I take the Toyota?"

"You've still got the keys." I hoped.

"I'll go take care of it." Kurt made the ninety-mile round trip sound like a jaunt to the corner store. "And I'll be back in the morning to check on you before we head out." He caressed me again, leaving a kiss over each of my eyes. The right one opened a little more now.

I watched him leave, wishing desperately that I could accompany him, walking on my own two feet.

My nurse jabbed the syringe through the IV access port still poking into my hand. I hadn't asked for any pain meds, and I'd already coughed for her about an hour ago. It didn't hurt nearly so bad this morning—I felt the ache more in the muscles where

I'd been perforated than inside where the agony had been for the last few days. She hadn't premedicated me earlier, so why now?

"I'll just say good-bye to him," I heard through the squeak of the opening door. "I won't keep you." Kurt followed the doctor into the room. "Hey, Jake. Brought your car keys back." He placed them on the bedside table.

"Hey, Kurt. Hi, Doc." The dose might be a little more than I needed right now—I felt kind of woozy, and some strange wavy lines were trying to wrap around them.

Kurt crossed the room to me, his brows wrinkled. "Are you okay?"

"We gave him some morphine. We're going to pull that chest tube," Doc Schneider explained. "He'll be glad for it in a few minutes." The latex snapped evilly when he pulled on some sterile gloves. He listened to my chest, moving the stethoscope pickup carefully around the dressing on my arrow wound.

Oh boy, more fun for Jake. "Wanna stick around and see?" I really meant *Dear Lord, Kurt, don't leave me now.*

Pain, maybe fear, flickered across his face, or was that my wavy little hallucination? They must have given me a bigger slug than before—then I'd only stopped hurting. I reached to the tube, but the nurse pushed my hand away.

"Don't touch."

"I'll keep him from doing that again." Kurt took my left hand in his and placed his right on my upper arm. I hadn't done it intending to provide him with an excuse to hold my hand, but Kurt did seize opportunities. And I wanted his support right now—everything they'd done suggested I was about to hurt like hell.

"When we give you the word, we want you to bear down, or you can exhale hard. Yelling counts as exhaling hard." So

Dr. Doom thought yelling was a reasonable reaction. "We'll pull the tube and get a dressing on it before you can suck air into your chest cavity, which would put you back to square one."

I did so not want to do any of this over. I flexed my fingers into Kurt's, feeling him squeeze my upper arm. The nurse unwrapped a clear dressing and held it at the ready.

"On the count of three." The doctor placed one hand against my chest, gripped the tube, and counted down. Then he ripped three feet of barbed wire out from between my ribs.

I exhaled, all right. Loudly. And if Kurt hadn't been holding on, I'd have screamed for sure. The nurse slapped my ribcage.

"Done." She took her hand away, and when I could open my eyes, I saw the doc dangling a length of plastic.

"That piece of Saran Wrap is the only thing between him and doing this all over again?" Kurt gritted out, his hand still tight on my arm.

"The tissues will swell shut and start healing, but for now, yes." Doc Schneider shoved the tubing and his gloves into a medical waste container as if he hadn't just inflicted some violation of the Geneva Conventions on me. And that was *with* the morphine on board.

"Put another six layers on."

I owed Kurt a blowjob for that. Some time when thin whimpers weren't my only form of communication.

"That occlusive dressing isn't moving. It's glued to him." The doc listened to my breathing with his stethoscope and must have found it still satisfactory. "Jake, if you can sleep for a while, it will help. You'll feel a lot better after the shock has passed. Your lung is almost fully reinflated, still a little wet, but greatly improved. We'll get you up this afternoon for a little walk, keep you on partial bed rest another couple of days, and as long as you don't develop pneumonia, we'll likely have you out of here by Wednesday."

That last caught my attention—funny how the wavy lines disappeared when the wall of pain hit, now crumbled against the opiate. "And when can I get back to work?"

"When you can swing an axe again. It'll be at least three weeks of restricted duty," Dr. Doom pronounced. "That won't be too great a hardship, considering that you're going to hate your physical therapist at the end of every session."

"Three weeks of PT?" Three weeks of me in town, Kurt in the wilderness.

"At least. That arrow perforated a couple of big muscles, not just your lung. You're a lucky guy. Whoever shot you was trying to kill you." He stepped backward out of the nurse's way; she picked up the now-silent canister and left.

"No, he wasn't." I had enough breath to argue the absolute truth, if not enough to get up and clobber him for the accusation. Kurt's hands went even tighter on me. I clutched back.

"For not trying he came damned close to succeeding." The doc took a look at the bruising around my eye, making a perplexed face. Maybe I'd gone purple with wrath and it all matched. "But you'll heal." He turned to Kurt. "Let him rest." To me again, with a look like he ought to take my blood pressure because it was high enough to make me stroke out—"Take a nap, and when you wake, you can hike to the bathroom." He left, and good news or no, I didn't miss him.

Alone, finally. Kurt approached gingerly, but clasped me tighter once he'd pressed against me. "Oh, Jake, I'd take the pain for you if I could."

I lipped his ear. "You did, kind of. Glad you were here."

"I can't stay long. Sam's waiting downstairs in the tanker." Leaving a line of kisses across my brow, Kurt ended at my now-

spectacular shiner. "I think he'll be okay for a temporary partner." He met my mouth. "But he won't be a good patch
on you."

"Let me get this arm working again. Soon." I could whip
any two physical therapists, eventually. "I'll keep you posted."
Mrs. Chief would probably let me use the radio base station, as
long I kept it to things I didn't mind Sam hearing as they drove
around in my tanker. "And you'll be back in town within
a week."

"Yeah. Wish I didn't have to go."

I wished the same, lying in his embrace, however unsatisfac-
tory it was compared to our usual, and I had to let him go too
soon. Watching Kurt walk through that door felt like the chest
tube coming out all over again, only this time it was my heart.

"On your feet again! Good." The Chief's booming encouragement nearly toppled me.

This was my first unassisted trip up and down the hallway,
and I'd gotten over the worst of the shakiness yesterday when
they'd let me out of bed for the first time. Not unescorted,
though—Mom was trying hard not to clutch my arm while we
marched with miniature steps. She was doing pretty well, really;
she'd only seized me once and let go after a few seconds, though
our first circuit had required both hands on my upper arm.
Since she was about nine inches shorter and sixty pounds
lighter, and had never, to my knowledge, swung an axe, she's
probably have been more of a mat to land on than support in
keeping my feet.

Chief held the door for us and followed us in; no doubt his
errand had something to do with the sheaf of papers in his

hand. Mrs. Chief said worker's comp claims had way too much paperwork, and the Chief held a good tree and a half's worth. Maybe I could make my left hand produce a semilegible signature or six.

Once I was settled, the Chief seated Mom in the one available chair. Gallantry, maybe, but he seemed antsy, as if the chair wouldn't be terribly restful for him. What kind of bad news was he holding?

"Mrs. Landon, you may not be aware, but my wife and I are listed as medical powers of attorney for our rangers. Most of them don't have family nearby, and in these parts, nearby can be a hundred miles. I don't want either of you thinking I overstepped my bounds in talking to the doctors. Jake, Doc Schneider said you'd be out of here tomorrow most likely, and he'd discussed prognosis and rehab with you."

Maybe if I was wearing real clothing instead of this gown and bathrobe, I wouldn't feel so vulnerable to what was coming. "He said three weeks of restricted duty."

"Once you're out of the hospital, at least three weeks. And since your job requires heavy manual labor, it may be longer. We're looking at the middle of August or even later." His mouth took on a grim set. "We don't have a lot of restricted duty jobs, Jake."

My mouth went dry. "You had Kurt on command post when his ankle was sprained." That was last summer, and it had kept us apart for a couple of crucial days.

"The forest doesn't catch fire at need. We'd keep your position open until you were back if it weren't for the timing. Where are you supposed to be the week before Labor Day?"

My mother twigged faster than I did, but while her face changed, she said nothing. I had to puzzle it out a bit longer. "Patrolling."

"What!" from her direction made me flinch. I hadn't shared the change of plans with the parents. "When do classes start?"

"My point exactly. Jake, I can't take you back if it's only for a week or two, and I may not be able to take you back even then—it depends on your healing and rehab." He sorted through the papers in his hand, finally settling on the ones on the top of the stack after all. "This leaves me with a couple of ugly choices."

"Sounds like it leaves me with no choice at all," I croaked.

"It leaves you with a bad choice and a better choice. Your bad choice is to gamble on coming back and then bowing out of your academic plans—"

"Ja—" My mother chopped off.

I already knew she'd hate that.

"If you come back, ditch your schooling, and then collapse that lung again, which is a real possibility in a fire-fighting situation, you'd have nothing but a funeral allowance. I can't in good conscience let you do that." He met my eyes, and damn, he had to be channeling Dad, Gramps, and every other man of character I'd ever met.

I wanted to fight this—I wanted to claw my way back to our little cabin, walking the fifty miles into the wilderness to be with Kurt again if I had to—

And I said nothing. Because there was another man of character on the other end of that trek. I could hear his voice in my head now, even through the roaring in my ears, telling me *Don't be stupid. Listen to the Chief's work-around plan so I don't have to kick your ass all the way to the campus.* And I didn't doubt for a moment that he would. Because he'd do anything, including shooting me accidentally, to keep from burying me.

The Chief paused, letting me work all this through in my head, and I didn't tell him the worst part—after Kurt finished kicking me into the classroom, he'd leave me. Maybe only until I could ask him to come back, or—maybe forever. For being stupid as well as in the closet.

I had to at least hear the Chief's ideas.

"So what are you suggesting?" Steadying myself meant focusing on staying with Kurt if this worked. I tried to listen.

"Because of the highly physical nature of your job, Doc Schneider said he'd sign off on a partial disability. It would give you a small monthly payment, which will help you get through school, and will stop once you've qualified for other work. You have four years of tuition. This is the best help I can give you." The Chief pulled the rolling bedside table in front of me, and laid the papers out in a neat row. "I know it's not what you planned, but it beats the hell—excuse me, ma'am—it beats the heck out of what happens if I have to fire you."

I wasn't so lost in my misery that I couldn't see the advantage I was being offered. The boon the Chief probably had to work on Doc Schneider to get for me. I needed the money, even if it was only a small sum every month. The only cost was my pride.

And Kurt.

My future, my fear, and him—I could have two of the three, he'd said. *Choose wisely*. Any pair that didn't include my future—he wouldn't be shy about discussing my wisdom.

I looked blankly at the paperwork, knowing what I should do and hating with a white hot flame to do it. The Chief put a pen on the top of the stack, but I couldn't reach for it with my right hand. And maybe not with my left.

"I'm sorry, Jake," he said, "but we're invaliding you out of the Forest Service."

SIXTEEN

My elderly crudmobile labored to drag the rental trailer up the dirt road. The tension in Mom's shoulders showed she was urging the four-banger engine to get us all the way to our destination without blowing up. She drove, because I couldn't manage the stick shift yet. Going back down would be easier. For the car. Downhill, and there wasn't a lot to load.

Mom and I pulled up next to the split-log cabin that had been home for so long. The tanker ticked softly in its usual spot by the cabin in its clearing in the pines. Kurt and Sam hadn't been back long. Swinging myself out of the passenger seat, I looked around at our primitive but homey camp. Guess it wasn't "ours" any more.

A ranger-green figure came down the track that led to the bear box, hands full of whatever dinner would be. I hoped they weren't planning to offer us a meal—I couldn't bear to sit with them and pick at food I couldn't choke down.

Kurt came out of the cabin, his face going from bright smile to blank with a flash of horror as the implication of the trailer sank in. He maintained enough to greet my mother politely. "Soooo…?"

Damn. The Chief hadn't told him? "Out on disability." Shrugging used the damaged muscles, so there went the nonchalant approach. "It's something to go back to school with." Damned little compared to what I was leaving behind.

"There's that." Kurt sounded frozen. "Headed to Denver then?"

"Yeah. Get some PT before school starts so I can pick up my book bag." I wanted to run the dozen steps to him, squash him close in a one-armed hug, and tell him how much I hated to go. But we had an audience.

"Yeah." Kurt leaned against the doorway, and maybe anyone who didn't know him like I did wouldn't see it as the near collapse it was. This wasn't how he should find out.

The silence stretched out. A jay screeched from the trees. Camp robber. Nothing it had ever stolen compared to what I was taking from Kurt now.

I could see his nostrils flair before he stood straight again. "Do you need help loading?"

I had my arm in a sling, though it had stopped flopping willy-nilly. Control would return before my three weeks of therapy were up—was returning already—but I didn't enjoy stabbing pain at random intervals. I might manage to carry my sleeping bag and that was about it. "Yeah, thanks."

Sam offered greetings, depositing his handfuls on the picnic table. Bet he was enjoying the refrigerator we'd rigged in the lake. Most ranger teams didn't have that luxury. At least I'd leave Kurt with that comfort. Sam seemed right at home for only having been there three days.

I didn't know what the Chief had told Kurt about me—I

was desperate to talk to him, and how the hell was I going to ditch our two unwelcome listeners? With Kurt and Sam on either end of the plastic-wrapped couch and my mother toting cardboard boxes one at a time, the cabin emptied and the trailer filled. There wasn't much; the boxes marked "K winter clothes" would have fit.

"Want to take those with you?" Kurt asked quietly.

Yes. No. Yes, if nothing else had to change. Yes, if it was possible to live with him and never have anyone consider the depth of our "friendship." Yes, if.... No. Yes.

I'd dithered too long.

"I'll probably need them at the end of the season up here. It snowed before we headed out last year." He didn't look at me, turning instead to shove the boxes against the split-log wall.

Rescuing me from answering hadn't really solved a thing. I hadn't known the answer on the way up, and the quiet ache in his voice made me want to say, "Let's load them." Sam and my mother waited expectantly for further directions. "Go away, I need to talk to my lover" was what I should have said, but the words stayed choked inside. A floorboard creaked below our feet, sounding desolate.

"If we're done loading, I'd really like to look around. Didn't you say there was a lake close by?" Mom sounded nothing but interested. "Sam, where is that?"

"I'll walk you down, Mrs. Landon," he said, and escorted her out.

The tiny cabin didn't seem any bigger for holding half as many people. Eight hundred pounds of angry simian loomed between us, and we couldn't pretend it away any more.

"Where do I fit in here, Jake?" Standing next to the cardboard boxes of off-season clothing, Kurt's body thrummed with tension. Cords of muscle flexed in his forearms, as if he might reach for me—or swing at me.

"I didn't want things to be different between us. But...." But I was headed to the city.

"But? Am I coming with you or not?"

"You have to finish fire season." The lameness of that hung in the still air.

"I know that. But after?" The late afternoon light slanting through the small windows picked out the creases above his brows.

"I love you, Kurt, but...." Every word that could possibly come after that balled up in my throat.

"But. Should I plan on being your roommate? Or a friend who lives a few streets over?" He lifted his hand as if pouring choices from his palm. "Or should I plan on teaching at Wapiti Creek again this winter?"

"Not Wapiti Creek, but, damn it, Kurt, I don't know!" I'd been turning this over and over since I'd signed the papers, and I wasn't any closer to coming out than I'd been a week ago.

"Better figure it out, because you're going to be looking for a place to live in about twenty-four hours. I hoped it would be a place for us to live, but if you don't know, a one-bedroom apartment is going to be awkward." Practical matters came out of his mouth, but the hurt driving them were straight from his heart.

"I did okay at Wapiti Creek!" And I hadn't thought too hard about having a one-bedroom place with a queen-size bed in it because I'd never expected to invite people over. As rangers, if we wanted to see other people we went into town; no one ever came out here. Until Sam, and Kurt had made a special trip out to wrap our mattress in yards of plastic and stand it against the wall before he saw it.

"You did. You even kissed me under the mistletoe at a party. So why is it such a big problem again?"

"It's… it's…." I was really floundering now. "Because out here, and at Wapiti Creek, it was like a world apart. Like it was disconnected from the rest of my life. Time out. And now I'm going back."

"Sounds like I'm not going with you when you put it like that." His voice had gone painfully soft. "And I'd kind of tied my life to yours. How big a mistake did I make with that, Jake?"

"I don't want that to be a mistake, Kurt!" My voice rose, filling the small space. "But I don't know how we're going to manage in Denver."

"Financially, we'd do a lot better as a household. As a couple we'd do a lot better if we were out. Doing it the other way will be much harder, and a lot like the first steps to breaking up. Except maybe we've already taken those." He regarded me steadily with storm-cloud eyes. "Or you have." He slapped the cardboard carton behind him with an open palm, and it sounded loud as a gunshot. "My stuff isn't moving to town with you. And we didn't load your skis or your bow yet. Am I supposed to sell them once the season starts because you're done with skiing and done with me and just haven't said so?"

"No, Kurt, damn it! That isn't what I meant!" I wanted to grab him, smash him against my chest best I could, but I'd have a better chance of cuddling a burning pine tree right now.

"Your mouth is saying one thing but your actions are saying different. Which do I believe?" His anger echoed between the walls and through my heart.

"I don't know how to act so it matches!" I yelled, though volume wouldn't make up for the mismatch.

"Yes, you do," Kurt hissed and came closer, circling around

me. "But you're afraid to. I understand exactly why you didn't say anything in the hospital. You were wounded, and we were all terrified, and it wasn't a good time for dropping bombshells. But now we're on your home turf, you're a lot better, I'm here, one of the most important people in your life is here"—he stabbed a finger toward the lake—"and she's so happy you're mending that you could probably tell her you like tentacle sex with aliens and she'd just say, 'keep the green goo off the carpet, dear.'"

"You said you wouldn't push, damn it!" I took a step back away from him and his take on the situation.

"I'm not pushing. I'm pointing out you have an opportunity here." He took a step forward to keep the distance between us equal. "Use it!"

I only had so many steps back to take before I hit a wall. "You made sure I had a lot of opportunities. I'm out of the Forest Service, headed to school, with some money coming in, all with one arrow."

Kurt halted as if I'd punched him. "I did *not* shoot you on purpose! I *did not* plan any of this, and I would not have hurt you for the world!" He turned away from me, and his shoulders dropped. "That was low, Jake."

It was, and I felt like a rat, but I'd said it because I was cornered. "Yeah. I know you didn't do it on purpose." Approaching him, I tried to lift both hands high enough to rest on his shoulders, but the pain lanced through my upper chest. I rested them instead on his waist, and at least he didn't pull away. "I shouldn't have said that."

He relaxed a little under my hands, but he didn't turn to face me. "I thought I knew how much you love me, at least enough to overcome your fear. But maybe I didn't know how huge your fear really is. Lord knows you're brave—there's nobody who's braver in the face of danger, but this is different. Lots of battles for the rest of our lives, but I thought—we'd face them together. And then I couldn't even get into your hospital room until your mom okayed it. Because I'm not anyone official in your life.

"All of those fights are going to be hard enough, but they'll be even harder if we're pretending we don't even have to fight them." He looked over his shoulder at me, and then down to the floor again.

"And I'm making it harder." I had to admit that much.

"Way harder than it needs to be. So you go to Denver and start classes, and you tell me what we're doing and how, but, Jake, you have to give me enough notice to make other plans if we aren't going to be together somehow. I can't deal with Denver if we're 'just friends.' I'll be there as long as you need to be, but only if we're—whatever we are to each other." He swayed under my hands, like our prospects were sucking away his strength.

"I love you, Kurt." I pressed my lips to his skin where the tan of his neck met the paler skin peeking from under his T-shirt.

"I love you too, Jake." He leaned back against me. "Even if I think you're being an ass right now." Turning his head to nuzzle against me, he planted a tiny sideways kiss. "Try to get over it, okay?"

"Yeah."

He broke away to reach for the bows hanging on the far wall: his compound bow for hunting, his longbow, and my longbow, unstrung and likely to remain that way for a while. "Load this. I'll bring your skis." He counted out my blue-fletched arrows and bundled them carefully. "Don't let your skills get too rusty."

Before we left the cabin with our armloads of sporting equipment, I caught him at the door for a kiss. I kissed him like I meant it, and he met me equally ardently, but he pulled back when I thrust my stiffening cock against him.

"No. Not like this."

I didn't know what he meant—he'd been getting erect too; I could feel it through his utilities.

"Not something to remember me by. You remember all the other times when we did it because we loved each other or because we were horny and happy together. I don't want sex when it just might mean good-bye." He slid out the door, and all chances of kissing him evaporated.

Kurt closed the door to the trailer once we'd stowed my equipment inside. "Give my regards to your mom. If I do it, I'll give you away without meaning to. Sorry. Keep in touch. I get my e-mail Friday at the library. Good luck, Jake." He thumped my good arm with the side of his fist. "You'll do great."

He spun and was halfway up the track to the archery range before I could say anything, but not before I saw the glitter in his eyes.

I needed a minute to dash my good arm across my face too, before I headed down the track to the lake.

Twilight wouldn't come for another few hours, but the sun filtered through the trees across the lake. Mom and Sam sat on the fallen log that had been the scene of so many good times for me and Kurt. Their chat came to me indistinctly, but Sam pointed at the stream emptying into the lake where deer would come to drink. My mom had probably picked up another "son" already.

A far cry from the usual activities there. I'd given Kurt my first ever blowjob while he'd reclined on that log, and countless more since. We'd rolled around on the grassy spot at their feet

—Kurt had lifted my ankles to his shoulders there and taught me the joys we could share. There, too, I'd lain on my back and watched him rise and fall above me, plunging himself down on my cock, another thing I'd never done with anyone but him and never wanted to. This was our lake, our special place, and we'd never have it to ourselves again.

Sam rose and put out a hand to me when I approached. "I'm going to go up and start dinner. Want to join us?"

I hesitated to take his hand, having feared this very invitation, and reached with first my right hand, which didn't go far, then my left. "Thanks but no. We need to travel with the light."

"Gotcha." He glanced at the sky. "You go safely. Good to meet you, sorry about the circumstances. I'll try to look after things here for you."

The man I was entrusting my partner to stood tall and square, confident and with an air of decency. I might have liked him had I met him some other way, maybe called him friend. Now he was the man who'd taken my place. He marched up the gravel single track to the cabin that was now empty of all that had been mine. I was entrusting two of the most precious things in my universe to his care—the forest and Kurt. I hoped he did better than I had.

I said silent good-byes to our lake, the tiny, deep blue jewel set into the mountain. Tracks, ranging from tiny claw marks to the broad pad marks of a coyote, marked up the muddy edge near the rock-lined track where we filled the tanker. Other creatures favored the lake as much as I did, depending on it to drink. The big cottonwood leaned out over the water, the Tarzan rope and the refrigerator rope anchored to its trunk. More cottonwoods clung to the shore, defending the liquid from the pines that stood back on drier ground. A few clouds scudded above, pushed by stronger winds than the breezes that licked my face and made the pines mumble and creak. A splash marked with growing ripples announced a trout that would be forever safe from me and my fishing pole.

I don't know how long I stood there, trying to absorb enough beauty to sustain me in the city. Some of the very best moments of my life happened here with Kurt. I would take away only memories—in my mind he swung, naked, from the Tarzan rope to splash in the frigid water, and emerged, shaking stinging droplets from his hair and coming toward me, arms open, to warm his chilled skin against mine.

If I could get my head out of my ass, he'd come to Denver. I could turn around and say, "Mom, before we go, let's say good-bye to my lover." The words clogged in my throat.

I felt warm hands slip into the crook of my good left arm; Mom had come up to stand beside me, her head against my shoulder. "It's very beautiful here," she murmured. "Hard to leave such a place."

She had no idea. I slipped my arm around her shoulders and tried to make myself believe that I could tell her the truth and she'd still think I was her golden son.

We watched another trout rise to ripple the still waters, and a red-winged blackbird trilled from the cattails at the mouth of the stream.

"We need to be on pavement before dark," I finally said, and we trudged up the gravel track to the cabin where Sam was setting plates out on the picnic table and Kurt was nowhere to be seen.

"Good luck," he called, and we waved on our way out, the remnants of my life shredding with every foot we put between the cabin, Kurt, and me.

Conversation was impossible rattling up the dirt track, and still impossible for me on the smoothness of I-70 once we reached the interstate highway. Mom let me brood, only breaking the silence to ask if I was hungry when we approached Eagle and ignore my "no" when we neared Vail. She pulled in to a gas station and came out with turkey sandwiches and bottles of juice. Hardly the best cuisine the resort town offered even at this late hour, and I was glad for the cover of darkness, because Vail looked way too much like Wapiti Creek.

You can eat it, or I can shove it up your nose, but it's going into you one way or another echoed in my head—Kurt had forced nourishment into me more than once. He'd pinch my nose and pour if he had to cope with me now. I drank the juice and felt marginally better, enough to respond in monosyllables when Mom spoke, although I didn't really want to hear encouragements on getting started on this new phase of my life. I wanted my old life back far too desperately.

Kurt would be the first to tell me I could have the best of both. But if there ever were a good time to shock my mother, it wouldn't be while dodging eighteen-wheelers on a six-lane highway, shortly after midnight. Not even when she gently urged, "Is there anything you'd like to tell me, Jake?"

"There's a long stretch of six percent grade between here and Golden, so gear down instead of riding the brakes." I had to trust my mom's driving. I wouldn't have said a word if Kurt had been at the wheel.

Sometime after 1:00 a.m. we collapsed in a motel room on the east side of Denver for the first of what could be way too many nights alone in a double bed. I dreamed of Kurt, who stood just beyond my extended hand and wouldn't come closer.

The next few days were a whirlwind of finding a place to live, unpacking the trailer into the cheap one-bedroom apartment we'd found, with hired muscle humping my giant green couch up two flights of stairs, and trying to turn the shoebox into a semblance of home. That required a couple of trips to thrift stores for ten-cent forks and twenty-five cent mugs, because most of last winter's kitchen lay in a cardboard carton in the storage shed in Meeker, right next to Kurt's motorcycle.

We'd even located a physical therapist within walking distance, which wasn't all that hard since my apartment wasn't far from the old University Hospital. That would be no help at all in getting to classes, since the University Hospital medical complex, including the pharmacy school, had moved east to a new campus, leaving a lot of orphaned practices and empty dwellings.

After coming back from my first appointment, Mom announced her intention to fly back home that evening. "You're settled as well as I can settle you, and your arm is healing enough that I'd only be sticking around to drive, and I'm afraid we're going to drive each other crazy soon."

"The therapist said he'd probably clear me on the stick shift next week, and I'm doing a lot better." I stuck my arm out straight from my shoulder to demonstrate. Not that I could have lifted it higher or swung a shovel yet, but I'd given up on wearing the sling. When I'd realized I had that much movement back, my first thought was to tell Kurt, and my second—that Kurt wasn't nearby to tell. Every time I turned around, I had one more detail to share with my lover who wasn't there, and as for e-mails—I didn't think he'd really care if the coffee pot fit better on one side of the sink than the other. If he wasn't there to pour a cup, it didn't matter.

"Is there anything we need to talk about before I leave,

darling?" She sat next to me on the big green couch, where I'd flopped down to mope some more.

Maybe I could tell her, and she'd stew about it for a while, and land in Detroit only half loathing me. I pushed myself upright, finding a forgotten bottle of lube making a lump between the cushions. Maybe that reminder of Kurt should have strengthened me, but—"No, Mom."

She patted my hand and went to pack.

I carried her bag to the curb left-handed, ready to put her in the taxi, and managed to hug her with both arms. "Thanks for coming out, Mom."

The horrible irony of that statement hit only after she'd hugged me back. "I'd do anything for you, Jake, even if you are a man grown and don't need your old mom so much. But you'll always be my son, and I'll always love you." She pulled me down for a kiss on my cheek. "Always. And give my regards to Kurt when you talk to him next."

I thought about that, watching the ride-share sedan pull away from the curb. I could almost believe her about the "always," even if I came out to her. But would she still have a kind word for Kurt? And what about Dad? Or Gramps? Great-Aunt Elaine was a lost cause, had been since I mowed off three sprinkler heads about ten years ago, so no change there. Only a couple of the aunts and uncles were raving religious types, and Aunt Beck could usually take the starch out of them with a well-placed comment, and when she and Mom ganged up on them, whew! Maybe....

The few nights I'd spent alone in the last year didn't prepare me for the quiet within the apartment. The silence absolutely echoed, aside from bumps, thumps, and muffled conversations from the neighbors.

I was the one who broke the stillness in the night. The bear breathed putrid fumes down my neck—I ran but not fast enough to evade the claws that sliced my clothes away. Naked, I turned to yell my last defiance. Gouts of red spattered over me, splashing into my eyes and mouth, tainting the air with the reek of hot copper. Explosions pummeled me; another wave of blood knocked me to my back. Sarge stood over me, the muzzle of his gun and his hard prick both the size of logs. Both pointing at me. "Give me an excuse," he said, and I crabbed away from him, backing into something solid and rough....

The solid whack of my head against the wall woke me, bringing me out of the hell that Kurt should have wakened me from. Another whimper escaped through my clenched teeth, and I'd swear that Kurt should have heard my heart banging against my ribs even if he was in the other room. The chest tube site and the arrow wound throbbed with each thud, and breathing hurt in a way I'd hoped was past. The sheets stuck to me in the river of sweat from my evil dream, and Kurt? Where was Kurt?

Miles away, and he wouldn't come unless I asked him. Rolling to his side of the bed, which comforted me only by being dry, I held the pillow and wished for him until the sun came up.

I sent an e-mail to Kurt, knowing it would still be a few days before he'd see it. A lot of daily stuff, but ending with:

... I got a one-bedroom place, because with you and me, it will be all or nothing. I won't try to make you live some half-assed life. But I haven't found the way out of this closet yet, though it stinks of old shoes.

Love you,

J

I got an e-mail back Friday morning.

Sam's okay to have around, even if he's not as good a cook as you.

That made me smile—he didn't consider my cooking all that fabulous, more "mostly edible," so I decided to read that as code for a lot of things I was to him that his new partner was not.

Glad to hear about the apartment. It's hard not knowing, but this has to be what you can do. I'll throw all my dirty socks into the closet if it'll help you decide.

Miss you,

K

Oh Lord, I'd better find my own path out before he started chemical warfare. Damn but I loved the man, and why couldn't I do this for him? For us? I wrote back:

I held a ten pound weight out straight for thirty seconds at PT today. Orientation starts week after next. Classes the week after.

I miss you too. Give the aspen tree and the hay bales my regards.

Love you,

J

We'd both leaned against that aspen tree to pleasure ourselves last summer, and I was spending almost as much time with my cock in my own hand now as I had when I was pining for Kurt and not sure he was interested. My imagination was a lot better this time around, because I knew how good we could be together.

I didn't have a lot else to do besides kick back, do my physical therapy, and check out all the online information about classes and buying books. I met my neighbors and even liked some of them, though questions about "Are you seeing someone?" were sort of awkward—I really didn't know how to answer that. "It's complicated" sufficed to bring knowing nods.

That still left plenty of time to walk around and get to know Denver the way I'd learned the Uncompahgre National Forest. One cheap sushi joint, an Ethiopian restaurant that smelled interesting, and a place billing itself as "The Home of the World's Best Burger" all went on the list of places to check out when I had the money and the companionship. Having a freezer at home to store the carton didn't keep me out of an ice cream shop that churned every one of its forty flavors. I'd have to bring Kurt here for sure.

Everything in the city got filtered through the lens of "would Kurt like it?" Cheesman Park made the list, maybe not so much for the expanse of green grass covered with people and Frisbee-playing dogs, some in bandanas, but because so many of them were men. Gay men. Had to be, they were holding hands, kissing, and several couples lay on top of each other, making me blush for park abuse. Honestly, when Kurt and I humped all over each other on every handy boulder, we didn't have an audience.

A few of them whistled at me, and I probably could have had a fine old time in the shrubbery three or four times over if I'd responded to some of the invitations. Did "out" have to be *that* "out"? Someone might have turned a fire hose on me for the way my face burned. Definitely not coming back this way without Kurt to cling on to.

But he would like it for the way it made me think. Every man there who'd touched his partner, or kissed him under the warm sun, or pushed one of the several baby carriages, had admitted to himself and the world what he wanted. Even the man who'd suggested sex without names was more honest with himself than I was.

I came home from that walk with a head full of thoughts chasing themselves around my brain, and collected the mail without really looking at it. A light box about six inches square stopped me—I hadn't ordered anything, nor had Mom mentioned sending something. Most of my mail came addressed to "Resident," but this had my name on it, a Meeker postmark, and handwriting I recognized.

I slit the tape with trembling hands. What had Kurt sent me?

A pine cone nestled in a bit of white tissue. A pine cone, no note. Why? I examined it for the message Kurt meant it to convey.

The scales flared widely; most of the seeds had fallen out. The tip stayed stubbornly closed, the prickles jabbing into my fingertips as I turned it over, finding the scorched spot. This cone had come from a lodgepole pine, and its resin had melted away, shedding the start of new life on the forest floor. Until disaster had befallen it, it had stayed tightly furled, all potential locked up. A serotinous cone—the word I'd searched for at the year-old burn site floated up unbidden—would not release its seeds until it had passed through fire.

Kurt and I had passed through fire once, becoming lovers. And then we'd had another disaster, but would I let it remain tragic, or would I let something new and wondrous sprout?

Growth. I would go for new growth, and my new life, with the best part my recent past coming with me. I loved Kurt, and he loved me, and the world in general could kiss my ass. Right now his opinions and mine were the only ones in the universe that mattered.

I had no faster way to reach him than an e-mail, unless I wanted to share too much with the world. Out was out, but having Mrs. Chief, or worse, the Chief himself, relay a message to my lover over the radio was just a little too far out. Getting my laptop open needed three tries and booting up took at least a year. When I could start a message, I wrote:

Kurt, I love you, I'm sorry,I've beenm such an idsiot I'm sorry. I love you. If peopl get weird that's their problem, I don't ever wamnt to hide you and us again. Come lifve with me when fire seasons done. I msis you so much and I dont want to miss you anyu more

Jakw

I managed to click on everything but "send" at first, but I got the message off at last. Today was Wednesday; he wouldn't see that note until Friday morning at the earliest, because that's when he and Sam would make their weekly trek into town. I could hope he'd hit the library first thing—he blogged and did all his other electronic business then. The waiting might kill me.

Looking at the message again, I realized I'd hit everything but spellcheck. Trying again produced:

Sorry, that was gibberish, but it's heartfelt gibberish. I love you, I miss you, I want to spend my life with you if you'll still have me, and I miss you terribly. I don't want to hide that away any longer. Please tell me I haven't fucked us up beyond repair.

Jake, who loves Kurt

I woke with the dawn on Friday morning, knowing Kurt would too. Still, the library wouldn't open until nine o'clock, and he couldn't see my outpourings until he'd opened the messages. Making coffee was a three-attempt project—the first time I forgot the grounds, the second time I forgot the carafe and had to swab counters and floor. It served to eat up another fifteen minutes. Then I ran back to the bedroom to make the bed, a task I always forgot, though Kurt tucked his blankets tight every morning. He might have been throwing his socks in the basket with memories of my teasing.

The laptop would not disgorge an e-mail, not for begging, pleading, or threats. I didn't need any of the crap it did produce —Viagra by mail offers and get rich quick schemes got deleted with extreme prejudice, but nothing with Kurt's address appeared in the window. Maybe shaking it would help. Maybe not. I settled for clicking send/receive fourteen times in quick succession. At 9:22 I did it again.

The pine cone helped keep me centered. Kurt would respond—he *had* to—that pine cone was far too explicit a message for one who could read it—unless he meant he was a part of my life that had burned away. No, if he meant that, he'd have said it. The cone's prickly end jabbed me when I turned it over in my hands, so I used a couple of paper clips to hang it from my desk lamp. It swayed with my next assault on the send/receive button.

Doing my home physical therapy exercises at least got me away from the keyboard, though every ping and chime made me look up with hope. I stretched, lifted, rolled, and arched, feeling the burn in the perforated muscles. The arrow wound below my clavicle had knitted and scabbed over, as had the entrance for the chest tube, leaving shiny pink polka dots to let me locate the twinges exactly, as if I needed help. I poked the send/receive button, only to be mocked by a notice from the school of pharmacy that I was too anxious to pay attention to.

Nothing from Kurt. Maybe he'd despaired, thinking I was taking too long, and he wouldn't visit the library until late in the day, after the grocery shopping, laundry, and reports to the Chief were over. Maybe he didn't know how to say *You blew it, Jake* and deleted the notes. Maybe... maybe... I could envision a lot of horrid scenarios, and had a couple dozen stored up before noon.

Running through the PT moves again at least made me feel stronger. Maybe some pushups? In another fit of hopefulness, I tried hoisting my upper body away from the floor in good form, although if Kurt was beneath me, I wouldn't have to keep my body straight. But if he didn't respond to my *cri de coeur* there'd be no point to straining this hard. I collapsed hard to the right on the third lift, my bad shoulder not up to the strain, and nearly missed the knock on the door.

SEVENTEEN

Not entirely certain the knock had been more than wishful thinking, I dragged myself off the floor and reached for the doorknob. What if I'd invented it out of the thump of my own fall? My pulse sounded like a freight train in my ears.

I opened the door slowly, and oh Lord, I saw a blond vision in ranger green. Kurt. My Lord, it was Kurt! Colorado sky-blue eyes filled with uncertainty glowed in his tan face, his lips parted with hope and fear.

Perfect for kissing. I flung the door the rest of the way open and dove into his arms. Kurt. Warm and solid and really in my doorway—I found his mouth, searching for the welcome I knew I'd find. His arms wrapped tight around me, and mine around him, though I took one hand to cup his cheek, needing to feel, to look, and to crush my lips to his again and again.

"You're here, you're really here," I gasped out, catching at his lower lip, running my fingers through his short blond hair.

"You sound—" He paused to scrape his cheek against mine on his way to nibble my earlobe. "—way too surprised. Didn't you get my e-mail?"

"I've been beating the crap out of the computer to make it give me a message." We were chest to chest, belly to belly, groin to groin. I pulled him tighter and ignored the sound of a door opening and shutting down the hall.

"Guess we're out to the librarian, because I was trying to reply 'I'm on my way' and may not have hit 'send' before I blew out of there." He found that sensitive spot on my neck long enough to make me groan, and returned to my mouth.

"She'll get over it."

He had to have been driving from the moment he'd read the message, and broken every traffic law to boot. I enjoyed the vision of him leaping away from the keyboard to pound out of the mountains, to be with me.

With me. In my arms now. I wanted to grab both hot globes of his ass and pull him tight against my now-throbbing erection, but if I got his utilities off first—some things still needed to be behind closed doors. Pulling him through the door and hauling his T-shirt off in nearly one motion got me started, and with the door closed, I could push him back onto the big green couch.

If we'd gone slower, we could have stripped Kurt faster—he got the zipper down and his butt up to let me peel him, but I should have gotten his boots off first. He was wearing new ones, not the pair Jonesy had stolen, but he wasn't wearing them for long, once I managed the laces. My own clothes bounced off the far wall and then I was on him.

Oh, I'd dreamed of this, I'd imagined us together again, but to feel the heat of his skin against mine. To press against his muscled frame, and grind against his cock, as hard and yearning as my own. Someone's precome slicked against my belly—mine or his, I wasn't stopping to check. Both. My lover, my partner, my love—he pulled me tighter against his body.

Just as I wanted it—with hands, mouth, and skin I explored him, as if he might have changed in the days since we'd been able to touch one another. But no, the familiar hollows and bulges of muscle and bone, the scent that was part pines, sweat, unpolluted air, and man, all I could find was Kurt, and it was like coming home.

Empty days and lonely nights fell away in the press of his flesh against mine, licked to nothingness in the dance of our tongues. I'd had the choice to embrace my fear instead of him, and I'd been stupid enough to take it, but if wisdom had come late, it had returned before Kurt gave up on me. Now we clung to one another, and letting go would never be a choice again.

That stray bottle of lube was still making a lump in the cushions, but using it meant unwrapping from him, and even a moment was too much. I lifted my hips enough to slip a hand between us, my fingers barely long enough to wrap around both of our cocks. Kurt wormed a hand in too, to help me hold us, and my fingertips rubbed against his wrist with every thrust of our hips.

Hope, yearning, and love exploded out of me, smearing between our bellies in shattering pleasure. I throbbed in Kurt's hand—pulsing against his skin was more important than my enjoyment, and I had time to open my eyes again before his orgasm rippled through him. To hold him through it was new again, but familiar. I'd missed Kurt terribly, but that chasm seemed deeper now that it had been healed. I traced his nose and cheeks with my lips, feeling his warm breath huff against my face.

"Convinced I'm here?" he teased.

"Almost. Maybe." I nibbled softly at his lips. "Might have to do this again before I'm sure." We'd done something pretty convincing, but I wanted one kiss for each of the thousand deaths I'd endured waiting. He seemed willing to provide, with his unsquashed hand kneading my ass. Kurt licked a drop of sweat that threatened to fall from the tip of my nose, reminding me of other drips.

I peeled myself off him and helped him to his feet, not that he needed it, but that I didn't want to lose contact with his skin for a second. Then I could give him a sloppy, upright hug. "Welcome to your new home."

His arms tightened around me at the word. "This is our living room. We have the smallest kitchen in North America over there, and here—" I maneuvered him three steps to the door. "—is our bathroom." We had just enough space in front of the sink for me to wash us off. He let me give him the tour, a grin spreading across his face with every obvious bit of introduction, until his dimple showed and I paused to probe it with the tip of my tongue. "Our bedroom, and our bed, which I shall acquaint you with far more intimately."

"That bed is made—are you quite sure you've been sleeping in it?" He leaned against me, surveying the truly novel change in my habits.

"How many socks has Sam kicked across the floor?" I suspected "none," though he only chuckled. Funny what missing someone will make you do.

"They're all sitting in the hall," he observed, turning in my arms. "Home is where, if you show up with a duffel bag, they have to let you do your laundry."

That was one of our important tasks to do on our weekly trips into town. And he was home in all important ways. "Washers are downstairs. Damn."

"Why 'damn'?" Kurt raised one eyebrow. "That's better than fifty miles away. We could get the loads started and then come back to explore this very inviting bed." The burgundy-striped sheets called *come slide in* where I'd turned down one corner.

"This isn't such a great building. If we leave stuff unattended, it gets stolen." I could just swap all my clean clothes for Kurt's dirty ones and launder them at leisure. If Kurt could get through the next week or two with my T-shirts flapping on him and my utilities threatening to fall off his hips. He had a belt, didn't he? His clothes might look like spray-paint on me, but if I stayed out of Cheesman Park, I should be okay.

"If someone took my duffel already that solves one problem," Kurt mused.

But created more. I could at least drag it inside. If I could reach it without exposing my naked hide in the hallway. Which I couldn't—he'd dropped it a good two feet farther than modesty would let me reach. Sliding my jeans back on was the only way to retrieve it and keep from flashing the world.

"If you're going to get dressed even that much," Kurt observed after watching me slide my commando butt into denim, "then let's just go down and sit with the laundry. We can talk and defend my underwear at the same time." He eeled back into his clothing.

He had a point. I picked up his duffel bag in my right hand, just to prove how much stronger I'd gotten, and Kurt extracted detergent from under the sink. We walked hand in hand down the stairs, and I didn't have to see his face to know his dimple was showing from that small contact. Some neighbor I didn't know passed us going up, and his face didn't change on seeing us. When he came around the landing, I clutched Kurt a little tighter but didn't let go. First step of being out, completed.

We filled two of the four coin-operated washers with Kurt's stuff—all the mud, blood, and dirt from our hideous adventure had been laundered away but a couple of garments reeked of smoke. "You and Sam had at least one fire, huh?" I poured blue slime on top of his clothes and shut the lid while Kurt fed quarters into the slots.

"One, nothing bad. We didn't even suit up." Kurt peeked out the garden level window, watching a pair of legs visible only to the knee go by. He turned back to me with a lopsided grin. "Nice little one to train the noob with."

"He can't be that big a noob, can he?" Sam was Forest Service, after all, even if he was a LEO. "All your partners can't start from total ignorance." Not like me last year.

"Nah." Kurt turned back to me and lifted my shirt to trace the healing pink disks on my chest. I tried not to flinch under his touch, which was gentle. "I really got you, didn't I?" His voice broke a little.

I didn't want him focusing on the past. "You did." But not how he meant it. Flexing my knees so I could lift him with my hands under his armpits, I demonstrated my recovery and what I meant by hoisting his butt onto a washer. Disguising the stab of pain if not the weakness on my right side by worming between his knees, I lay my head against his chest. "I am all yours."

"Mine. Okay." He wrapped those bronzed, whipcord arms around my shoulders and leaned his cheek against my head. "I like that." He seemed willing to stay like that a long time. The washer hummed against us.

"You're not still angry with me?" he murmured into my hair.

"No, Kurt. Not for any of it." He stiffened a little in my arms. "You were right." He relaxed a bit, but some tension remained, like he was totting up just how much I had to be angry about.

"I got past all that somewhere in this last lonely week.

Because you were right about everything. A little of the problem was money, but you showed me that money would turn up—it's a detail. Some of it was being spooked by the competition, but if we could survive Tubbs and Jonesy, a bunch of college kids with notebooks and pens just aren't that frightening." I talked into his chest, and could feel his little snort of recognition against my cheek and through my arms.

"And as for being spooked about us in the city and people knowing—" This was the hardest to say because I was still kind of jumpy. "I'd rather be out with you than alone in my closet."

"I had to let you see how stuffy it was in there." He ran a thumb around the orbit of my eye, where traces of chartreuse lingered. "That was damned near as hard as leaving you at Sarge's camp. Or knowing that I'd nearly killed you. And you thinking I might have done it intentionally."

"We're done with that, Kurt. Honest." I turned to kiss him full on. If he'd gotten me into Denver, aimed toward a classroom and a little better off financially, it was nothing he could have predicted when he drew back that bowstring—he was good, but nobody, not even Kurt, was that good. And I didn't want him beating himself up any longer.

I might have about had Kurt convinced when footsteps stopped behind me and someone cleared her throat. "You have an apartment for that, don't you?"

I turned without moving my hips or letting go of him—I was his fig leaf and he was mine. "Hi, Eleanor. Kurt, this is my neighbor down the hall. Eleanor, this is my partner, Kurt Carlson."

She raised one eyebrow toward her salt-and-pepper hairline. "Is this the 'It's complicated' fellow?"

"Not any more. It's simple now—Kurt's going to move in with me after fire season." Telling Eleanor seemed like good practice for telling the rest of the world. In fact, telling Eleanor was a lot like telling the rest of the world—she could give Max at Rendezvous Lake Lodge a run for the title of "Area News Conduit." I gave Kurt another squeeze and flashed her a smile.

Every piece of nylon in her laundry basket should have melted from her glare. "And when he hits you again?"

Fwump went the need for a fig leaf. "Damn, Eleanor, is that what you've been thinking?" I whirled around, furious, and Kurt went rigid behind me. "Kurt *saved* me from the guy who did hit me—he fucking *saved my life* and the only thing complicated was me being an idiot about being out!" I wanted to shake her 'til she rattled for even thinking that. Kurt put his hands on my shoulders, his strong grip my anchor to staying in place.

"My apologies, but you frankly looked like hell and have been the picture of gloom and doom since you moved in. It didn't seem like a large step that you were running from an abusive situation." She set her laundry basket down on the next washer.

"Eleanor, if you have been telling people that, then you were way off base." It didn't occur to me that new acquaintances would look at the remains of truly spectacular bruising on my face and imagine that was the complication. "No one has ever been as good to me as Kurt."

"No, Jake, I have not been spreading that around. That was my unwarranted assumption, and as you can plainly see, assuming has made an ass out of me. I'm sorry." There was no give in her, no fear, just a straightforward apology. Kind of like Kurt would do. I stopped shaking with the need to obliterate her notion.

"I've been down because we were apart and my life got

turned upside down, that's all." I found Kurt's calves by reaching back.

"That, apparently, was enough. As the two of you were clearly having a happy reunion before I barged in, why don't you go upstairs and enjoy yourselves while I take care of the laundry by way of apology for the interruption?" *So I don't have to sit through half a wash cycle and an entire dry cycle of silent recriminations* or maybe *So I don't have to watch you start from the beginning* might have been her motivation, but I didn't care, I'd take it.

"Thank you," I found my tongue to say, and Kurt echoed it.

"Three o'clock then," she said, and shooed us away.

Didn't have to tell us twice—Kurt and I pelted upstairs for a couple of hours of privacy.

EIGHTEEN

Chirping from my phone, which lay abandoned on my desk, greeted us when we got back inside. I would have ignored it save for a sense of foreboding that it was important. With one arm around Kurt, I slapped the device to my ear.

Good thing. It was the Chief.

He spent a word and a half on greetings and got right to the meat of his call. "Jake, have you seen or heard from Kurt today?"

I gave my lover the raised eyebrow of *Do you want me to admit to seeing you?* Kurt nodded.

"He's here now, Chief. Um, why did you think he'd be here?"

"Because he took off like a bat out of hell, and I got a call from the highway patrol about one of my trucks exceeding the speed limit outside of Eagle and where was the fire?" The Chief sounded more amused than annoyed. "And if he wasn't on his way to you, then I have a rogue ranger and a stolen truck, which doesn't match what I know of Kurt Carlson."

Good Lord, what did he know of Kurt Carlson? Or Jake

Landon? A fragment of a conversation from earlier this summer came back to me. *You have this opportunity, and you hired on with the expectation that you'd pursue it. I planned for it, rather than lose you both this season.* So the Chief had known months ago that Kurt and I were a couple. Was it that obvious?

"He'll be back." What else could I say? "Do you want to talk to him?"

"No. You can deliver the message that he's responsible for the diesel fuel for the round trip, and that Sam is here at Head-quarters, eating all of Mrs. Chief's brownies." The Chief snorted. "The chewing-out can wait 'til he gets back, and I'll check in with you later about school and such." His good-bye was more nearly a chuckle. I pocketed the phone to hug Kurt with both arms.

"Did you ignore all radio contact on the way down?"

"Yeah," he admitted into the hollow of my throat. "Forgot that the GPS transponds. Nice of him to call instead of sending the cops."

"Won't get you out of a hefty fuel bill and a lecture. Nicer of him to be agreeable about us as us."

That got me a funny look. "What do you mean?"

"I think he's known about us for a while. Something he said before everything went to hell. And it hasn't been a problem." The more I thought about it, the more I realized the one with the problem was me. Although discretion in the middle of the rodeo chutes would probably still be a good idea. "He probably would have worried more if you hadn't come here."

"Huh." Kurt thrust his groin against me. "Let's go take a shower."

Fine by me. Naked again, I let him stand under the spray alone for a few minutes, enjoying the warmth, while I found a bottle of lube. Never know what we'd find to do in there.

We shared the spray, wetting Kurt's hair. Massaging the dollop of shampoo into his scalp gave him a cap of foam. He curled like a cat into my hands, and I could keep both arms up now. He closed his eyes to better luxuriate in my touch, and it was so easy to tip his face up for another kiss or five when I backed him into the spray to rinse. The foam ran down our bodies, slicking us, and we used each other for giant washcloths, rubbing with bodies, hands, arms, and enough soap to clean us six times over.

I had lathery fingers wrapped around Kurt's cock when I sipped the flat of my other hand between his cheeks, luxuriating in this intimate touch, our mouths together. Stroking against his hole, I could feel the coarse hairs sliding by, and his twitches for the stimulation. Teasing him became a game, but I didn't want him coming too soon, so I turned his back to the water and let the suds rinse away with our cocks trapped tall and proud between our bodies.

Kurt opened his mouth against mine, tracing short paths along my lower lip with his tongue. Giving me ideas. I turned him to face the tile and dropped to my knees.

He helped, once he knew what I wanted, thrusting his hips back to give me access. I couldn't get enough of him, and he knew it, spreading his feet and moaning soft encouragements. *Mine!* I'd roared the first time we'd done this, but we both knew that to our very souls now, and I could save my breath to caress him in spite of the water sheeting down his back.

Some bad combination of licking, inhaling, and moving sent a pint of water up my nose, and I plopped back on my butt before I wanted to stop. Kurt waited out my choking before giving me a hand up, the slackness of his face telling me he hadn't lost the whole mood in spite of my undignified snorking.

I managed another lick across the head of his cock, so stiff and perfectly aimed at my face, before I clambered up and turned him around again. I could nip and lick at his neck while getting the lube open.

Some for him, some for me, and Kurt backed against me, taking me slowly but completely within. Again, like coming home—I had to mumble his name and a dozen *I love yous* with each slow stroke. He bent, and I bent over him, every possible inch of our skins touching. I wanted to last forever, knowing I wouldn't so we'd just have to do it again and again until it became our forever.

His own quiet litany of "Jake, I love you" mixed with moans and went in time with my hips and my hand, which I'd wrapped around his cock—my right hand, which I could again move well enough to give him pleasure.

My orgasm roared through like consuming flames the falling water did nothing to slake. I convulsed and poured into Kurt, who shoved himself back against me, taking me deeply within, letting me all but meld with him. Without disengaging, I managed to get us upright once the waves had receded, devoting my full attention to stroking him to the same joys. Not faster, but more attentively, and with my arm across his chest and my lips at his neck. When he cried out and pulsed in my hand, I kept him from falling.

And then Kurt turned in my arms and we held each other until the water lost its warmth.

NINETEEN

We had a few minutes to find our britches and forage for sandwiches before Eleanor would turn up. I certainly hadn't eaten today, and Kurt admitted to running on empty too. Maybe I was maudlin, or maybe hypoglycemic, but even something as silly as plopping sliced turkey on bread together felt like good omens for the future. We lost a few crumbs on each other's chests, and licked away streaks of mayonnaise that might have been imaginary in a couple of cases, but damn, did it all taste good.

"Thanks, Eleanor," Kurt said when she knocked at the stroke of three. "You didn't have to fold stuff too." He took the basket from her.

"Think of it as a peace offering," she said, and stumped away.

"I like at least one of our neighbors," Kurt told me, tossing a ball of paired socks my way. I flipped it into the duffel for three points. "I have a couple of hours before I really need to head back. Anything you'd like to do?"

"Oh yeah." I knew exactly what we could do and started to pull on my shoes. "You'll love this."

"Okay." He followed me out the door.

So maybe what I wanted to do wasn't so much what lay at the other end of our route, but the walk itself. I pointed us west on a pleasant tree-lined street that went one way, past turn-of-the-century homes and some newer apartment buildings. The street was pretty and not too busy, and the perfect place to try my newest signal of affection.

I took Kurt's hand to walk the mile or so I meant us to go. He laughed when I did, and we had to sort out whose hand went where before we were comfortable, but I was going to take a walk with my partner. I was out—there was no going back.

Of course Kurt figured that out. "Going whole hog, aren't you?"

"Yeah." I gave him a little squeeze and kept him from stepping off the curb into the path of a murderous Pontiac. One of us had to pay attention to our surroundings. Not that I didn't almost walk us right past the ice cream shop in a love-induced haze.

"You've been exploring the terrain, huh, Jake?" Kurt didn't quite press his nose against the glass while trying to decide which of the endless flavors to choose.

"Of course." Ice cream didn't survive in our wilderness fridge, which made this an uncommon treat. The diner in Meeker offered vanilla or chocolate from the market. We hadn't been willing to pay resort prices for the good stuff when we lived in Wapiti Creek, nor was a frozen sweet particularly enticing after a day outside in the snow. The clerk offered him samples on wooden paddles, and I enjoyed the sight of my confident lover reduced to dithering.

"We can come back and try the others another time," I

pointed out after the clerk handed over yet another sample, this one a deep orange which made Kurt's eyes go wide and then close.

"But they might not have mango-peach that day." He licked the paddle clean in a way I'd only seen him do when he was kneeling over my groin. Give me another ten minutes to recover and I'd pop wood over it.

"But they'll have ginger-honey or adobe pie or thirty-eight other delights." I could see us spending a lot of time and money here over the next four years. Maybe Kurt could get hired on and taste test to his heart's content.

"This." Kurt waved the mango-peach paddle.

I ordered a single scoop in a cone and handed over enough money to buy a half gallon of a grocery-store brand. Kurt gulped but didn't reach for his wallet—good. We'd get this "who treated whom" stuff worked out. Maybe I could get a part-time job here. Or a pharmacy intern position, which would pay for ice cream and some other essentials. I'd seen something about that flash by on an e-mail I'd been too nervous to read fully earlier.

We took our ice cream outside, taking turns licking. Damn that was good. Tart and creamy, with flecks of fruit pulp. "We could walk over that way a couple of blocks and become more or less invisible because of the high concentration of affectionate gay men," I told him between slurps. "Unless we attracted a lot of attention because of the way you're enjoying that."

Kurt really did look orgasmic during his turn to lick. Maybe this was a little further out than I'd meant to head. Um, wasn't going to interrupt his treat. He opened his eyes. "You too, Jake. Let's go the other way, because I'm going to have to go back eventually and I don't want to spend precious time heading off suggestions."

We walked back down Thirteenth Avenue with my hand on his shoulder and Kurt holding the cone for us to alternate bites. The ice cream was marvelous but tasted a million times better because Kurt fed it to me.

Once back at our apartment, we had to kiss the drips off each other, and of course one thing led to another, and I got to see Kurt wearing his mango-peach ice cream face again.

We were drowsing afterward when Kurt mumbled, "Does this total turnabout mean you'll reconsider going to Wyoming for Thanksgiving?"

"I'm out, and I'm staying out," I told myself as much as him, "so I'll just brace myself to meet the in-laws. But maybe we could do it sooner, on a not so emotionally charged date?" Didn't matter if I was frozen with fear—no one was ever going to frighten me as much Jonesy and Tubbs had, and Kurt had already assured me of his family's basic goodwill. I could do this.

"I'll check with Cliff and Vanessa. We can catch Larry and Polly on our way through Casper." Kurt trailed his fingers up and down my torso, playing dot-to-dot with my nipples, birthmarks, and scars. "They'll like you."

I'd trust he was right. Kurt's orientation wouldn't come as a surprise to them. Unlike my family. Kurt left them unmentioned.

"We need to figure out some times when we can see each other before the end of fire season." I caught his hand and held it tight before he could circle the arrow scar again.

"When does school start?"

"Week after next. I have a couple of days of orientation next week and then the White Coat ceremony on Friday, but I thought I'd skip that." It seemed sort of pointless. Yes, we were embarking on schooling that taught us how not to kill people accidentally; I didn't need a big deal made of it to understand the importance.

"Why? It would be like missing the opening ceremony at the Olympics just because you don't expect to win." He lifted on one elbow to stare down at me.

"I won't have anyone there. If it's just me, what's the big deal? I could come up and see you instead."

"Nope. What time is the ceremony?" His dimple suddenly showed to the right side of his smile.

"One o'clock. Why?" I suspected I knew why.

"Because instead of hijacking a piece of federal equipment again, I'll get my motorbike out of storage and come." He leaned down to smooch me, and laughed at my wide eyes. "I can be here a lot earlier that way. It's your first milestone with school. You should be there. I want to be there for you."

I rolled him over to control the next kiss. "I wasn't planning on making you sit through anything until graduation, but okay." Better than okay. I wanted to shine in his eyes, prove that all my stupid objections were behind me, and if this ceremony was the way to do it, we'd get there early. I'd introduce him as my partner, and if anyone got snarky about us, well, that would be my early-asshole-identification system. Because my class-mates could just go bite rocks if they objected—we weren't living our lives for their comfort. I was going to tell myself that enough times until I really believed it.

I kissed the end of his nose again, knowing that there was one huge gap in this coming out business. "So... that just leaves my family."

"I'm not going to push you on that, Jake. It seems like fami-ly's the hardest to tell." He wrapped his arms around my neck.

"Yeah." I leaned my forehead down to his. "I have no idea how to bring it up, and it really should be face to face. 'Hi, I'm gay and this is my partner.' At least Mom's forgiven you about the arrow."

He groaned. "I may never live down that arrow."

"I probably should have told her before she left, but…." I had an idea, one that would make it possible to get this last cloud out of my sky and make Kurt happy. "Want to come to Detroit for Thanksgiving?"

He froze. "You mean that?"

"Wouldn't have said it if I didn't." And it gave me months to figure out how to break the news. Also a deadline. I needed the deadline, because without it, I'd been running on a timetable of "never." I swung up to sitting and fished my phone out of my discarded jeans.

"Hi, Mom, yeah, things are fine…." We ran through some social talk about my arm, buying books, and was I cleared to drive yet. Kurt curled around me, listening as if his future depended on it. Guess it did. "Uh, Mom, I didn't make it home for Thanksgiving last year, but I'd like to plan for it this year."

"Wonderful! We missed you, and we have so much to be thankful for this time." Her voice held extra warmth, which helped a little with the ice in my guts. Kurt listened gravely. I swapped the phone to my right hand so I could stroke his hair while Mom and I talked.

"And, Mom, is it okay if I bring someone home with me?" I got the question out without a stutter.

"Certainly, Jake. Your friends are always welcome, and it's easy enough to mash another potato." The frozen lump in my middle grew so large that turkey and fixings couldn't possibly fit any time this year.

"Okay, great. We'll plan for it." My endurance for this chat was nearly done.

"We'll be delighted to have you, and tell Kurt I'm looking forward to seeing him again."

"What?" I flipped my head back so fast I knocked the phone out of my own hand and had to scrabble on the floor for it. Kurt sat bold upright from my alarm, and put a warm hand on my shoulder when I finally got reorganized. "Why are you so sure it's Kurt?"

"Darling." Mom tutted at me. "Please. I was born at night, but it wasn't last night. He's been your constant companion for over a year. The two of you plan your jobs together. Jobs that require living together. You speak of him constantly. And even without that, I saw how it was killing him that you'd been hurt, and how you got stronger when he came into the room. It isn't that you weren't discreet—you were. But I know you, Jake, and it was perfectly clear to me that you two matter a great deal to each other. If I'm wrong, you can tell me."

Since she wasn't, I made some gaffed-fish mouths that weren't exactly an answer. "You knew." And she'd given me opportunity after opportunity to say something. *Is there anything you'd like to tell me, Jake?* Kurt had called me the stupidest smart man he knew. Guess he was right.

"Well, call it ninety-eight percent sure. And it's okay. You're my son, I love you now and always, and you have good taste in men."

Damn but Mom could cut straight to the chase. I continued my trout impersonation. Kurt began to chuckle behind me.

"Are you all right, dear?" she asked after the silence grew.

"I'm fine," I croaked, and cleared my throat. "I thought you were the one who was supposed to be speechless after this sort of talk." I turned to throw an arm around Kurt's shoulders, and squished a kiss on his temple.

"Oh, give your mom some credit for an open mind. And —" She laughed. "—I couldn't leave you in your previous state of grumpiness while you waited 'til Thanksgiving to tell me. You'd be unbearable, and no one deserves more of that."

I probably had been a surly bastard. Good thing she loves me. "What about Dad? Does he know too?" This might be easier than I thought.

"That's a discussion you'll have to have with him—this isn't my story to tell. But I don't envision any problems." She sent my heart pounding with one statement and calmed it with the next, but only about halfway. Then she cranked me back to max. "You definitely need to have a talk with Gramps."

"Uh, right. Yes. Well. Um." I could stand to wait a few months for that. "Okay. Um. Talk to you soon. Bye."

"That went well," Kurt said for me.

Falling over and hyperventilating was as much response as I could manage for a while. I pulled Kurt against my chest and held him tightly. "I really am an idiot." I finally mumbled into his hair.

"Nah. Just human. And scared. Now it's not so scary." He hugged me back. "And I'm here."

For a little while longer now, and only now and then for some time to come, but Kurt'd be back full time when the snows came to the high country. This bed would feel too empty, but then we'd have years. Years with Kurt. And I no longer had to live in fear of anyone noticing we were lovers, because they'd been noticing all along. I felt ready to wrestle wildcats, but Kurt was a lot more fun and much handier, so we rolled over the bed, tussling and tickling. Not sure what the endpoint was supposed to be, but we wound up in a liplock.

"I wish I didn't have to go," he told me when we broke for air. "But I have a long drive ahead of me."

More than four hours back just to collect Sam, and another hour to the cabin, and Kurt would have to be up with the sun tomorrow. I didn't want to let go either, but I understood.

When he was dressed and ready to go, I walked downstairs with him. Our old familiar tanker with the scratched Forest Service logo sat next to my crudmobile just like at the cabin, but only Kurt would be in the mountains tonight.

He fired up the engine, getting the throaty diesel grumble that had been our accompaniment to two summers, and I remained on the ground. I wouldn't be riding along this time.

One more kiss, one more touch—I needed enough to get through until Kurt came back next week, next month, until October when he could stay. I jumped up on the running board to put my head through the open window and meet his mouth. I kissed my beloved once again, but—I wasn't kissing Kurt good-bye.

ABOUT THE AUTHOR

P.D. Singer lives in Colorado with her slightly bemused husband, one proto-adult, and twelve pounds of cats. She's a big believer in research, firsthand if possible, so the reader can be quite certain Pam has skied down a mountain face first, been stepped on by rodeo horses, acquired a potato burn or two, and will never, ever, write a novel that includes skydiving.

When not writing, playing her fiddle, or skiing, she can be found with a book in hand.

Follow the adventures at Pam's website.

Keep current with Pam and the Rocky Ridge gang by joining the newsletter.

ALSO BY P.D. SINGER

Fire on the Mountain

Snow on the Mountain

Fall Down the Mountain

Return to the Mountain

Running to Him

Spokes

The Rare Event - returning soon

A New Man - returning soon

Diving Deep - returning soon

Concierge Service

A TASTE OF RETURN TO THE
MOUNTAIN

GARY AND SETH, CHAPTER 1

The leather strap bit into Gary's shoulder, the clubs clanking behind him. Ultralight, ultrathin fabrics might be a mark of wealth in some sports, but the heft of cowhide still ruled for golfers who didn't have to carry their own bulky bags. The clubs would probably stay in the Beemer's trunk until the owner got home, unless some other low-paid, strong-backed flunky lifted them out at the hotel. Gary'd had eighteen holes of hauling, and the twenty-dollar tip in his pocket wasn't making up for the crick in his spine.

He scanned for the burgundy convertible, expecting to find it near the end of this row, but enough luxurious vehicles filled the Wapiti Creek Golf Club parking lot that a brand new BMW M3 didn't attract nearly as much attention as the owner might hope. If Gary'd parked his 1984 Cutlass on the members' side of the lot, now *that* would stand out. There. Second from the end. Gary hoisted the golf bag into a more comfortable position and started walking.

He'd dump the clubs—well, wait patiently by the BMW until the fifty-five-pretending-to-be-forty-five-year-old man with the tanning booth tan came out to unlock the trunk. Maybe he'd offer another tip if he kept Gary standing a while, but not a lot of hope there; Gary already knew how much this kind of guy valued the time of an eighteen-year-old caddy. Maybe he'd lean the bag against the paintwork.

Gorgeous car, though—all rounded curves and supple leather, a real penis extender. Probably good for three inches in the eyes of whatever liposuctioned, botoxed blonde the owner was fucking this week.

Damn but Gary wanted to find Seth and get back to Phippsburg, where people wore their own faces. Mostly.

He heard Seth before he saw him, and that pleading note in Seth's voice made Gary break into a run. Lord, who was picking on his buddy here? Back at school he'd know if it was TJ Stone-breaker stuffing Seth into a locker, which Gary *thought* his mice had put a stop to, or that scumbag Eddy who'd liked to catch Seth's hand in a come-along grip until Gary explained the error of his ways using a bench vise. Gary'd fixed Eddy's bucket but good a year ago; he'd shied away from both Seth and Gary ever since, so not him, but none of those guys would hang around here anyway.

He didn't have as much leverage on adults, and he sure as hell didn't have much leverage on old rich ones. But Seth shouldn't ever have to sound so scared. Gary ran.

Seth cried out again—"No!" Damn, Seth's "no" should mean no like anyone else's. There he was, in the open door of a big black SUV, its windows tinted as deeply as its paint.

"Seth?" Gary stepped into the gap between the vehicles. "What's happening?" He tried to look big and threatening, but that wasn't ever going to happen unless he got lucky with another growth spurt and a hell of a lot of gym time. But just showing up should help.

"Gary!" Seth's big green eyes looked even bigger under his shaggy fringe of chestnut hair, his face turned over his shoulder. "He won't let me go!"

"He" was an older man in a lime-green polo shirt sitting sideways on the bench seat, with both hands on Seth's arms. "Twink-boy here made some promises and now he doesn't want to follow through." He gave Seth a shake.

"What kind of promises?" Gary would talk before he rushed in to get physical—he could probably get Seth out of this with nothing more than a scare. He'd managed with TJ, hadn't he?

"Said he could show me how to make a hole in one, and took a lot of money on the promise of it." The old fart leered. "And now I want it."

"Gary...," Seth whimpered and tried to break free, but flinched when the man's hands dented his biceps.

"If Seth said he could show you that, you'd be on the golf course for it. He's just that good." Good Lord, how had Seth phrased that offer? He didn't always understand the nuances of what came out of his own mouth. "Probably on the fifteenth hole on this course."

"This punk kid? Come on. The only holes he's gonna make are the one in his face and the one in his ass." His laugh was ugly, heavy with lust and disbelief. "And that's what I paid him for."

"He didn't, Gary! He gave me forty bucks, and you know that's just a good round tip!" Seth protested.

"It is, you tightwad, and you probably cut eight strokes off your game for having him caddy." The wave of fury coursing through him left Gary feeling a foot taller and fifty pounds heavier, too big for the narrow space between the SUV and the next sedan. "Let him go."

"Don't think so." The man pulled backward on Seth's arms —Seth struggled away.

"Know so." Gary had a pack of weapons on his back to make sure of it. He dropped the golf bag, pulling one pom-pommed iron out as the rest fell. Hefting it like a southpaw with a baseball bat, he glanced at the rear windshield, more darkly tinted than he thought was legal. "Think the car alarm will go off when the glass breaks?" He waggled the club. "Or should I aim for the sheet metal? Or both?"

"I'll tell the cops some punk kid just started whaling away at my truck, officer, no idea why," he sneered. "Maybe just rage at wealth. Have fun making bail."

It might almost be worth the jail time for vandalism, but not the beating from his dad. Gary had to break the stalemate somehow. "You hand Seth a hundred bucks and let him go—" Oh Lord he didn't want to offer this, but he'd be a hundred bucks closer to getting away from his old man, and Seth would be safe. "—and I'll make good on whatever you think he offered."

"A hundred?" The man lifted one side of his mouth.

"What did you think you'd get for forty?" Gary countered, waggling the club behind his head. Maybe he could get some noise out of the backhand strike and then shift around to get more leverage with a forehand swing.

"I'll take a kid with some fire to him." The old lech kept a grip on Seth's right arm and dug his wallet out of his pants, stretching out one leg to do it. He dropped the billfold on his lap, fumbling out the bills. A great flash of green winked at Gary from within the leather. The man handed Seth two bills— he took them without really looking.

Gary had to prompt Seth to check. "Is it right?" Maybe someone would come along and interrupt this strange scene, but everyone seemed to be back at the Nineteenth Hole, no doubt sucking down screwdrivers and salty dogs, telling themselves the orange and grapefruit juices counted and the vodka didn't. A little humiliation for this old shit would be handy right about now, but no one came by with curious looks.

"Uh, yeah." Seth stumbled backward, clutching the money.

"Okay. You keep it for me." Gary didn't trust the man not to demand it back once he was in grabbing range. "And this." He handed Seth his wallet, too, and the golf club in its ridiculous hat. "Take the clubs to the BMW convertible at the end of the row. The owner should be there soon, and if I'm not there in fifteen minutes, come back and scream bloody murder, okay?"

"Uh, yeah, sure, Gary." Seth looked totally confused but took the club and the wallet. "Fifteen minutes."

"We'll be longer than that, boy," Old Lech interrupted.

"Only if you can't get it up, old man," Gary fired back. "We aren't going anywhere—that thing you drive is a traveling bedroom." He turned back to Seth, needing to calm those frightened eyes. "Go on. It'll be okay." He smiled weakly. "If the convertible guy comes soon, wait at my car."

"Okay." Seth jerked the bag of clubs off the blacktop and ran, stealing a look over his shoulder.

It would be okay. He'd deal with whatever he had to do, and Seth was safe. Gary advanced into the SUV's open door. "Scoot over." His khaki slacks swished against the buttery soft leather as he followed the man into the back seat. The rewards of being a rat bastard were pretty good.

He closed the door, the interior darkening as the deep-tinted window filtered the light. Anyone not looking straight in through the windshield wouldn't see them. Maybe the guy had chosen the vehicle for just these traits.

"Get busy, boy." Old Lech jingled his belt open and unzipped his golf slacks, which at least weren't a plaid that might blind Gary from close range, though he'd never like lemon yellow again. "Start with your mouth."

And finish with my mouth, Gary thought. He'd make that happen somehow; he wouldn't give this fucker a chance at the rest of his body, and he sure as hell didn't expect the man to return any oral favors. He stared dubiously at the first real erection he'd ever seen besides his own. Gary'd dreamed of sucking cock, but not this one.

"Bite and I'll rip your ear off," the man warned him.

"Might be worth it to bleed all over this interior." Shaking away Old Lech's insistent hand from the back of his head, Gary closed his eyes and got started.

Pretend it's Seth, pretend it's Seth… kept him going, and experience or not, they were done in a lot less than fifteen minutes, even with the choking. Gary'd barely finished swallowing when Old Lech started trying to zip his pants and shove Gary from the SUV all at the same time, accomplishing neither very fast, but frantic in his demands. "Get out! Get *out!*"

Was that his wife? A woman in pale peach ambled down the row of parked vehicles, chatting with another man in pastels meant for the course. *Or maybe that's his partner?* Didn't matter. "It'll cost you everything in your wallet for me not to say, 'Hi, your pal has a tan mole on his hip.'" Gary exhaled hugely on each vowel and *H*, making the point about the scent his breath carried.

"Fuck, okay, yeah, here." The man dug in his pocket, extracting bills. "Go! *Go!*"

Bad time to hold back. "All of it." Once he'd slapped the last bill—a fifty, nice—into Gary's hand, Gary slid out the door and closed it with a last-second slam. He could go greet the advancing pair, but he checked for Seth instead. The glossy convertible's slot contained a silver Audi now, so Gary abandoned his idea for a double cross and went in search of his friend. Seth needed some reassurance more than Gary needed revenge. More revenge. He shoved the bills into his pocket and headed to the employee section on the outskirts of the lot.

He could see Seth pacing near the faded salmon Oldsmobile that got them to and from the little town down valley where so many of the resort's staff lived. Maybe one day he and Seth could have an apartment in the three-story buildings Wapiti Creek maintained for seasonal workers, but for now, they both lived with their parents and dreamed.

Or Gary dreamed. He wasn't sure what Seth saw as their future; he seemed content with their present.

Gary could tell the exact moment Seth saw him coming across the asphalt—he stilled and slumped, waiting in one place for Gary to finish his journey. Standing tall would show even at this distance that everything was okay—Gary found another inch in his spine and worked up a smile.

"Thirteen-and-a-half minutes when I saw you, Gar." Seth waited for Gary to unlock the passenger door, a matter of reaching across the vehicle and lifting a knob. He got in, his eyes still wary. "You're okay?"

"Yeah. I'm fine." Not really, but he'd walked away with a pocket full of cash, and he wasn't going to bitch and moan to Seth about how he'd earned it. Nor would he count his bonus for silence here. "Let's go home."

"He didn't—" Seth started to ask, about ten miles into a silent drive on the two-lane highway, but either ran out of words, or maybe ideas.

"He didn't hurt me, he didn't even get my clothes off, and he was way off on how much time he needed." He wouldn't lie to Seth, but if the mistaken impression the old bastard had creamed his jeans in the mere presence of a teenager got out there, Gary wouldn't correct it. "It's okay. He's less of a problem than TJ, even."

Seth laughed without humor. "We'll see if TJ's a problem again in a week."

"Think we should start trapping mice?" Good, something to distract Seth, maybe even make him laugh. "It'll take me about a day and a half to get his locker combination once classes start." Maybe less, if he could sweet-talk Mary Ellen; she had a job in the office and didn't like TJ much more than Seth did. This could liven up the start of their senior year. Well, Seth's second senior year, but Gary wouldn't comment on that. "I can rig it so the box pulls apart when he opens the door. Be even better than last time."

"Oh my Gawd!" Seth threw his head back, his eyes closed and lips curved with his laughter. "I can still see his face. When that mouse fell on his foot. He danced around screaming like a little girl." Most of the junior class had seen that performance.

The memory floated them most of the way home. TJ had ceased being a problem after he'd connected pushing Seth around with finding vermin in his belongings. Gary'd been a bit concerned about the one mouse chewing its way out of TJ's backpack too soon, but no, it had made its appearance in second hour English, where only half the junior class had seen and snickered. If he reverted to his old ways, Gary would reduce him to class joke.

The highway became the main street of Phippsburg, making Gary slow to what felt like a crawl after the last twenty-five miles at speed.

"You want to come by the house? Make some hotdogs or

something?" Seth offered. "Mom'll be home in another half hour or so."

If Mrs. Morgan didn't work at the Pamida, hotdogs would be about as scarce at Seth's house as they were at his. Somehow Dad always had plenty of beer. Gary checked the time and calculated how many cans might have disappeared down the parental gullet so far. Not enough to make sure Gary didn't have to talk with him if he went home now, and it wasn't worth it, no matter how desperate he was to clean his mouth. "Sounds good. But I want to make a stop first."

He chose Ray's Drug rather than the grocery store where he might encounter Seth's mom. Right now he didn't want to have to exchange pleasantries with someone who'd worry about him or wonder about his purchase. Seth offered Gary's wallet and Old Lech's two fifties once they'd pulled up, saying nothing. Taking his billfold and one of the bills, Gary left Seth holding the other and didn't wait to see what he did with it.

Once inside, Gary knelt at the bottom shelf of the oral care section to select the least awful of the stiff, cheap toothbrushes better suited for cleaning grout than teeth.

No.

Not this time—Old Lech was buying. Gary would choose from the bright white brushes with the colorful, squashy grips that would feel very strange after the hard, thin handles he'd used all his life.

He'd never had a red and white toothbrush before.

Read the rest.

ALSO FROM ROCKY RIDGE BOOKS

The Diversion Series from Eden Winters

Diversion

Collusion

Corruption

Manipulation

Redemption

Reunion

Suspicion

Decision

The Wrestling Series from D.H. Starr

Wrestling With Desire

Wrestling with Love

Wrestling With Passion

Wrestling with Hope

The Dark Angels Series from Z. Allora

With Wings

Tied Together

Finally Fallen